KU-419-659

"A beautifully arranged tackle box of everything Watkins does best—cut-through-the-bone narrative of family apocalypses; custom blending of the historical, the unimaginable and the impossible; enchanting, terrifying encounters with the American West." —*Los Angeles Times*

"An audaciously candid story . . . Watkins's book sparks the same electric jolt that *The Awakening* must have sent juicing through Kate Chopin's readers in 1899."
—*The Washington Post*

"A tour de force . . . Much of motherhood literature can radiate a sort of wounded egotism, as if the greatest crime that society might commit against a woman were to think ill of her. Watkins, though, neither stews nor panders. She just follows her light." —*The New Yorker*

"Unequivocally triumphant . . . Watkins shows readers—and perhaps proves to herself—that one does not have to choose the lesser of two evils. A woman can want motherhood *and* the rest of her life." —NPR

"There's some kind of genius sorcery in this novel. It's startlingly original, hilarious, and harrowing by turns, finally transcendent. Watkins writes like an avenging angel. It's thrilling and terrifying to stand in her wake."
—Jenny Offill, author of *Dept. of Speculation* and *Weather*

"[A] surreal autofiction masterpiece . . . written in sharp language that is both deeply funny and painful. Completely absent any navel-gazing or self-pity, it is a book that probes questions of family, feminism, ecology, and home, and refuses to settle on easy answers. . . . Absolutely original." —*Los Angeles Review of Books*

"Intense, intelligent, and bristly . . . angry and alive . . . A virtuoso performance."
—*The New York Times Book Review*

"Our most significant rising writer of the American West . . . *I Love You but I've Chosen Darkness* is a road trip story gone wild. . . . It's career redefining and absolutely bonkers in all the best ways." —*Vulture*

"The brutal, arid, electric terrain of remote California and Nevada crackles across almost every page. . . . Trippy and beautiful, slippery and seductive—a unique psychogeography of a region that is integral to the American vision and yet seems to have too few literary chroniclers." —*Vogue*

"A beguiling, biting exploration of motherhood (and personhood)." —*Vanity Fair*

"Darkly funny and poignant." —E! Online

"This book is stupendously good. It practically vibrates in its ferocious frankness, and is so funny too that one can't help falling for this voice, even in the pain, because of the pain, with the pain. A marvel."
—Aimee Bender, author of *The Particular Sadness of Lemon Cake* and *The Butterfly Lampshade*

"Daring . . . Boldly imagined and authoritatively told, this ambitious novel reminds us that Watkins is one of the most visionary writers working today." —*Esquire*

"Dark and edgy—but also dazzling." —*Entertainment Weekly*

"A wild, hilarious novel, told with a contagious, unchained ferocity. It's a wonderful book by an author who's quickly proven herself indispensable to American literature." —*Star Tribune*

"Worth the wait. A bracing and reckless piece of autofiction set in the crackling terrain of the American West, it's the work of a writer at the top of her game, her hand remaining steady even as her narrator's life spirals exhilaratingly out of control." —*Chicago Review of Books*

"A dark, and darkly funny, work of autofiction from [a] gifted writer." —*USA Today*

"A knockout of a book. Alternately funny and heartbreaking." —*POPSUGAR*

"Funny and fearsome." —*The Philadelphia Inquirer*

"If the evocative name of the book doesn't grab you, Watkins's stylish prose likely will." —Thrillist

"The author's wry writing style shines . . . [painting] a detailed, colorful portrait of life after grief, and the powerful cycle of generational trauma."
—*Pittsburgh Post-Gazette*

"A simply incredible title, and the novel within definitely lives up to it. . . . A compelling portrait of a woman on the brink." —*Hey Alma*

"[A] surreal, hilarious, and sneakily devastating hybrid of autobiography and fiction . . . [with] a voice that blazes with ferocious wit and candor." —*Lit Hub*

ALSO BY CLAIRE VAYE WATKINS

Battleborn

Gold Fame Citrus

I Love You but
I've Chosen Darkness

Claire Vaye Watkins

Riverhead Books
New York

RIVERHEAD BOOKS
An imprint of Penguin Random House LLC
penguinrandomhouse.com

Portions of this book have been published previously, in different form:
"10-Item Edinburgh Postpartum Depression Scale," in *Sex & Death* (2016);
"Some Houses," in *Tales of Two Americas: Stories of Inequality in a Divided Nation* (2017);
"I Love You But I've Chosen Darkness," in *Granta*'s *Best of Young American Novelists* (2017);
"My Bitch Mama," in *StoryQuarterly* (2018); "Naked in Death Valley," in *Guernica* (2018);
"Trespassing," in *Tin House: True Crime* (2017).

Riverhead and the R colophon are registered trademarks of Penguin Random House LLC.

The Library of Congress has catalogued the Riverhead hardcover edition as follows:

Names: Watkins, Claire Vaye, author.
Title: I love you but I've chosen darkness / Claire Vaye Watkins.
Description: New York : Riverhead Books, 2021.
Identifiers: LCCN 2021009728 (print) | LCCN 2021009729 (ebook) |
ISBN 9780593330210 (hardcover) | ISBN 9780593330234 (ebook)
Subjects: LCSH: Autobiographical fiction—21st century.
Classification: LCC PS3623.A869426 I3 2021 (print) | LCC PS3623.A869426 (ebook) |
DDC 813/.6—dc23
LC record available at https://lccn.loc.gov/2021009728
LC ebook record available at https://lccn.loc.gov/2021009729

First Riverhead hardcover edition: October 2021
First Riverhead trade paperback edition: October 2022
Riverhead trade paperback ISBN: 9780593330227

Printed in the United States of America
1st Printing

BOOK DESIGN BY LUCIA BERNARD

I often wondered where I'd have been if I was in a city and a stranger to my neighbors, as I so often had been in Las Vegas.

—Martha Claire Watkins

I Love You but

I've Chosen Darkness

I've tried to tell this story a bunch of times. This will be my last try, here in my garden with Moana, Lucky, Abigail and Boomerang, each naked except for Boomerang, who is cinched into a blue plastic saddle. The "garden" hardly merits the word by the standards of the house-proud resource-hoarding whites I must count myself among. My garden is mostly rock and dirt, wild, needless as Moana with so many sticks in her hair. Lucky and Abigail are Netflix properties. They have no sticks in their hair, for my daughter gave them butch haircuts last time she was here.

The story starts at some point in my daughter's first year, the point perhaps at which I became aware of my inability to feel any feelings beyond those set to music by the Walt Disney Company. I'd banned Disney, its toxic messages and bankrupt values, forbid it my child long before conceiving her. Yet there I was listening to the *Moana* soundtrack a dozen times a day and digging it, screening the film as often as my infant's budding synapses could bear. No other text moved me as much, with the exception perhaps of *Charlotte's Web*, particularly the chapter called "Escape," in which Wilbur briefly breaks out of his pen and the Goose, soon to be yoked unmerrily to her eggs, urges him yonder.

. . . the woods, the woods! They'll never-never-never catch you in the woods!

Or maybe it starts before then. Like I said, I've tried to tell it a bunch of times. Each try takes me further from whatever it is I'm after. I finish on an alien shore with a raft of needs, reminded once again that books heal people all the time, just not usually the people who write them. I promise to need nothing from this last try. It's only a yarn for the dolls.

It starts with my husband, Theo. (I've disguised his name because he is innocent.)

It starts with Theo in a waiting room reading over my shoulder.

1. Since my baby was born, I have been able to laugh and see the funny side of things.

    a. As much as I ever did.

    b. Not quite as much now.

    c. Not so much now.

    d. Not at all.

2. I have looked forward with enjoyment to things.

    a. As much as I ever did.

    b. Not quite as much now.

    c. Not so much now.

    d. Not at all.

"That's kind of evasive," Theo says. "'As much as I ever did.'"

"Do you think I'm being dishonest?"

"No, but . . ."

"But what, Theo?"

The baby squawks. I rock the car seat with my foot.

"I'm just saying a diagnostic like this shouldn't be multiple choice," Theo says. "It should be short answer. Or essay. Don't you think?"

    "a. As much as I ever did."

Ten-Item Edinburgh Post-Natal Depression Scale

1. Since my baby was born, I have been able to laugh and see the funny side of things.

We tried to find you a nickname in utero but nothing fit so well as the ones we had for your father's scrotum and penis, your brothers Krang and Wangston Hughes.

An app dinged weekly with developmental progress and fruit analogies. Some weeks I wrote my own.

This week your baby is the size of a genetically modified micropeach, which itself is about the size of a red globe grape. Your baby's earholes are migrating this week. Your baby can hear you and may already be disappointed by what it hears.

This week your baby is the size of a medjool date dropped from the palm and left to soften in the dust. Your baby is now developing reflexes

*like lashing out and protecting its soft places. It is also developing para-
doxes, and an attraction to the things that harm it.*

*This week your baby is the size of a navel orange spiked with cloves
and hung by a light blue ribbon on the doorknob of a friend's guest bathroom. Your baby is developing methods of self-defeat this week, among
them boredom, urgency, and nostalgia. It may even be besieged by ennui!*

*Your baby has begun to dream, though it dreams only of steady
heartbeats and briny fluid.*

2. I have looked forward with enjoyment to things.

Pain-free bowel movements, sushi, limitless beer and pot brownies,
daycare, prestige television events, everyone going home.

My sister visits and asks how much a doula costs. Does a person
really need one?

No, I tell her, not if you have an older woman in your life who is
helpful, trusted, up to date on the latest evidence-based best practices
and shares your birth politics, someone who is not all judgmental,
won't project her insecurities onto you, is respectful of your boundaries and your beliefs and those of your spouse, carries no emotional
baggage or unresolved tensions, no submerged resentment, no open
wounds, no helicoptering, no neglect, no library of backhanded com-
pliments, no bequeathed body issues, no treadmill of jealousy and
ingratitude, no internalized misogyny, no gaslighting, no minimiz-
ing, no apology debt, no *I'm sorry you feel that way*, no *I'm sorry you
misunderstood me*, no *beauty must suffer*, no *don't eat with your eyes*, no
I cut the ends off the roast because you did / I did it to fit the pan.

"That's a *steal*," Lise says. "Seven-hundred and fifty dollars for the
mother you wish you had."

3. I have felt scared or panicky for no good reason.

There are little white moths drifting twitchy through the house, sprinkling their mothdust everywhere. I cannot find their nest. I brace myself each time I take a towel or a sheet from the linen closet.

You are born jaundiced. We wrap you in a stiff so-called blanket of LEDs, to get your levels right. She's at twelve, they tell us, without saying whether the goal is fifteen or zero or a hundred—not telling us whether we are trying to bring them up or down. I don't know which way to pray, Theo says. Little glowworm baby, spooky blue light-up insured baby in the bassinet, hugged by this machine instead of us. A gnarly intestine-looking tube coming out the bottom of your swaddle. Jaundiced and skinny though neither of us are. *Failure to thrive.* In the car Theo agrees that a ridiculously lofty standard. Haven't we every advantage—health insurance and advanced degrees, study abroad and strong female role models? Aren't we gainfully employed, and doing work we do not hate no less? Didn't we do everything right and in the right order? And yet, can either of us say we are *thriving*? I remind myself it's not so bad, the jaundice, the smallness. Lise says, I was little and look at me! I remind myself of the nick-u and pediatric oncology, which we must pass on the way to our appointments. I remember the apparatus we learned about in breastfeeding class that the lactation consultants can rig up for a man. A sack of donated breastmilk and a tube taped to his pectoral, positioned to deliver milk to the baby as though through his nipple. I comfort myself with the dark, unmentioned scenarios wherein this rig would be necessary.

A box on the birth certificate paperwork says, *I wish to list another man as the baby's biological father (see reverse).* I see reverse, curious what wisdom the hospital has for such a situation, what policies the board has come up with to solve this clusterfuck of the heart, what discreet salve for-profit medicine might offer the modern woman's roving loins, but the reverse is blank.

Theo has hymns and spirituals, but I can remember only the most desperate lines from pop songs.

If you want better things,
I want you to have them.

My girl, my girl, don't lie to me.
Tell me, where did you sleep last night?

4. I have been anxious or worried for no good reason.

Lise says, "Your phone is ringing."

"What's the area code? There are certain area codes I categorically avoid."

"What about home?"

"Especially home."

In my Percocet visions, our blankets are meringue-thick and quicksand, suffocation-heavy, the baby somewhere in them. From the toilet I shout it out.

"She's not in the bed," Theo says from the hallway.

"How do you know?"

"Because she's in the bassinet."

"But how do you *know* she's in the bassinet?"

"Because I am presently looking at the bassinet and I see her in there."

But how does he know that he is truly *seeing*?

5. I have blamed myself unnecessarily when things went wrong.

A postcard arrives from Lake Tahoe. Addressed to the family but meant only for me. *Funny how some people feel like home.*

6. I have been so unhappy that I have had difficulty sleeping.

On video chat people say things about the baby I don't like—she seems small, she seems quiet, she is a princess, she will be gone before we know it—and I slam the computer closed. After, I send pictures of the baby and small loops of video, to prove I am not a banshee. I am a banshee, but cannot get comfortable with being one, am always swinging from bansheeism to playacting sweetness and back. The truth is I cannot play nice and don't want to, but want to want to, some days.

7. I have felt sad or miserable.

I can hear the whispers of my own future outbursts. *I wiped your ass, I suctioned boogers from your nose, I caught your vomit in my cupped hands and it was hot! I pruned the tiny sleep dreads from your hair and blew stray eyelashes off your cheeks.* I can feel the seeds of my resentment as I swallow them. *When you couldn't sleep I lay beside you with my nipple in your mouth. For hours I did this!*

I can feel lifelong narratives zipping together like DNA, creation myths ossifying. You would smile, but only if you thought no one was looking. Your hands were always cold, little icicles, but pink and wrinkly as an old man's, little bat claws, little possum hands. Your dad cut off the teensiest tip of your finger while trying to trim your nails, and after that we let them grow. That's why you have socks on your hands in all your pictures, to keep you from scratching yourself. When we took the socks off, you had little woolly worms of lint in your palms, from clenching and unclenching your fists all day. We have a machine that rocks you and another that vibrates you and an app that very poorly replicates sounds from the world you've not yet heard—breakers and birds, rain on a tin roof. Robo-baby, I worry you'll become, since you like the machines so much more than me.

8. I have been so unhappy that I have been crying.

Ours is not even a bad baby! She's chill. She sleeps so much I have to lie to the other moms, pretend to be a different kind of tired than I am, commiserate lest they turn on me. In truth ours sleeps through anything, even two adults screaming at each other crying begging saying things they can't take back making up and screaming again— our baby sleeps through all of it, waking only when we stagger into bed.

Creation myth, his: He broke his collarbone falling off a fence. He was trying to get to the neighbor girl.

Creation myth, hers: When they brought her baby sister home from the hospital she tried to put the bundle in the trash.

9. I have thought of harming myself.

But more the profound pleasure of sitting in the backyard on the last warm day of fall, you and your dad on a bedsheet on the grass, me in a lawn chair because I cannot yet bend in the ways that would get me to and from the grass, in my lap a beer and a bowl of strawberries.

10. Things have been too much for me.

On Christmas Eve the Ann Arbor Whole Foods is a teeming, jingle-bell hellscape. I take deep belly breaths. I decide to play nice for once, an exercise, my Christmas gift to the universe! I strap the baby to me and do not pretend not to notice when strangers gape at her. I stop and let them say oh how cute and even oh how precious and when they ask if the baby is a boy or a girl I do not say, Does it really matter? nor, A little bit of both! nor, You know, I'm not sure, how do I check? And when they ask how old? I do not say, Two thousand eight hundred and eighty hours, nor, A lady never tells. I round up and say, Three months today! I wag the baby's hand and make the baby say hi and bye-bye. I spend too much money on stinky cheeses and chocolate coins, stovetop popcorn, armfuls of fresh-cut flowers, muffin tins I will never use, pomegranates that remind me of home. I do not use self-checkout, the misanthrope's favorite invention, and when the nosy checker asks me to sign my name on the electronic pad I do not write 666 or draw a big cock and balls and instead I sign, in elegant cursive, the baby's name. And outside I do not look away when more lonely people ask me with their eyes to stop so that they might see the baby and touch the baby and instead I do stop, in the fresh snow padding the parking lot, let them hold the baby's hand and tell me how I will feel in five years or ten years or twenty years or this time next year, let them tell me where I will be and what will be happening and how I will cherish every minute.

Vagina Dentata

Theo took the baby to her first Christmas Mass. I stayed home to read a little and masturbate a lot. How I'd missed masturbation! I'd beaten off like a maniac throughout the pregnancy—watched filthy porn with headphones on so the fetus wouldn't hear—but this was my first self-love session since giving birth.

It wasn't long before I noticed something alien in my vagina. A node in the wall. Left side—my left—about half a finger in. My first thought was *birth injury*, though I'd had a c-section so that didn't track. The node didn't hurt, but it also didn't heal. It seemed over time to harden. I did some research. A vaginal dermoid cyst, I decided, a condition so rare and unlikely I would never ask my doctors about it. They already thought me drug-seeking and insane.

Cyst. Such a soft, sisterly word, all air. It allowed me to nearly forget the nub for months, until the day my daughter cut her first tooth.

Absently letting her gum my index finger, I felt an edge and recoiled. I put my finger immediately back in her wanting mouth and found a spearhead of enamel. I thought: if *this* is tooth then *that* is tooth. More research revealed that vaginal dermoid cysts are in fact sometimes teeth. I found mine inside me that night and pressed it, confirming.

Naturally, at first I felt myself a mutant. I was afraid and disgusted. But most vaginal dermoid cysts are benign, I read. They come from DNA the baby leaves in you. I admit I did not entirely grasp the science. But rather than hate or fear the tooth, I resolved simply to monitor it. Observe without judgment, as the yogis advised. I ministered to the tooth. I fetched the green glass jar of olive oil and the ceramic fingerbowl Theo had used while stretching my perineum throughout the third trimester. It had been a source of great anxiety for me during pregnancy, the fate of my woefully inelastic perineum. My fear of episiotomy was right up there with fear of death and c-section, though it was the c-section that ultimately rendered my dutiful stretching regimen for naught.

I dipped my finger pad in the olive oil and stroked the tooth with the same forced fondness with which I applied ointment to my stretch marks, trying to practice the self-love encouraged by my therapists and budtenders. I deleted certain apps in hope of replacing the shocking image search results for birth+injury or vaginal+dermoid+cyst with the throbs of my own body.

Miraculously, it worked! The tooth was hard and unequivocal, but not unpleasant to touch. It did not at all interfere with masturbating, neither with digits nor with toys, and Theo and I were not really having sex at the time, so the tooth was truly no bother. Neither were the others, as, gradually and at about the same rate as my daughter, I cut a ring of them.

Tooth enamel is the hardest substance in the body, I read, understanding myself to be mythical and rare. Possibly it was my imagination (and what does it matter if it was? what is any of this—love *especially*—if not imagination?) but after my teeth came in, my orgasms became longer and stronger, more intense and easier to come by. I filled my alone time with them.

Yes, I said *love*. I loved the teeth and was unafraid of that love. I loved freely, as the poet advised. The teeth became my secret companion. I told no one, not Theo and, as I've said, not his colleagues tasked with evaluating what sort of risk I posed and to whom.

I did not want to hurt the baby or myself. I stressed this. We were the only people I didn't want to hurt.

How long have you felt this way? was a question they all liked.

Since my baby was born. No, before. Way before. Since I was clouds pressed against a mountain. Since Tecopa.

I was okay. If I stopped breastfeeding and started meds and kept going to therapy and called my sister every day and journaled and beed a lizard at hot yoga four or more nights a week and took a lover or two, I would be okay—would survive my child's first winter, a sludgy era of despair, bewilderment, and rage passed in the palm of the mitten.

A Personal Narrative of
People and Places

The Amargosa River is one of the world's most remarkable water courses. . . .
You may cross and re-cross it many times totally unaware of its existence, but in
the cloudburst season it can and does become a terrible agent of destruction.

—William Caruthers, *Loafing Along Death Valley Trails:*
A Personal Narrative of People and Places

The Amargosa River begins as rare rain on the proving grounds, Pahute Mesa, not far from the made-up place where California becomes Nevada. The rain braids in washes down the alluvial slopes of Frenchman Flat and Yucca Mountain and seeps into the rock, flows south underground for about ten thousand years and sixty miles under a desert basin splashed with turquoise, aquamarine, smears of amethyst, rose quartz, folds of charcoal and onyx sparkling above dry lake beds of bleached bone dust. The river is ephemeral, sometimes there but mostly not, its few oases guarded by impenetrable thickets of thorny, black-barked mesquite.

However, near the town of Tecopa, the Amargosa surfaces to a surprise party of riparian wonders. Mesquite, as ever, but also endangered pupfish and voles, bobcat, coyote, cattails, mint, aspirin bark and other medicinal plants. Here the river turns, wends west then north in what my biologist calls the J curve, and in its wending digs a canyon. All along this canyon there are springs, water rising hot from the rock year-round. The jade mud at the springs is bentonite, good for the soul, skin, upset stomach or snakebite. A mask of it sucks the poison out. The water itself is said to heal. Fossil water, my biologist calls it.

We considered this place ours, my family and I, its names hints we did not take. *Amargosa* is Spanish. *Tecopa* is Paiute, after a Paiute chief. A mining company's way of asking to dig. Yucca Mountain, the site of the would-be Yucca Mountain nuclear waste repository, genus *Yucca*, subfamily *Agavoideae*: agave, yucca and Joshua tree. *Joshua* comes from the Old Testament by way of the Mormons, as in leading whoever needs leading out of the desert. The Amargosa River never gets out. It dies below sea level somewhere beyond Tecopa, baked into the sky above Death Valley. *Death* as in death as in no one gets out alive.

THE SUMMER OF 1967, the summer called the Summer of Love. My father turned seventeen and hitchhiked from his parents' house in Thousand Oaks up to Haight-Ashbury and from there to a commune in Taos. In September he went home to LA to start his senior year. But he *couldn't handle school anymore.* So says his 1979 memoir, *My Life with Charles Manson* by Paul Watkins, cowritten with Guillermo Soledad, *the pen name of a member of the faculty at University of California at Santa Barbara.* Paul dropped out, forfeiting his position as class president, and once again fled back to the Haight, only to find the weather had turned and the scene soured. By March of '68 he was back in LA, living in a pup tent in Topanga Canyon, hiking, smoking pot, jamming all day on his flute and French horn.

One day, Paul was tooting his heart out amongst the butterflies, bees and mustard weed when *two blue jays joined in*. That's how he likes to tell it. The jays reminded Paul of his friend Jay, who had a house up the canyon. Paul followed the creek up the canyon to Jay's, where he discovered Jay's car gone and in its place a school bus painted completely black.

Paul knocked on Jay's front door. *Two naked, wispy-legged teenage girls with waist-length hair stood in the doorway.* Jay doesn't live here anymore, said Brenda and Snake, welcoming Paul inside. Ten or twelve people—most of them girls, and those mostly naked—sat on the floor around a low table topped with candles. A fire in the fireplace. At the head of the table, a shirtless man holding a guitar.

Brenda introduced Paul. Charlie said, *Won't you stay and make music with us?*

They played, Charlie talked, and then the rap session gave way to an orgy—*we moved together in a kind of harmonious, inventive slither.*

As harmonious and inventive as the slither may have been, Paul woke at dawn the next morning, slipped on his moccasins and split. He hitchhiked up to Big Sur and camped alone on the beach for three months, did some housesitting, then once again gravitated back to Los Angeles. Thinking he'd hitch to his camping spot, Paul stood with his thumb out on the corner of Topanga Canyon and Ventura for mere minutes before a battered green Plymouth pulled over. Snake and Brenda, fresh off a dumpster dive, invited Paul to come see their new digs.

Want to smoke a number? he asked from the backseat of the Plymouth.

No thanks. We'd rather make love.

Snake drove the Plymouth up Santa Susana Pass to Spahn Ranch. Paul unloaded his stuff and joined a group playing music in the woods. After, Paul and Snake—fifteen years old and dispatched by Charlie for this purpose—spent the rest of the afternoon balling in a eucalyptus grove. That night Charlie drove the Family to Bel Air to play music with Dennis Wilson. This reads like easily the best day of Paul's short life.

Everything at Spahn's was seen through a veil of dust, Paul writes of the movie-set ranch where he lived with the Family. The very next day they knocked out the wall dividing the jail from the saloon. The girls brought in mattresses and tapestries and turned the space into a giant bedroom. The boys installed a toilet in the corner, as no one was to leave during the evening ritual of music, lecture and orgy—*the heaviest psychosexual therapy imaginable*—which for the most part my dad makes sound like a lot of fun.

Charlie's rap in those early days urged egolessness, surrender and other Eastern precepts cribbed from the Beatles. Plenty of acid that first summer, and group sex where casual rape was disguised as radical body positivity, but no talk of violence. Not even as much talk about the revolution as Paul would have liked. He'd been busted in Big Sur the summer before, tripped on acid all through a roadside beating from the cops, did some time in jail. *Some time.* That's how he put it to Charlie, eliding the specifics of his two-day incarceration. Charlie had done time, real time, and it was this time that made him brilliant, more serious, more committed than the burnouts Paul had lived with in the Haight and Taos.

Which is not to say the scene at Spahn's was no fun. The girls cooked and cleaned and embarked on thieving expeditions to keep everyone in zuzus, Charlie's word for junk food. The boys smoked dope, played music, took Dennis Wilson's Ferrari on a joyride on Santa Susana Pass and totaled it. Sadie had a baby. Minus a few bad trips—freak-outs, choking, confusing requests (*Paul come over here and show this girl how to give head*)—this was a beautiful time.

But the friction between the Family and Spahn's wranglers, once easily lubricated by alcohol and dope, began to chafe. Charlie and Paul tried and failed to infiltrate Fountain of the World, the tantric monastery over the hill. Three new girls joined the Family: Juanita, Leslie and seventeen-year-old Catherine "Cappy" Gillies, whose grandmother owned a ranch in Death Valley. That's when Charlie began *rapping in earnest about moving to the desert.*

The family spent October rebuilding the engine of their fifty-six-passenger International school bus and remodeling its interior, adding plush carpets, satin tasseled curtains, a refrigerator and a stove. On Halloween they loaded the black bus with *mattresses, blankets, clothes, musical instruments, food supplies, five cases of zuzus, a kilo of grass, and fifty tabs of acid* and lit out for the Mojave. They camped comfortably in the bus the first night, candy and drugs for dinner and sex for dessert. By dawn the next morning the bus was northbound, their magical mystery tour headed into the Panamint Mountains.

They found Goler Canyon, the only route to Cappy's family's ranch, treacherously steep, too narrow for the bus, strewn by flash floods with immovable boulders. Forced to ditch the bus, they loaded their backs with all the supplies they could carry plus two infants (another baby had joined) and hiked for miles up the canyon.

The Family tried to settle into the bunkhouse of Cappy's family's ranch, known locally as the Myers place, but Charlie grew increasingly paranoid. Cappy had told her grandma it would be only girls camping up there. Charlie and Paul scouted for other homesteads and soon found one farther up Goler Canyon, seemingly abandoned. Paul and Charlie tracked down its owner, Ma Barker, in Ballarat, the nearby ghost town. Together they convinced Ma Barker to trade them the Barker Ranch for one of the Beach Boys' gold records.

DEATH VALLEY MARKED *a turning point for the Manson Family*, my father "wrote." Our family lore credits this desert with saving his life, but first it tried very hard to kill him. *The cosmic vacuum of the desert was a perfect place to program young minds.* The vastness of scale offered by the stars, the treeless mountain ranges and plunging valleys urged surrender. *With infinity so close at hand it was easier to give yourself . . . Ideas that would have seemed utterly inconceivable to me in West Los Angeles were perfectly understandable on a crystal clear morning from the peaks of the Panamint Mountains.*

Death Valley inspired the particulars of Charlie's apocalyptic thinking, particularly its ghost river, the Amargosa, here flowing, here raging, here dried to nothing. He became obsessed with one spring in particular, Devil's Hole, bottomless, waves in its waters from earthquakes on the other side of the world.

This phenomenon always perplexed Charlie, who, from the time we arrived began speaking of "a hole" in the desert which would lead us to water, perhaps even a lake and a place to live. Charlie's mythic hydrogeology sent him and Paul on grueling night hikes in search of *a subterranean world, a cave, a place where we might take the Family and make our home when the shit came down*. They hiked, smoked, Charlie rapped. Paul collected rocks and gaped unscientifically at the shock of stars overhead. Had they been there this whole time?

Nights got colder. Supply runs to LA and Vegas demanded hours of hiking down and then back up the canyon lugging plunder. Gas was scarce. Isolation invited madness. Paul watched the deterioration of his friend Brooks Poston, who took to chopping wood from sunup to sundown to avoid Charlie. Charlie himself struggled to adapt to the desert, hanging comatose in a hammock all day and raving like a demon after dusk. *The flower child in Charlie Manson was dying, wilting away in Death Valley day by day, freezing by night.*

Then, all at once, things changed dramatically. Charlie went to LA for a meeting with Dennis Wilson and Terry Melcher and returned euphoric, having heard *The White Album* and found in it a name for his doomed prophecy: Helter Skelter. Race hate was palpable in the city, Charlie said, perfect conditions for the Family's album. They would lure young love to the desert while the rest of the world burned. The Beatles had *put the revolution down to music.*

Later, after, Charlie said, *Why blame it on me? I didn't write the music.*

He summoned the Family minus Brooks and Juanita back to LA, to the Yellow Submarine, a yellow two-story house on Gresham Street in Canoga Park. *Suburbia . . . mellow enough when compared to L.A. proper but hectic after living in the desert.* With his Family submerged in the Yellow Submarine, Charlie kept on with his *grisly raps* and tests. Paul enrolled in Birmingham High School to recruit teenage girls. The *macho brigade* moved in: *mechanics, bikers and ex-cons,* Vietnam vets, men tutored by the state as Charlie had been, *men content to do*

what they were told in exchange for sexual gratification and good weed.
Charlie sent *Sadie, Ella, Stephanie, Katie and Mary to work as topless dancers in clubs in the valley. To buy vehicles and outfit them properly, we needed money. The girls went to work willingly.*

On Gresham Street the Family focused on their music. Recording sessions at Brian Wilson's studio went poorly. Charlie arranged for Terry Melcher to come hear them play in the Yellow Submarine. The girls cleaned the house, set up the instruments and made dinner: *vegetables, lasagna, green salad, French bread and freshly baked cookies. Then they rolled some good weed.* Melcher didn't show. *That motherfucker's word isn't worth a plugged nickel,* said Charlie.

Preparations for Helter Skelter accelerated. The Family moved back to Spahn's, hoarded dune buggies and Harleys, listened to *The White Album* nonstop. Charlie rapped on the Book of Revelation, chapter 9, locusts and scorpions, electric guitars and the coming holocaust the Family would ride out in their hole. *"When all the fightin's over,"* Charlie said, *"the Muslims will come in and clean up the mess . . . cause blackie has always cleaned up whitey's mess. But blackie won't be able to handle it and he'll come over and say, 'You know, I did my number, man . . . I killed them all and I'm tired of killing. The fightin' is over.' And that's when we'll scratch blackie's fuzzy head and kick him in the butt and tell him to go pick the cotton."*

AROUND THIS TIME Charlie instructed Paul to steal *a big heavy duty Dodge ambulance-weapons-carrier* and take it on a supply run to the Panamints. Paul thought of Brooks, *zombied-out* and withdrawn last Paul had seen him. He hesitated only a moment before hot-wiring the Dodge. By four a.m. he'd loaded the stolen truck with supplies and *several girls . . . still in their nighties and T-shirts.* By dawn this band was back in the desert, thinking themselves free.

Instead they were busted, the stolen truck pulled over outside the town of Mojave, the group thrown in jail. The next morning, Paul was bussed to the Los Angeles county jail. He was booked for car theft and, after a couple of days, released.

Returning to Spahn's so suddenly, after anticipating a stay in the desert, made me even more aware of how denigrated things had become. Guns and Buck knives and bad vibes from the wranglers. Charlie, too. *Gotta get a goddamn truck up there man. Something's stopping us.* One afternoon in late June, Paul and Charlie walked to the corral. Charlie climbed the fence and sat watching the horses. Paul asked how much longer. Charlie winked down from the top rail. *"Helter Skelter is coming down,"* he said, *"but it looks like we're going to have to show blackie how to do it."*

Another Panamint run—another bust. Released again, and newly appreciative of Charlie's rule that only the girls carried dope, Paul ached for the desert. What was the barrier keeping him away? He felt it hitchhiking out of his city, felt it all the way to Ballarat. It was with him hiking up Goler Canyon, until the moment he saw Brooks *bounding down the hill like a frisky goat.*

Been climbing mountains, Brooks said. *Met this far-out old prospector dude.*

Paul Crockett, Big Paul, the man my father credits with deprogramming him. The three men wandered the desert for three days. Crockett showed Paul and Brooks the velvety texture of bentonite clay, how to find opal, lapis, gold. He showed them how the desert is an organism. At a mine called Gold Dollar he taught them that everything was by agreement.

Paul said, *Charlie says everything is in your imagination.*

Yeah, that's kind of how it is . . . but it's there because we agree to it . . .

The Panamints had agreed to Paul, offered clean air and water, sobriety, meditation, dark skies and deep sleep. His mornings passed billygoating up and down the mountain with a backpack full of that same mountain, his afternoons helping Juanita in the garden, making food from the mountain or grinding the mountain with mortar and pestle to pry gold from the quartz base. Evening meant dinner and making music.

This was the scene when Little Paul embarked on a mystical scavenging expedition to Las Vegas that would eventually cleave him from Charlie. In Vegas he stole a motorcycle and *three live chickens, a rooster, two watermelons and two dozen eggs.* Struggling to carry his loot up Goler Canyon on the motorcycle, he wrecked deep in the canyon. It was 125 degrees.

When at last Paul limped back up to Barker Ranch, dehydrated and deranged, the surviving poultry squawking under his arms, something strange happened. Big Paul healed Little Paul. Crockett laid his hands on Little Paul's busted body and talked the pain away. My father felt his hurt evaporate into the dry air, a mist of agonies that belonged, he saw plainly now, in the past.

HE WAS IN DEATH VALLEY during the murders. He returned to Spahn's soon after, unaware, and asked to be released from his agreements. Charlie said, *Sure, Paul.*

Snake crawled into his sleeping bag that night to say goodbye. *I knew Charlie had sent her but it didn't matter.*

THE FAMILY FOLLOWED PAUL into the Panamints. Little Paul, Big Paul, Brooks and Juanita could hear them coming all night, war whoops and the engine screams of dune buggies echoing up the canyon walls. The Family moved into the Barker Ranch while Crockett and his apostates stayed a quarter mile down in the Myer bunkhouse.

Charlie started in on his creepy crawlies, saying, *You ain't released from nothing.*

Saying, *we cut him up real good.*

Saying, had they heard about Bobby and Mary? *They're in jail, man . . . for murdering Gary Hinman.*

Did they do *it?*

Sure they did it . . . you did it, I did it . . . we all did it.

JUANITA SPLIT. Brooks wanted to. Crockett wouldn't be run off his claim. Charlie sent Snake to Paul again. It was August in Death Valley, 120 degrees by eight a.m. Someone brought the mail from a forgotten post office box. The U.S. Army had summoned Paul to Los Angeles for a physical.

After *a well-thought-out spiel on the virtues of drugs in expanding consciousness* and his arrest record got him classified as unfit for service, Paul hitched a ride back to the desert with Brenda and Clem. Brenda sat in the middle. Clem drove. He drove and he talked. All night driving into the desert Clem talked about killing Shorty Shea. *Yeah, it was a trip, you know. I never seen so much blood.*

So when Charlie told me, I took the machete and chopped his head off so he'd stop talking . . . and it just rolled off the trail, bloop . . . bloop . . . bloop . . . into the weeds.

27

Paul did not tell Crockett or anyone what he'd heard from Clem. If he told it he would have to hear it again, would have to know it and live it. The Crockett camp feuded with Charlie through the summer of 1969 and into the fall, when leads on Tate–LaBianca ran dry. Charlie and Tex took to bringing their guns down to the Myers place for target practice. Nights, Brooks or Paul would open the door of the bunkhouse to find Tex and Charlie crouched in the darkness with knives between their teeth.

At last, the apostates decide to scoot. They hike fifty cold miles through the night to Shoshone, population thirty. Gas station and post office on one side of Highway 127, a bar, restaurant and an Inyo County sheriff's substation on the other. Paul and Brooks tell the deputy everything they know. The deputy tells them to stay put. He asks the patriarch of Shoshone for a favor. Find these boys a place to live—somewhere secret. The man's wife leads the boys out to the tufa caves at Dublin Gulch, a place still mistakenly called the Manson caves. (Manson himself never set foot there.)

Dug originally by itinerant miners, prospectors, and other vagabonds, who, over the years, found the town a convenient oasis in the scorching lowlands of the Amargosa Valley, the caves were *for a long time the site of a thriving hobo jungle.* The patriarch puts them to work. They are not particularly useful, wracked as they are by shock and withdrawal. When the Amargosa jumps its banks, Paul is ordered to hose mud away from the gas pumps. He stands catatonic, hose running, staring at nothing in awe and terror. Periodically someone takes Little Paul by the shoulders and turns him a bit, so the water from the hose might wash away more mud.

Eventually Charlie was arrested, charged with murder and indicted. Sadie and Leslie too. More bodies surfaced.

Sometime around Christmas, shortly after Charlie had been granted the right to defend himself, I felt the urge to go to LA and see the Family.

When I told Crockett, he said it didn't surprise him. He said it would take a long time to get free of Charlie's programs and my ties to the Family, and I wouldn't ever do it by avoiding the issue.

I wanted to see Charlie. I wanted to see the others. At a deeper level perhaps, I wanted to extricate some meaning from all the horror and carnage, to step back into the nightmare and find something worth salvaging.

Once in LA, Paul tried to reach Snake at the Patton State Hospital. *They said Diane Lake was there but that I couldn't see her.*

Next he went to the LA county jail. *I'm just here for Christmas,* Charlie told him. *I always come for Christmas.* Charlie wanted to talk about Crockett and the album. He wanted Paul to come back. "*We're getting the album out. You got to help them out, keep things together.*"

Paul had already made full statements to the Inyo County sheriff and the DA. Yet he went back to the Family. He *met with Charlie, discussed strategy, helped the girls secure new lawyers; I spoke to Sadie and Leslie and conveyed Charlie's messages. Meanwhile, . . . I reinstituted therapy sessions and love therapy and began indoctrinating the new guys in the arts of sex. For a time I did become Charlie . . .*

Paul moved the Family back to Spahn's. They had an acid trip and orgy to celebrate their return. The next day Paul went to court to help Clem change attorneys. The day after that, unaware that documents including his statements had been delivered to Charlie per his motion for discovery, Paul himself went to court for a traffic violation. Brenda and Squeaky went with him. After receiving his sentence—sixty-five dollars or five days in jail—Paul sent the girls outside to get the cash from his stash under the dashboard. The girls left and never came back.

Paul went to jail for five days. *Charles Manson had spent 23 years in prison. To me, five days seemed an eternity, particularly since I knew I'd pushed my own games to their limit.* Released, delirious and exhausted from five nights of insomnia and searching, Paul hitchhiked back to Spahn's, where the girls waited with copies of his statements. They threw him out, calling him Judas.

I had reached the end and the beginning at the same time, Judas said.

Exiled from the ranch, Paul slept up the canyon in a van that night. More accurately, he lit a joint, lay down on the bed in the back of the van, and *I guess that's when I fell asleep.* When he woke the van was full of white smoke, flames melting the seats like wax.

Paul threw himself from the burning van and called for help. Someone drove him down the mountain to the emergency room. *Before the hospital did anything they wanted to be certain I had medical insurance.*

Blisters swelled his throat closed, *more pain than I could ever remember having felt.* Pop the bubbles! he begged, but his vocal cords were charred. No one could understand him. At last he grabbed a surgical instrument from a tray and jammed the handle down his throat, bursting the blisters.

Three days later, he woke in Santa Monica Hospital, without a voice. His mother, my grandma Vaye, was beside him, cutting his hair. *She said everything was going to be okay and for me to rest.*

When he was well enough, he went to Big Sur. *I wanted to sit on the edge of the cosmos and watch the sea in silence.* From Big Sur he went back to the desert to look for gold and grow his voice back. Brooks and Big Paul took him for a steak dinner in Vegas his first night back.

The Gold Dollar was off-limits, the whole of Goler Canyon now state's evidence. The men lived in the Manson caves and did whatever work they could find, bussing tables, maintenance, fixing roads, construction, mining talc. They laid pipelines, played music, wrote songs and scripts and poems, cooperated with the prosecution, told and sold their stories in various ways over the years. Crockett met a woman and moved on down the road. Brooks, too. That's the lay of the land when Paul finds an abandoned shack in Tecopa.

1980, THE BEGINNING OF THE END. See my father naked in a hot spring, mask of bentonite mud tightening on his face. He has followed the Amargosa from China Ranch—formerly "The Chinaman's Ranch," after Quon Sing, according to *Loafing Along Death Valley Trails: A Personal Narrative of People and Places* by William Caruthers, originally published in 1951 by Death Valley Publishing Co. My mother had a copy. She left it to me. Well, she left it and I took it. It was not really an inheritance scene.

The land was in the raw stage, with nothing to appeal to a white man except water. . . . The industrious Chinaman converted it into a profitable ranch. He planted figs and dates and knowing, as only a Chinaman does, the value and use of water the place was soon transformed into a garden with shade trees spreading over a green meadow—a cooling, restful little haven hidden away in the heart of the hills. He had cows and raised chickens and hogs. He planted grapes, dates, and vegetables and soon was selling his produce to the settlers scattered about the desert.

From a wayfaring guest he would accept no money for food or lodging.

After the Chinaman had brought the ranch to a high state of production a white man came along and since there was no law in the country, he made one of his own—his model the ancient one that "He shall take who has the might and he shall keep who can." He chased the Chinaman off with a shot gun and sat down to enjoy himself, secure in the knowledge that nobody cared enough for a Chinaman to do anything about it.

The Chinaman was never again heard of.

Having pilfered Quon Sing's dates and figs, Paul filled his canteen at an irrigation pump and pressed on to this secret spring. Now, his mud mask dries to cracking. He scrubs the crust from his face, emerges, dresses. He wets his handkerchief and ties it around his neck. Rivulets of water stream between his shoulders and evaporate as he picks his way into a slot canyon, where the trail disappears. Paul pauses to eat a gooey date in the canyon shade, spits the velveteen pit into the dirt and doubles back, finding the tracks of the old railroad. He follows these deeper into the canyon.

Cliffs of calving sand rise on either side of him. Soon he can no longer see even the tallest date palms at China Ranch, their seeds ordered from a catalog by a pioneer daughter and mailed from Iran. He scurries up the canyon and emerges onto a treeless plain. Before him rises a hill of crenulated ore of a curious burnt-orange color, where the other hills are dun, pungent green-gray after rain, pink at sunset, splashed with yellow verbena in spring. At the base of this peculiar mountain a hole opens into darkness—a mine.

Paul ducks inside, in search of opal, lapis, gold. The mine is cool, not deep enough for him to stand. Yet, stooped there in the darkness, he sees a thousand promising glints. He emerges sometime later, his knapsack heavy with finds. Giddy, he continues until stopped by an unambiguous omen: black volcanic boulders arranged in a somber ring, a cross made of scarce timber blackened by the sun, an untended grave shimmering in the heat. The mine's previous owner, presumably.

Did my father kneel? Did he pray?

Let's say he prayed. Say he said sorry to the body, sorry that it did not get more time on this rock. Say he whispered, "God keep him," though he does not right then know God. That's another thing he's looking for out here.

Lapis is the original blue. When I am in the emotional place my mother called *no-man's-land* I wear a pendant of lapis from this mine, a specimen rutilated with an oxbow of mica, the stone pulled from the earth by my father, ground and polished by him, set by his hands in ropy gold cooled by his breath. That's how I like to tell it.

It is the hottest part of the day now, Paul's canteen light. He takes leave of the grave and hikes up the sandy wash toward shade. A clump of salt cedars. (Tamarisk, says my biologist, invasive.) Around the trees Paul discovers a broiling boneyard of heavy equipment: broken-down mining rigs, water tanks, rusted oil drums, gutted cars and a shot-to-shit dump truck with tires crumbling like old cake. At the heart of the junkyard he finds an abandoned shack. He cups his hands at the shack's one window, spies a sink, a shitter, the springs of a burned mattress.

Another thatch of green beckons Paul up the hill, which he finds bristling with technicolor stones splotched with lichen, barrel cacti, sage, horny toads and Gilas. Canyon views at the summit, a wink from the river. China Ranch is to the southeast, a mile as the crow flies, and if that crow kept flying it would cross a mountain range and a Joshua tree forest, the site of a future solar array, and then a larger mountain range on its way to Las Vegas, the meadows.

As I've said, it's the eighties. There is not yet an industrial solar array in the valley between Tecopa and Las Vegas. No surveying bird will mistake the array for water only to combust upon descent and streak flaming to the ground like a daytime comet. We have not yet whizzed gasping through certain deadly thresholds. The cane grass has not yet overtaken the spring at the top of the hill, the tamarisk has not yet brined the earth below.

For now, a desert miracle: a spring. Paul does not yet know this is Tecopa's old stamp mill, only that someone has installed an iron catchment pool and it is full of clean-enough water. He fills his canteen, drinks, rewets his handkerchief and lays it across his burned neck, envisioning the pipe he'll run from the pool down the hill to the shack beneath the salt cedars, the place he already thinks of as *mine*.

THE TAMARISK IS A RACIST TREE, a well-documented instrument of redlining. Lines of the shaggy, deep-barked trees were planted to cut off Black neighborhoods from golf courses, mountain views and other desirable features of desert living in Palm Springs and without a doubt beyond, thereby redistributing wealth to whites, says my biologist.

PAUL MOVES NINE MILES down the road from the Manson caves to Tecopa. He works the mine and expands the house with whatever he can find, adding a bedroom of scrap plywood and railroad ties from the Tonopah and Tidewater, a greenhouse of chicken wire windows from the old borax mill. He masons a fireplace from rocks he finds on the long walks he takes in the canyon when he's trying not to drink. He installs plumbing of sorts—scorpions come up through the drains and soon there is a soft, stinky depression behind the house.

The house, the stars, the astonished earth's absorbing. Tecopa becomes his salvation, the love of his life. In one version it remains so for a decade, until a girl walks into a bar.

THE CROWBAR IN SHOSHONE. Paul has worked his way up to bartender. The girl is leggy, freckly, a redhead. Bright coppery hair feathered out from brown, wide-open eyes. Huge glasses, huge boobs, beige smock top with puffy sleeves, no bra. Younger than him but not at all a *girl*. She is wearing a ring but not acting married. Paul asks where she's from.

"Vegas. My ma and stepdad took a ride out here yesterday. Said the bartender was a good-looking hippie with no friends."

Paul remembers them immediately, the old bikers who came in on a hog and dry-humped on the pool table until last call. He nearly had to pry them apart with a cue. The man's white belly bulging from beneath the snug leather vest, the parting insults as the hog peeled out, spitting rocks, the other barflies grunting in admiration from the parking lot.

"It's true I've got no friends," Paul says. "Half the locals don't like hippies and the other half don't like narcs." He studies her face, wondering how much she knows.

She smiles, says, "Sorry Joe called you—what was it?—'Pinko flower power pussy'?"

He shrugs. "I'm not even all that pinko."

"Fuck him," she says, burning suddenly. "He's a bad man. I know a thing or two about bad men."

She gets up, plays Carole King on the jukebox. Joni Mitchell. Elton John. He asks what she does for work.

"Camera girl at the Sands," she says. "Where you from?"

"LA."

"I got a cousin in LA." She shrugs and ashes her cigarette on the floor. "Used to be real apeshit about the place. Now I'd rather be out here."

Paul pours himself a beer and Martha another. There is definitely an orb forming between them. She says, unprompted, "I'll be a friend to you."

He can't think how to respond. She's suddenly very pretty. "What's a camera girl?"

"Vegas for photographer. Souvenir photos. Skeezeballs and their mistresses get dressed up to see a show on the Strip, we take their picture before curtain, run downstairs and develop them in the darkroom in the basement, rush our asses back upstairs and sell them at intermission. All in heels and basically underwear." Makeup too, lots of it. She's always getting written up for not having enough on. That's why on her days off she wears none, no bra, no socks. She slips off her Keds and rubs her bare feet on the barstool—pretty loaded all of a sudden. ". . . then I lived with my sister in the Haight for a while." By "lived with" she means "visited." How did she get on this?

"You weren't a hippie," he says. "You're too young."

He notes the freckles across her collarbones, splashed down her shoulders, neck and breasts. She notes him noting and smiles. Maybe she doesn't care about Manson. Maybe she just likes coming out here. A city girl but a sympathizer, a new convert to the Old Testament scene. An honorary desert rat, like him. Paul reaches across the bar and rubs her bare arm, smooth and sparkling with minerals.

She crushes her cigarette into the ashtray he's fetched for her and raises her jaw. "I'm not a hippie," she says, "but I would ball a hippie."

They don't ball, not that night. The camera girl does not even get his name.

Her mother is a change girl at Caesars Palace. When Martha was a child, some feminists printed the names of the casinos that didn't promote women in the newspaper. Caesars Palace, the ads said, was the worst of the worst. NOW and the unions marched on the Strip, shut it down for a day. At last Caesars capitulated, promoted a few of the white change girls from the floor into the cage, including Martha's mother, Mary Lou. With this raise and what she managed to steal, Mary Lou bought a ranch house walled with breeze-block on Fairway Drive, the sewer side of the public golf course. Martha's older sister, Monica, lived in San Francisco with her husband. Her older brother, Jack, was a valet at The Sands. Her stepdad, Joe, sat at the bar at Caesars through Mary Lou's whole shift, watching. They fought, then Jack and Joe fought. Someone in that house was always beating the living hell out of someone else, and the moment the hell started spilling out, Martha rode her ten-speed to a ditch that would one day be the Meadows Mall, to her friends' houses, to school or work, to Harry's, good enough reason to marry him.

Harry is in New York, working. He doesn't write and he doesn't call and he doesn't send money like he said he would, and Martha does not mind a bit, drunk-driving her VW Bug back to Vegas beneath a smear of stars pointing west. The hot springs have melted the work from her muscles. On Harry's mattress like a raft on a sea of dirty clothes she sleeps the deepest sleep of her life. She dreams a black orb and wakes knowing its message. She packs her shit, loads it into the Bug and drives to her mom's house, to the bedroom she and Monica once shared, where all her favorite things are still, things she has never brought to Harry's. Her perfect reading chair made out of raw wood and hide, the garage sale mirror, the full bookshelf and two big, thirsty ferns. Her acoustic guitar from Sears on a carved wood stand, a rug almost half the size of the room, an aloe plant in a macramé sling, a maroon and gold tapestry.

Behind the tapestry is a hole punched in the wall some time ago by some man. Inside the hole, waiting down in the darkness in a Crown Royal pouch hung on a nail, are all of her earthly treasures: ticket stubs to *Jesus Christ Superstar*, Bob Dylan, *Rocky Horror Picture Show*, Joni Mitchell, and Elton John, a fat ounce, and some whites. She adds her tips, rehangs the velvet pouch on the nail, replaces the tapestry and waits.

She lives again in this room in her mother's house on Fairway Drive for two weeks. Mary Lou doesn't come home, or if she does, she comes while Martha is at work. Martha listens to the radio and tends her plants and practices guitar with the chords she'd long ago drawn on the wall of the bedroom near a yellow submarine and Kilroy and Charlie Brown and Snoopy. She goes to the laundromat and into her mother's bathroom (silver Marilyn Monroe print wallpaper) to smell Mary Lou's cold cream. She rides her old ten-speed to her ditch, reads there and writes in her diary. She types a letter to Harry and another to her cousin Denise, buzzing with clarity. Obeying an arbitrary but nonetheless rigid timetable she's assigned herself, on the second

Saturday Martha loads the Bug with her now-clean clothes, her toiletries, her best books, her guitar, Denise's typewriter, her cameras and equipment, her portfolio, her plants and her sack of treasures. After work, aloe and ferns buckled into the passenger seat, Martha drives back to the Crowbar.

There he is, her nameless love, polishing a glass at the bar.

He looks up. "What took you so long?"

Things are complicated, then they aren't.

She moves to Tecopa.

THEY RAISE A PARACHUTE on a telephone pole for shade, grow grapevines, dates, figs, palms, bamboo. Martha grows mint from cuttings taken from Quon Sing's patch. She feeds the soil coffee grounds, eggshells, bonemeal and menstrual blood. Ice plant and carrots, onions, corn, tomatoes, hollyhocks and honeysuckle. Her darkroom had been Paul's workshop, and her chemicals and equipment share space with blades and bits and cracked five-gallon buckets of rocks until they open a rock shop in town, next door to the post office. Visitor's Center—Rocks Maps Gemstones, the sign says. They sell postcards, maps, Paul's rocks and jewelry, Martha's photographs—landscapes, Paul in the mine, the dogs—and copies of *The Amargosa News and Views*, the newspaper they make with their friends.

Lise and I are born less than a year apart, Irish twins. Me in 1984 at the hospital in Bishop near the lake LA drank, Lise in 1985 in the back of Mary Lou's Datsun 280Z on the side of the road in Death Valley. Around this time we whiz unknowingly through various deadly thresholds.

Well, Exxon knew.

MOM WOULD OPEN our front and back doors so randy tarantulas could migrate through. Don't bother them, she said, they were here first. Lise practiced shaving with our dad's razor. I remember them holding her down in the kitchen, lots of red-black blood on the green linoleum. She remembers me walking on a cinder-block wall in front of the post office. *Calif.* had just become *CA* but *lif.* was still sun-stamped on the block wall. I slip and catch my chin on the cinder block, my blood lit red-orange in the late-day sun. Lise watches them sew me up, nine black stitches ants along my jaw. The scar still pulls a little, making my smile look sarcastic.

One planter box in the garden is surrendered to any tortoises we catch. We feed them iceberg lettuce until they tunnel out. Horny toads we tag with nail polish, cataloging them in a locking diary, until Mom says they breathe through their skin. "You're killing them," she clarifies.

A lump on my father's neck. He goes for rides in airplanes. Lise and I sleep together beneath Raggedy Ann and Andy bedding bought on layaway. We lie before the swamp cooler, splayed naked in the sun with Dad cross-legged beside us, coated in mud.

We become the leaders of a small pack of dogs—Barry, Spike and Garfield. A pack of coyotes on the far ridge yipping, cackling, waiting. They get Garfield, then Barry, but not Spike and not us, not yet. Rattlesnakes at dawn and dusk. We never see but at times can feel the bobcat up at the spring, watching.

I'VE SEEN THE FOOTAGE and the reenactments. I've seen a video of my father on *Larry King Live* wearing a tan button-up shirt and a bolo tie. I've watched him fiddle with his malfunctioning earpiece and talk about his friends in the Family. *They were sick. They thought they were righteous angels on a wave of revolution that was cleaning up the world.*

In another video he is in Malibu, propped up with pillows in the bed where he will die of leukemia. He looks into the camera. He says, *Here I am, my girls. I want you to know how much I loved you. I want you to know who I was.*

Did he know then that he was asking too much? I was six years old when he died. Lise was five. We have none of the memories he so hoped we would have. We have CNN, *Helter Skelter. My Life with Charles Manson.* I look for him there. I play his interviews over and over, listening to his voice rasp and tremble in all the familiar places. I listen, listen like I listen to nothing and no one else, especially myself. But he never says what I need him to say.

Malibu had flowers that looked like birds and had the names of birds. Slugs and snails and dew, everything glistening. One neighbor's house was a giant barrel, another's a geodesic dome. The drained swimming pool behind the guesthouse we rented throbbed with frogs. Paper dolls on Lise's birthday. The zoo, the tar pits, the beach, Disneyland.

Malibu. The place our father came to die and did, while I was doing somersaults in a busted hot tub and my sister was beside me, counting.

AFTER, Mom ran the rock shop and sent us both to kindergarten at the trailer school—a dozen students in a single-wide trailer, grades K through six in one room, seven through twelve in the other, two bathrooms in between. It was early for Lise and she clung to me until we twinned. Our classmates, white boys and a husky Indian named Winston, liked to catalog our likenesses: same hair, same eyes, same laugh, same voice. Only our sizes were different. Was Lise a little little or was it me a little fat?

Winston was not good at reading. Something had happened to him as a baby and it made him slow, his voice hoarse. Sometimes our teacher would hit him across the face with his reading textbook. This was 1990. I had a bad singing voice too. For this reason Winston and I were put together in a closet at music time, the door cracked so we could hear the others sing. The crack let a little light in. It caught Winston's top teeth, four silver ingots gleaming. I wanted them.

SISTERS IN THE BACK of the rock shop after school, coloring with highlighters, making happy birthday banners from dot matrix printer paper, bird's nest crowns with the shred bin. Mom is nicer to kids in the shop than she is to us, gives them TV rock or pyrite she never calls fool's gold. Outside we pick pomegranates and split them open on mining equipment or glaciers of talc with holes bored in from a long-ago drilling race. We build forts in the salt cedars, venture deeper into the mesquite groves and then, bravely and at the urging of an older girl, into the grasses, the alkali soil crunch underfoot. We watch out for rattlesnakes—for that river that is sometimes there and sometimes not.

Little twin, fat twin. Mom says we're sturdy stock, black Irish on our dad's side, crazy fairy folk, jockeys and alcoholics. From Mom's side came our freckles, bad vision, more alcoholism, more crazy.

It seemed we three were alone a long time, but it also felt immediate that we girls were no longer allowed to sleep in Mom's bed, not allowed the Mountain Dew or the Kraft singles not ours in the fridge, a hard hat and an Igloo lunch box on top. Her boyfriend Ron was sober, recently released from prison, an apprentice in the carpenters' union. They met at an AA meeting. He built parking garages for casinos in Vegas and needed to be closer to his jobsites. We moved to Trout Canyon, a wrinkle on the west-facing slopes of the Spring Mountains ("Las Vegas's sleeping porch," Caruthers called them), where my father's parents owned a one-bedroom cabin.

Trout Canyon was a spooky, sensual place, the plot steep, rocky and alive with wild juniper, cherry and apricot trees, blackberry brambles climbing the chain-link. At the bottom of the property, near the dirt road that came up the mountain, sat a slimy pond ringed by weeping willows. Ponderosa pines sticky with sap, a patch of lamb's ear I liked to walk on with bare feet. Inside the cabin, between two stones in the fireplace, was a secret door. When we opened it a tiny animal skull peered out at us, something with teeth. In Trout Canyon I told my mother that all I wanted was for us to be normal, a normal family.

She said, Oh honey, there's no such thing.

I would have liked to stay in Trout Canyon forever, but it didn't belong to us. We moved again, down the mountains to the valley floor to Pahrump, an unincorporated smattering of innumerable Libertarian retirees who refused the census, its northern boundary Yucca Mountain, its southernmost point a dry lake bed rimmed with two legal brothels and a commercial military-grade artillery range where you could shoot bazookas. On a clear night, from the front door of our wood-paneled double-wide on the north end of the valley, we could see the lights of Vegas over the range, our neon aurora borealis.

At the bus stop on the first day of second grade, Lise and I met our first best friends, Ty and Kevin Chen, real twins who looked nothing alike. If they were twins, we were twins, we all agreed. The Chens' dad was dead too. The four of us made an elaborate fort near the bus stop, a tumbleweed midden surrounded by a labyrinth of trails through the sagebrush. Me and Lise and Ty and Kevin were in the fort early mornings well before the school bus came and after school until dark. We were in the fort all weekend, unless we were breaking into houses with Mom.

She'd read the real estate listings in the newspaper, copy down the addresses of the listings that interested her, and we'd head out. These were boom times in southern Nevada, so many houses being built, stucco and drywall on bare desert lots off unpaved roads, no trees or sidewalks or city water. And best of all: no neighbors. Mom liked her space. There was no worse slur she could sling at a house than "too close to the road." She was not quite a hermit but easily a misanthrope. She liked to see people coming a mile away, alerted by a dust plume billowing across the valley.

If a house was not too close to the road, we entered in various ways. The front door was sometimes unlocked, or the garage door. We rolled it open and ducked under. More often Lise, runty and cunning, slid through the doggie door and let us in. Mom could pop a screen in seconds, so sometimes Lise went in through a window. Or we came through the front door: one of the local realtors used the same code for the digital locks on all her listings and never changed it, so that was worth a try. We walked around the house, picking out our rooms, enjoying the way our voices bounced.

Mom went to the kitchen sink and held her fingers under the water, sensing the pressure, timing how long it took to warm up, feeling how hard it was, looking through the window for the mountains.

She discussed with us the carpet decisions, the tile decisions, the drywall job, the foundation. We shut ourselves in the walk-in closets, opened and closed all cabinets, fridges, sliding glass doors and blinds. Lise and I fantasized aloud about what colors we'd paint our rooms. Mom fantasized about central air and skylights. Once, we all three lay in a dry Jacuzzi tub and sang. Then we left everything more or less as we had found it and drove home across the desert, briefly invigorated by the lives we might live.

It was around this time that Mom took Lise and me to Outback Steakhouse and announced she was going to have another baby. We ate a Bloomin' Onion and watched her cry.

My mother lived by her own code, something like: you won't see it all if you don't trespass a little. She had little regard for the concept of private property, but after her third baby was born—and with help from G-ma Mary Lou, who tapped her pension from Caesars—Mom and Ron bought land in Pahrump: three and a half acres shaped like Nevada, mostly mesquite with a beautiful big cottonwood shuddering at the tip. Mom customized a double-wide for the property and we were there the day its two halves were trucked in.

MY MOTHER'S CAREER was a bit of a con. She didn't graduate from high school and had no formal education in museum studies, yet she expanded the rock shop into the Shoshone Museum. She was a self-taught historian—meaning she read a lot—and learned photography in the basement darkrooms of the Strip. My father had taught her a little about mining and lapidary work, and she taught herself a lot more. She began to make her own jewelry and sell it at the museum and at gem shows. She was an artist, a naturalist, a writer, though she never used those words.

At some point she stopped taking pictures. I know she did not always love being a mother. She loved her garden and smoking and work. When she got home we were not to ask her any questions for an hour. She wanted, more than anything, to be left alone in her garden on unpaved Lola Lane, bordered by open desert and alfalfa fields. She cultivated the property with a technique known by the family euphemism "view it at night," a specific subset of theft, typically the stealing of landscaping elements from a corporation by cover of darkness. She might say, "They just put century plants in in Summerlin. Perhaps we should view them at night," and in no time we'd uproot a few ornamental agaves from the freshly landscaped median and take them home. She might back up her Bronco over a new curb and load it with baby date trees waiting to be plugged into the sod lawns of an unfinished subdivision. She might, with Ron's help, roll expensive decorative boulders from the outer banks of the parking lot of a union-busting casino and into my dad's old truck. She might persuade Ron to spend his weekend digging her a pond then stock it with lily pads and koi skimmed from a golf course water feature. In this manner the Lola property bloomed. Frogs moved into the pond with an elusive turtle we got from the fair and never saw again, only heard plopping himself into the water when we opened the front door first thing in the morning.

Other wonders appeared. A bench swing in a grove of screwbean mesquite, their curly-fry seedpods falling silently into a bed of mint. A fence, a deck, a patio off the master bedroom shaded by climbing roses. Dogs from the pound to keep Spike company: a Rottweiler we named Vash after Captain Picard's girlfriend and a lunkhead golden retriever I got to name Oberon because I was just back from Shakespeare camp and Mom had missed me.

One day, driving on the ribbon of highway between Tecopa and Shoshone, we passed a house that Mom knew to be vacant. We stopped to take a look. Behind the house we saw a pen, and in it two donkeys, one iconic brown with a black cross of Bethlehem on its back and a bristly Mohawk mane, the other entirely white, an albino.

I didn't even notice the animals' ribs or the empty trough turned over in their pen, but as we drove away, Lise began to howl. She didn't stop until Mom borrowed her sponsor's horse trailer and we took the donkeys home. Around this time and in a similar manner our household came into a gigantic potbellied pig. Lise named him Wilbur and almost as quickly came home from school to find him killed and partly eaten by Vash. It was not Vash's fault, Mom said. She was made that way.

The donkeys fared better than Wilbur. Ron built them a corral and we fed them sheafs of alfalfa from the farm at the end of the road. Not long after their arrival Lise and I took the brown one—mine, Buckwheat—out into the desert for a ride, playing Mormons. Her donkey, the albino, was skittish and mistrustful and would not tolerate mounting. As we circled back, a strange sound echoed into Deseret, a keening. The white donkey, braying for her brother. The moment she caught sight of him, she tried to jump the corral. But she was tired, malnourished, afraid. We could see all this in her eyes as she writhed on the corral, stuck, her hooves screeching on the iron bars and sending up sparks. That's how Spark got her name.

You must remember that this was real. Real hooves, real sparks.

Mom and Ron got married in the garden of the Lola house on Super Bowl Sunday. They served sub sandwiches from the Blimpie inside Terrible's Town. The men watched the game during the reception. Lise and I jumped on the trampoline with our cousin Darren, sailing high over the garden, our sunflowers, ice plant, water lilies, roses, much of it viewed at night, though some of Mom's acquisitions had occurred in broad daylight. I leapt into the air, spying on my mother in her garden. Her shoulders were wrapped in creamy lace—a curtain she'd transformed for the day into a gauzy shawl—and her hair shone in the sun like some new metal. She was surrounded by women she loved and who loved her. She was holding her baby. When the vows came she had assented to every word save one.

Obey.

MY MOTHER NEVER got to make everything she wanted to make, to build even a fraction of what she wanted to build. Still, she built a lot. When she learned that a fantastically preserved skeleton of a woolly mammoth had been dug up from the bed of the Amargosa near Tecopa and taken north, she convinced Sonoma State to give it back. She built—well, Ron and some of his AA buddies *built* but Mom fundraised, lobbied, agitated into existence—a one-room wing on the back of the Shoshone Museum to house the mammoth. Then she took us to Sonoma to get him.

He was on display in the sunny atrium of some sciences building, presented as he'd been found, lying on his side with his ribs arched skyward, his spectacular tusks unfurled in the mud. Mom and Ron dismantled the display, wrapping the mammoth bones in moving blankets and sleeping bags we'd brought from home. It was not unlike viewing things at night, except for the graduate students helping under the direction of Kathy, a geology professor my mother had gotten to know during the repatriation negotiations. Kathy was boyish, not married. She and Mom had something between them, something I wanted the way I'd wanted Winston's silver ingot teeth. But my job was to look after baby Lyn, just learning to walk. I spent mammoth moving day with baby fingers in mine, watching Lyn bumble back and forth across the lawns of Sonoma State in bare feet, the grass's giving softness a magic to me, as well the wide fronds offering shade in a courtyard, the ancient trees and the birdsong everywhere—all of it became on that day the smooth cool lush shelter I would ever after attach to the word *campus*.

MOM WANTED A REAL HOUSE. She said so on our early morning runs down Lola Lane. Past the cottonwood where the gravel road went dirt, then right on the ranch road, irrigation ditch and alfalfa fields on one side, wild desert on the other. I held a knob of silvery cottonwood as a marker and dropped it when we slowed to a walk, so that each morning we ran a little farther, deeper into the alfalfa fields, toward the dairy.

She was done living in trailers, she huffed, even a trailer called a *manufactured home*, even a double-wide on acreage with an apron of cinder blocks obscuring its wheels, even a trailer with a pond.

We moved into a house on Navajo Road, in the Indian streets on the southernmost end of the valley. Navajo, Paiute, Savoy, Comanche,

Pawnee, Cheyenne branching off Homestead Road with two brothels down on the end of Homestead, the Chicken Ranch and Sheri's. I learned to parallel park at Sheri's, which boasted one of the few curbs in town. The other option was the Mormon church, but my mom refused to set foot there. My school bus had passed the brothels every morning and afternoon, turning around in the Sheri's parking lot. It was a moment I waited for, that slow view of the Chicken Ranch—stick-built, painted hot pink and baby blue, gingerbread embellishments and dormer windows, a white picket fence. I wanted to live there.

But I lived with Mom and Ron and Lise and Lyn in Pahrump in the Navajo house, stick-built, two stories in the style Mom called Cape Cod. Cape Cod was not a place any of us knew or wanted to know. Whatever the Navajo house was supposed to be it was clearly not. Something was badly off in the proportions. Everything seemed to change for the worse the day we moved in. In fact I came to consider the Navajo house cursed. It had no insulation, it had a pigeon infestation. Pigeons fucking day and night, Mom's words. Evenings she sat outside in a lawn chair with a pellet gun, smoking cigarettes and picking them off. Spike got the carcasses and did his thing with them.

Spike died of old age in the Navajo house with his head in my lap on the floor in front of the bookcase, an institutional metal rig my mother had coated in FlexStone, a mainstay of her decor repertoire. The bookcase was crammed with what seemed like every kind of book, one whole glorious wall arranged in no order and by no rule except to keep the encyclopedia sets together. *Encyclopedia of Rocks and Minerals, Encyclopedia of the Supernatural, Encyclopedia of Greek*

Myth. I ransacked this shelf one summer when all I did was work and read and tan. Out on the blazing trampoline I read Zane Grey, field guides to rocks, addiction memoirs, second-wave feminist manifestos, N. Scott Momaday and Tony Hillerman. Orwell's essays plus *1984* and *Animal Farm*, which I thought was about an animal farm. I reread my old Goosebumps and Boxcar Children and Updike's *The Witches of Eastwick*. I read *Cadillac Desert* and *Silent Spring* and several anthologies of local color and Manifest Destiny propaganda. I read the *Pahrump Valley Times* every day starting with Sports, looking for pictures of hot boys playing anything. I read the clippings from the *Amargosa News and Views* in my mother's dusty portfolio, her short-lived column of plainspoken Caruthers-style pieces about zany desert folk, half of them dogs. I read her letters to the editor about chemtrails and Yucca Mountain and domestic violence.

We buried Spike in the backyard.

We watched a lot of VH1.

G-ma Mary Lou bought Lise a porcelain doll and Lise was too gracious about it so G-ma kept buying them, *collector's items* she said of what even we knew was daytime TV junk, Kewpies and Precious Moments and a themed doll for every holiday. Lise's room filled with smooth glass heads with curls painted on, drowsy eyelashes and deathless plastic eyeballs. She stopped sleeping, got into feng shui, broke the bad news. Our front and back doors were perfectly aligned, inviting the worst kind of energy. The stairs were positioned in such a way that they shot all our blessings right out the front door.

Too hot upstairs, too cold down. Old pink-gray carpet downstairs with a threadbare trench leading to the bathroom. One morning Mom woke me before dawn. She was watering the downstairs carpet, that smoker's-lung color against the green garden hose. "Get dressed," she said, "I'm scamming the insurance company and I need your help."

The scam worked! We got new carpet. But the trench came back. Nicotine stained the walls, stamps of white when you took a picture down. Off acoustics. High ceilings paneled in pine so sound couldn't find a clear path. No one could hear anyone, ever, nor the phone ringing, so by the time you got someone's attention you were already screaming.

Bad vibes indeed and these confirmed for me that we'd always be two families, two houses. The Tecopa house and the Navajo house. One family of four, one family of five. We—my mother, Lise and I—missed the Tecopa house as we missed my dad. Grief was a river running under the three of us, all but invisible to Ron and Lyn. We couldn't help it. We longed for Tecopa, each in our own way, my mother's mostly private. I only ever saw it out the corner of my eye. Between Pahrump, Tecopa and Malibu I tried to triangulate who my father had been. I developed various small, secret fantasies about him meeting boys I liked or walking me down the aisle. At night he might speak to me through my stomach gurgles. If I prayed, I prayed to him.

I said, *Dad, I wish you were here. I need you.*

Or, later, *Dad, I wish you were here. Mom needs you.*

DARKNESS DESCENDED on the Navajo house. One by one, we each became deeply unhappy there. Mom had lost Spike and a bunch of other people. Cancer, mostly, and suicide. She was sick all the time. I became an angry, overachieving teenager completely obsessed with one cruel boy after the other—the worse he treated me, the better.

Lise and her born-again boyfriend lost their virginity to each other and then the boyfriend asked Jesus to give his back. Lyn had lava dreams, wrote a report on Martin Luther King Jr. winning the Nobel Peas Prize. Ron left the house at four each morning to drive to job-sites in Vegas. For breakfast Lise made him horchata rice cooked mushy with butter, sugar and cinnamon. He got home a few minutes before dinner, sat speckled with concrete at the table and nodded off while we ate Mom's Marie Callender's or Hamburger Help Me. After dinner Ron showered then collapsed in his recliner upstairs in the den and we all watched TV. Some nights he stayed downstairs on the computer. He got deep into Age of Empires. We all got deep into *X-Files* and *Coast to Coast AM*. Art Bell lived and broadcast from a few dirt lots away. Our desktop computer helped NASA look for UFOs. Mom monitored the Test Site and Yucca Mountain and Area 51. Aliens, lunatics with guns, cancer clusters. What was crazy about any of it? Lise and I were taught to identify chemtrails by the distinct pattern and pacing of their dispersing tail. Sometimes we were not allowed to play outside because, Mom whispered, *They're spraying*. Her belief was blinding, too bright to behold. We started looking at her only through the big picture window. There, she stalked across the front yard in her nightgown, camera raised to the midday sky.

THE NAVAJO HOUSE had a few rules. We could not say *shut up*. We could not call someone stupid. We could not say *I can't*. We could not answer the phone during dinner and never if the caller ID said UN-KNOWN. All mail went unopened into a drawer by the back door and that drawer was never otherwise opened. If someone came to the door we were to sic the dogs on them.

Her hands began to shake there. One Christmas I waited downstairs at the picture window for a boyfriend to pick me up. While I waited, Mom's reflection said nonsense things to me, silly things she seemed to know were funny though not why. She amused and frightened me.

I suppose she must have been in a great deal of pain—even now I struggle to simply say: she was hurting. Struggle to say: she was sick.

Many evenings of my childhood were spent in the common areas of twelve-step clubs; many weekends passed at AA picnics or round-ups. I have sat in open meetings and eavesdropped on closed ones. Miles and miles of lonesome desert road has folded beneath my mother, my sister and me as we listened to rock bottom stories on tape. I have read the literature. I have attended my fair share of Al-Anon meetings. Addiction is one of those concepts I cannot recall ever learning. A notion I seem to have been born knowing. Words my mother had been taught to say too late. She'd had to learn for herself, and told us when and where and how she'd learned, was learning. She told vague stories about the years she drank, gestured to things she'd done to us when we were little, described Lise protecting me, me protecting Lise, shameful incidents neither of us girls remembered but which our mother confessed to anyway. AA was as close to a church as our family would ever get. My mom was careful to never say she *was* an alcoholic or *used to be*. I ached for her to say it—the present tense frightened me. For years she had cigarettes, coffee, work, gardening, building, making jewelry, making dinner. She was never still. She never played. I asked her often how come if people replaced one addiction with another, like she said, she couldn't just get addicted to playing. That's not how it works, she said. You can't get addicted to anything that's good for you.

She kept a rainbow of chips in her jewelry box, sobriety medallions in every gleaming color commemorating days then months then years. I was allowed to touch them but never to remove them. I often opened the jewelry box to stroke them. I liked how they stacked up, how they slid. They called to me, budding kleptomaniac, but I never took them. All I knew for sure as a girl was that if my mother wasn't sober, my sisters and I would be the kids in those rock bottom stories: lost, taken or dead.

Today I know even less. I don't understand her at all. I can't. She is a void. She goes suddenly very still. Hurting all over, she said, and no one could say why. No one believed her, she said, and she was right. Too late, they diagnosed her Lyme disease. A tick had bitten her in Sonoma, she thought she remembered, while she was getting the mammoth. She was given OxyContin for her chronic pain.

Soon, with help from the internet, she became her own doctor.

She quit the museum or was fired, we didn't know which. I read the accusations in the paper. She took the money but only as a loan, she said, and what she took was nothing compared to what she was owed.

The Navajo house filled with rocks and bore down on us, that stick-built house with a brick-and-mortar mortgage. Cigarette burns opened like eyes on the blankets and cushions and on the couch where she watched *Star Trek: The Next Generation*, *The X-Files*, *Law & Order*.

We watched her fall asleep with cigarettes smoldering between her fingers. I remember my dad almost burned alive in the van. We developed a technique of intervening at the fabric's first singe but not before, for if she woke she'd accuse us of overreacting, and without a burn hole we'd have no evidence to the contrary.

On her arms were morphine patches and on her nightstand a mortar and pestle so she could grind her Oxy and snort it. Many mornings she did not wake up and some she could not wake up. Once she took so many pills that she passed out before she could swallow them all. She still had them on her tongue when we found her, in various stages of dissolve.

Lise and I took turns on those mornings. One sister walked Lyn down the road to a friend's house, asked Lyn's friend's mother to make sure Lyn got on her bus, then this sister boarded her own bus for high school.

The other sister waited at home for the ambulance. She greeted the EMTs. One of the EMTs was a few years older than me. Sometimes I ran into him at parties, sitting around a fire on old tires or tailgates, he and I usually the only ones not chugging Robitussin. He never acknowledged that he'd carried my mother naked on a stretcher down our bad energy stairs on more than one occasion.

(How many occasions?)

So many I lost count. So many the emergency wore off. Waiting for the ambulance was the worst job, and Lise and I bickered bitterly about who would do it, who had a test in first period, who had too many absences, whose teacher was more lenient and whose was a hard-ass. I often won. My first period was Drama 2 and I got a scholarship to Shakespeare camp. Lise's was Algebra and she failed it. I took Drama, Anatomy & Physiology, Civics, AP English. I was on the yearbook committee and put so many pictures of myself in it that the class of 2002 called it the Claire Bitch Project. Lise got held back, needed glasses but no one noticed. She skipped class for the darkroom. I skipped class for Dance Dance Revolution at Mountain View

Casino and Bowl. My seasons were volleyball, basketball, plays, work. I answered phones at Domino's Pizza, lifeguarded and taught swim lessons at the public pool. I read at work and through various boyfriends' band practice. When I turned sixteen I was given my mom's 1970 orange Volkswagen Beetle.

Lise stayed home and basically raised Lyn. She read the *Golden Compass* trilogy and the Encarta encyclopedia and watched *Pop-Up Video*. She mastered first the SNES, then PrimeStar and finally dial-up. She barely graduated from high school.

I graduated easily but could not afford college. Ron had been slipping large portions of his paychecks into slot machines, I deduced after he finally agreed to fill out his portion of the FAFSA. The spring my classmates spent saving up to move out or dropping out to have their babies, I spent having risky sex with dullards and overexercising, baffled on the treadmill at how my stepfather's tax returns could tally up to over a hundred thousand dollars per year and yet every day at lunch one of my girlfriends loaned me two of her five dollars so I could buy Pizza Hut breadsticks or a seven-layer burrito. The mail drawer overflowed with envelopes that went white yellow pink. The phone rang and rang and we did not answer for the caller ID always said UNKNOWN.

MOM CALLED her overdoses *accidents*. I let myself believe her. Lise didn't, couldn't. But Lise wasn't unkind with her wisdom, allowed me my denial. So many years before, when our father was dying, Lise had been the one to tell me what dying meant. It's my first memory. She explained impermanence gently but exhaustively when I came up for air in the busted hot tub, so perhaps she thought she needn't explain it again. Still, it's a concept I struggle with.

I moved to LA, into an apartment with my cousins. Lise stayed behind in Pahrump with Lyn. That's when, Lise says, the wheels came off.

Mom made more trips into Las Vegas to get pills from her sister. On one of these trips she totaled her car by driving it off an on-ramp. Lyn was in the car. Years later, we found out it was Lyn driving. Lyn would have been ten.

After the accident, Mom took Lyn. They disappeared for six days. When she came back, out of money, Mom said they'd been in Utah taking a friend to a doctor's appointment, that she had wanted to show Lyn Utah, that it was none of our beeswax where she was she was a free woman.

She took out a restraining order against Ron and he took one out on her. He was at work the day the deputies served it, forcing Mom out of the Navajo house. She took Lyn with her. Lise was seventeen and could do what she wanted, Mom said. But Lise, who knew her capable of any insane thing, went with her, to protect Lyn.

Somehow Mom convinced someone to rent her a house, though she had no job, no money, bad credit. I doubt she even had a bank account at this point. But she was smart, knew how to manipulate the dirt farmers, as she called the men in our town. She told a landlord that she was being beaten by our stepfather. I don't know that she wasn't, but I never saw him hit her or be violent with any person. What I did see was my mother hurt herself, often and not always by accident. She would pass out on the toilet and fall face-first into the sink or throw herself down the stairs. In this manner she had broken her nose many times and the blood vessels there seemed permanently open, her nose squished and pink and blooming. It would not have been difficult for her to convince a landlord that she needed a place immediately, a battered woman and her girls. If you knew my mother you'd know it would not have been difficult for her to convince a man to let her live for weeks and weeks without paying him anything. This would have been a kind of sport for her, she who enjoyed a well-crafted scam, swiped letterhead and stationery wherever she went, who always said you could never have too many death certificates on hand. (At the time I was paying part of my rent in Mar Vista with fraudulently extended Social Security checks, survivor's benefits from my father that would have expired on my eighteenth birthday if my mother had not used my letters of recommendation to forge documentation to extend them for another year—my graduation present.) So while it isn't at all difficult for me to see how she got into the rental, I still find myself fixating on this figure: the landlord. Maybe he represents a sort of valve that might have closed, preventing everything that happened, after.

I WAS IN LA working as a roller girl at the Puma store on the Third Street Promenade, discovering yoga and Al-Anon, failing to learn to surf, taking English 101 at the community college and falling in love with California's legendary weed. One night, a Sunday, on my fifteen I used a calling card to call the Navajo house looking for Lyn and Lise. Ron told me Mom had taken them.

Where?

He didn't know.

How long had they been gone?

Almost a month.

The next day I called my old high school and the receptionist said Lise hadn't been there in three weeks. Lyn's elementary school said longer.

I'd like to say I started packing. No one knew where my sisters were. I'd like to say I went home to find them. If it happened now I would get in my car and scream across the country and drive up and down every road in Pahrump kicking in every door until I found them. But this was my mother. I loved her and she loved me, loved us. I was eighteen years old, a roller girl at the Puma store. Their disappearance was somehow the Fates, the natural and inevitable culmination of all the accusations and secrets and blood, so the situation seemed somehow inevitable, maybe okay. I could not say to myself: she is a drug addict and she has kidnapped your siblings. It was that and it wasn't. I did not drive home to the Navajo house. I did not go looking for them. I had class in the morning. I had to wake up early to find free parking close to campus. I had to finish *Heart of Darkness*.

IN THE RENTAL Lise and Lyn slept together on a mattress on the floor, Lise stroking Lyn's hair to get her to sleep. Lyn was in the third grade. Lise was a senior in high school. The rental was a two-bedroom duplex. Mom had her own room. Before she left for school, Lise told Lyn, *Do not go in there.* Lyn begged Lise not to go to school. Lise stayed as often as she could without dropping out. There was no food except what Lise's boyfriend brought from a gas station. Lise made sure they kept their shoes near.

One night, Mom passed out and Lise took Lyn's hand and whispered that she was to run and not to stop. Even if you get scared, she said. Together they ran into the desert night. It was dark. They stumbled over bushes and rocks. Lise pulled Lyn and together they ran toward the glowing neon tubes of the Mountain View Casino and Bowl.

Lise's boyfriend had snuck her a calling card. Trembling at a pay phone in the vestibule of the casino, she used it. She had to be quick, had to make the call before a security guard came and said *you kids can't be in here without a parent*. Lise called Ron and he cried and said where were they and to wait. They waited between two sets of black-tinted glass double doors, hoping security wouldn't come. They did not know whether Mom had woken up, and if she had, whether she would beat Ron to Mountain View. The slots chimed. Maybe some of their classmates were inside, bowling. If it was a Saturday the fluorescent lights would have been off, the black lights on, disco balls and rainbow lasers spinning crazily at a ritual we called cosmic. If it was a Thursday it would have been league night, every lane full. If it was a Tuesday it would be youth league, where in another life Lise and I had bowled on a team called Bob's Corner Store in identical royal blue T-shirts with pins screen-printed across the back. Lise found these shirts stuffed in a drawer at the Navajo house the night Ron brought them back. She and Lyn slept in them.

MOM WAS SOON EVICTED from the rental. She moved somewhere with some man none of us knew and shortly thereafter went to jail. The Navajo house was repossessed. Ron, Lise and Lyn moved into a double-wide trailer on Mesquite Avenue. When Mom got out of jail, she joined them.

We always took her back. We always believed her (insofar as we were capable of belief) when she said she was sorry, that she would get better. There was another stay in rehab, a place in the mountains, as Lise described it—I never went. I came back from LA for the summer. For a few weeks we all lived together one last time in the trailer on Mesquite. Mom and I fought; Lise and I fought. I bullied her, but she rarely got angry. When she did it seemed involuntary, a spasm, mostly physical, like a crack went through her and her limbs spazzed out and one of them, her arm, her hand, grabbed a knife from the wood block and threw it at me.

The morning after Lise graduated from high school she moved to San Francisco for art school. She left before the sun came up. Only Lyn and I saw her off—Ron was already at work and Mom was not getting up. The dawn was violet. Lise threw two garbage bags of clothes into the bed of her boyfriend's truck, ready to put some miles between her and all these houses. I was leaving again in a few weeks.

Lyn held Lise and asked her not to go. "Please," she said. She was eleven. "Please don't leave me."

What could Lise have said if not what she did say, the most humane and honest thing she *could* say?

"Get *off* me."

Lise remembers it violent but I heard the gentlest mercy. I remember she said it and it soared: *Get off me.* As in, *You cannot be on me because you are on your own.*

ONE WAY TO SAY all this is, My mother was an opioid addict and she overdosed.

Another way is, My mother was suicidal and she killed herself.

Another way is, My mother was poor and ignored, dismissed, called hysterical and hypochondriac by doctors who believed instead their well-paid colleagues who spoke on behalf of Purdue Pharma, believed the FDA who renewed and renewed Purdue's patent, and so despite her history of addiction, despite the fact that she was in recovery, that she had all those years sober, that she did not even have bananas flambé on Mother's Day, her doctors put her on legal and extremely profitable heroin.

Another way is, Medicine tossed her to the Sacklers and they sucked her dry, destroyed her and everyone around her, and blamed her for it.

Another way is, She needed help and no one gave it to her.

Another way is, She had her mother's pain swimming in her blood and her mother's and her mother's and her mother's and she was fat with it.

Mom always said Lise got her Dutch parts. I got our dad's fun Irish, his mean English. We both got the crazy because it came from both sides. She said we three girls had the same hands, artist hands. She taught us jewelry making, photography, breaking and entering. To scavenge and build and refurbish, to scam and steal and to bullshit. She taught us names of plants and rocks and the names of every part of our body. She taught us where the water came from. She died the way the Amargosa River dies, not so far from where it was born. Her whole life passed in the dusty outposts along the Old Spanish Trail. I see them now from above: Las Vegas, Tecopa, Trout Canyon, Pahrump, the dry and indifferent town where she died on the couch, or possibly on the floor in front of the couch, in the living room of a trailer too close to the road.

Her roads were Fairway and Tropicana, Stampmill, Lola, Navajo and Mesquite, where Ron and Lyn found her. Lyn was thirteen.

In the trailer when they found her: dozens of try-on eyeglasses from Walmart with the anti-theft sensors still on. A pack of six mail-order self-help cassettes about depression, tape number two missing, found later in the boom box in the bathroom. Books I had read in college and passed along, telling myself they would cure her. *The House on Mango Street* and *Love Medicine*. Every episode of *Star Trek: The Next Generation* on VHS, every episode of *The X-Files*. In a dish on her dresser a coin stamped *PAUL LOVES MARTHA, Disneyland, 1989* and a bb chain looped through a plastic fob with Lyn's school picture on it.

In the trailer when they found her: a hole where the flooring in front of the front door had rotted away from beneath, covered with carpet badly sagged and torn in one corner where many over the years had tripped. My first love fell in this hole once, rolled his ankle pretty bad. We are not a subtle people. This was the last time I saw her. She got him some ice. He tuned her guitar. She looked good. The trailer was clean. She had plants.

In the trailer when they found her: a dark stain on the living room carpet.

A couch with many eyes burned in.

An answering machine with no daughter's voice on it.

Plants in the bathtub. She must have watered them right before.

If It Isn't Grown
It Has to Be Mined

My plane touched down with a screechy jolt, pop rocks of wifi dopamine vanishing all these ghosts. One of the white boys from the trailer school had messaged me.

You prob know no one is living in your house anymore, he began. It took me a moment to know he meant the Tecopa house. After we moved to Pahrump my mom had rented it to an elderly Timbisha woman named Nadine for a hundred dollars a month, money Mom spent on gas, cigs and ice cream. At my mother's lurching funeral, held in a Quonset hut, Nadine had asked where she should send her rent. Lise was living in San Francisco, and I was moving every year, always in August, to another apartment or another college in another city or to live with another man. Neither of us had much of an address. And then there were the Paiutes scalped by Kit Carson in Tecopa in 1844, the one thousand and thirty-two nuclear bombs detonated on and in Newe Sogobia between 1951 and 1992. One hundred dollars a month seemed like a small price to pay to alleviate our white guilt. Lise and I told Nadine she could live in the Tecopa house as long as she liked for free, on condition that we be permitted to visit the garden there, where our mother had scattered our father's ashes and where we would scatter hers.

I wanted to be some kind of filial for once, bring some sort of serenity to someone. It had brought me genuine comfort since then to imagine Nadine living rent-free in the peaceful seclusion of the Tecopa house for all her years. But now I learned that Nadine had relocated to San Diego some time ago, to be with her sister. She had moved her body and belongings freely to the sea without regard for my white savior fantasies. I was nobody's savior, for in the years since my mother's death I'd unearthed no title, deed or mortgage, nothing in the way of paperwork demonstrating any ownership of the Tecopa house. If my father had pulled off another gold record swap, it went unrecorded in the ledgers of Independence, the county seat some two hundred miles away. There the property belonged to the federal government and always had. Squatters, I suppose that made us, nested squatters within the Great Squat.

BLM says if no one's living at the Watkins ranch they're going to tear it down, my classmate wrote. He needed a place to live and wanted my permission to move in. Although the permission was not mine to give, I refused him. I told him that *the Watkins ranch* did not belong to my family, had never belonged to my family, was *public land*, a place no one could live on or own but anyone could visit. I added that in my opinion my parents would have been happy to see the property restored to the commons and thereby contribute to the preservation of our beautiful desert, a place itself stolen. (This despite the fact that my mother considered the Desert Protection Act a land grab and Dianne Feinstein a carpetbagger.) If Nadine living at the Watkins ranch for free was an act of decolonization (a notion I secretly entertained), then the prospect of my white former classmate moving in on what turned out to be BLM land had I guess a Bundy vibe for me. I was suspicious of the boy though for no better reason than that he'd stayed. His social media phantoms suggested he rode dirt bikes, wrecked one, had no insurance and no car. These details could be wrong—in truth I had long ago erased this person from my feed because the occasional yowls from his difficult life interfered ever so slightly with me enjoying my comfortable one.

Anyway! that's how I came to learn that the so-called Watkins ranch was empty and awaiting demolition by the federal government. I thought, absurdly: What about the bobcat? What about the voles? I saw my father's spring run dry, the cane grass dead, the stone chimney rubbled. I saw the garden scraped away. I should have thought: Lise, who lived not far from Tecopa now, in Las Vegas, and would want to know. Deserved to know—our parents' ashes were there. But if Lise knew she would want to do something about it, and this I could not bear.

Besides, I reasoned, the informal demolition of the house was doubtless already under way. Rocks smashed through windows and the swimmy glass of the greenhouse. The warped green linoleum peeled up in strips. The chimney toppled. They'd spray-paint the place, tag it, shoot it up, burn it down. People do these things to desert ruins and I don't blame them. They tug us.

Consumed by my feed, I gathered my things, waited my turn, moved down the aisle, through the jet bridge and the terminal, lifting my head finally where the exit used to be. Instead, a bighorn sheep stood before me, glass-eyed and gray on some fiberglass rocks. A stuffed black bear reached eternally for a beehive like birchbark nearby. I turned around and tried the opposite direction. A mannequin in a hard hat reminded me *If it isn't grown it has to be mined!*

It appeared I was trapped in the airport of a city where I'd once lived. I passed a classy McDonald's and a pub planked in reclaimed barnwood encouraging diners to *Ski in, ski out!* Slot machines went *ping ping ping.* Jesus pizza, how I'd missed them! Following a stream of purposeful-looking people, I finally came upon the exit: a frosted glass door with a severely highlighted sign warning that reentry was impossible beyond this point. Yet it was through this very point that I reentered the city of Reno, which was, for me, reentering the past.

Ty Chen, my oldest friend, was to meet me at baggage claim. Ty had been valedictorian of our high school, not exactly a feat in a rural Nevada county whose cultural resources include Yucca Mountain, Area 51, sundry abandoned mines, and a clown-themed motel oft featured on listicles like "12 Real Haunted Hotels That Should Not Exist!!!" Ty's overachieving and my friendly rivalry with him—a rivalry he hardly noticed except in AP Lit, where my essays were always xeroxed and distributed as exemplar—ended with both of us getting full rides to either Nevada university from a soon-to-be sabotaged slush fund the state created with the settlement from a major lawsuit against the tobacco companies on behalf of us Nevada children who enjoyed so much secondhand smoke while growing up, to say nothing of our cancer-dead parents.

Ty went to UNR right away. I spent a year in Los Angeles while my mother downspiraled, then I followed Ty and my boyfriend to Reno. We three shared a carriage house on Lake Street with two other roommates, lovebirds called Rust and Ivy. In fact, we were all in love with each other in different configurations and durations and to varying degrees of intensity and, very rarely, consummation. I don't want to get into the weeds here. Anyway, that was the college group, the five of us within a wider assembly of first-generation country mice, white trash would-be artists and musicians, emo Basques from Elko with radio shows and columns in the paper, snow bros whose parents insisted on college so they'd picked the one closest to Tahoe, metalhead dropouts who liked the pole and the hole, self-described alkies in combustible codependent relationships incinerated at every house show and rebuilt every industry night, for beyond all else what bonded us was our work, the tender and nostalgic upkeep of the city's decrepit casinos. Front of the house, back of the house, valet, buffet, hostess, cocktail waitress, concierge, sports book, dealers, all of us side by side with the lifers. Soon Ty would drive us north past the Hilton where I'd been a lifeguard, and just the memory of the shape of the building from the freeway, the silhouette of it against the tree-less hills, brought me the taste of the pink cake cubes demoted from the buffet to the employee cafeteria, and like a flavor my old, forgotten worry returned. Money, I mean. I remembered now the way I distinguished the economic strata of the old gang—I let myself think that phrase, going down the escalator to baggage claim, "the old gang"— you could afford to fuck up or you could not. Either you had parents waiting in the wings to remortgage their house for rehab, therapy, a gap year, or you were one DUI away from living under the bridge with the Juggalos.

Ivy could afford it. She had parents, rehab, backpacked through Tibet and married Rust. Ty and I moved away to our respective grad schools. Ty finished his PhD in mechanical engineering at Purdue, but instead of following the rest of his cohort into a lucrative life of tinkering to improve upon the horrors known as industry, he accepted a cushy post-doc in Boulder. He focused on various interests gone dormant while he'd been away from the West, among them psychotropics, backcountry skiing and the topknot. After Boulder, Ty moved back to Reno to work at Tesla. I published a coming-of-age novel set at the clown motel, swept the little kids' table at awards season and got a tenure-track job, the hardest thing I'd ever done and an accomplishment that meant next to nothing to the people I wanted to impress most in the whole world, namely Ty, Rust and Ivy.

I'd seen Ty here and there over the decade I'd been away—we'd get baked at a Friendsgiving in West Lafayette or he'd drive to Columbus to try to hook up with my friends at MFA parties—but I'd lost touch with Rust and Ivy completely. They had a bunch of babies now, the freshest not even a week old. Ty was taking me straight to them.

"What took you so long?" he asked.

I said, "There's more than one terminal now."

"Did you check a bag?"

"No, this is it"—I offered him my tote bag, unwieldy with my top-of-the-line Obamacare breast pump, ice packs, bottles, nipples, caps, power cord, water bottle, nipple pads, nipple butter, the old iPod I'd found alive at the bottom of a drawer that morning, headphones, wallet, phone, charger, toiletries, change of clothes, book and a pulverized granola bar.

"You got it," said Ty, not taking my bag. "Have you been crying?"

"I was watching something sad on the plane."

In truth I'd been experiencing uncontrollable spasms of grief since leaving that morning. All through the journey, on the first plane and the second, I'd absolutely lost it at the sight of any baby. Even a TV baby sent coursing through me a seizure of raw longing so severe that I had to stop and brace myself twice while walking through the airport.

"What were you watching?" Ty asked, uncharacteristically attentive. I must've looked puzzled or wobbly with feelings, some of them quite the opposite of suffering. "On the plane."

"HGTV," I told him truthfully. "One of these flipper couples had a baby."

Ty nodded. "A baby with flippers," he said. "That *is* sad."

It had been sort of lovely crying on the plane, or at least it was a relief not to have to deploy any of my standard crying camouflage techniques. On a plane, crying privately while watching a movie or reading a book didn't mean you were depressed or abandoning your family. Unfortunately, my first flight had lacked TVs, and I was traveling light on this overnight to Reno for an evening reading and a talk to some students in the morning before going home, room for only one book. So I'd had to open a copy of my own semi-new novel and cry into that. Embarrassing, yes, but also honestly kinda nice, because the book was not a smash and aside from being separated from my baby daughter indefinitely, aside from my heartbroken husband who knew I was seriously contemplating divorce, aside from my post-partum depression and the ring of teeth that had grown inside my vagina, it was the book that made me want to cry. I didn't feel like the person who wrote it. So there was a comforting symmetry at crying into my own disappointing pages, which in a way compensated for the embarrassment, so long as no one on the airplane matched me to my author photo on the back jacket. Lucky for me the photo had been taken when I was childless. In it I was so glowy that my hosts frequently assumed I was a vegan. I had been taken to so many salad bars and

71

vegan bakeries on book tour that I asked my speaking agent to include my indiscriminate eating habits in my contracts: *author is ethically omnivorous.*

So I did not worry about being recognized while weeping into my own novel, even with my fat face right up against my skinny face. These days I was a lot of things—an overweight and deeply ambivalent mother, a wunderkind burnout rethinking her impressive career, a white trash orphan spending her bourgeois salary with haste, deeply distracted by various dalliances about town and a serious so-called "emotional affair"—but I was no longer a glowy childless vegan.

In the car Ty announced that he was reading my book. "The new one. Reading the reviews, too. Do you read them?"

"Yes," I said. "But if anyone asks, no."

Ty observed that it was difficult to imagine a circumstance in which anyone would ask.

I said, "Let's talk about something else. How do you like being back in Reno?"

"I miss Boulder sometimes. Reno is rough."

I scoffed, an affectation I'd picked up. "Rough how?"

Ty sighed. "People here use so many plastic bags."

"The fact that a person coming from where we came from would be able to say something like that almost makes me believe in the meritocracy."

With that Ty and I launched into a retrospective on the violence that swirled like dust devils through our childhoods: hijacked school bus, Binion's gold, tweaker murders, busted his teeth out with a baseball bat, punched her in the stomach behind the bowling alley to get rid of it, the body of a fourteen-year-old stuffed into a beehive in a cottonwood. "That was my cottonwood!" I bragged, the one at the end of Lola Lane, where my mother and I once turned right into the alfalfa fields on our morning jogs.

"I don't know what they're thinking having another kid," I told Ty, changing the subject to Rust and Ivy. "I only have one and I'm losing my fucking mind. What did they name her? Gondolin?"

"Guinevere," said Ty. "Rust wanted something classic."

"Speaking of women's names," I said, "do you have any mary jane handy?"

Ty shook his head. "I don't roll dirty. You hard up?"

I said, "What 'roll dirty'? It's legal now."

"I know! Damn it feels good to be in the target demographic." He struck his steering wheel in triumph and spent some time on his prophecy that climate collapse would be reversed by Elon Musk and a northern hemisphere at last awash in psilocybin. "Anyway," he concluded, "we'll blaze it up with impunity after your reading."

I said, "Before would be ideal."

He raised an eyebrow. "Do you have, like, a problem?"

"It's not for the reading itself, just . . . the people after. They scrape me out."

"I think Rust has some old Burning Man weed at his house."

He took our exit, campus up the hill. We pulled up to Rust and Ivy's house, a funky gingerbread number with a dead lawn and two ancient cottonwoods rising from the easement. I got out of the car and watched a shirtless Baby Boomer in cutoff jean shorts with a harness around his junk ratchet himself up into one of the cottonwoods. Ivy came out barefoot with the newborn in her arms, looking thin and happy. She hugged me—tightly, intensely, maybe even desperately, I thought—but was that my desperation or hers? How much did she know about the mess I'd made? She presented me with her smush-faced, husky slice of a newborn.

"There's a man in your trees." I pointed by way of not accepting the child.

"It's my dad."

"Larry!" I waved up to him. "I didn't recognize you."

Larry waved disinterestedly.

"How did you get the pulley up there?" Ty called.

Larry said, "Slingshot," like it was a dumb question, and Ty nodded his engineer's approval.

"Where's Rust?" I asked.

Rust was inside, wearing a headset and playing a space war video game on their wall-size TV. He half hugged me, one eye on the screen. I heard men shouting in his ears. Joy, their oldest, sat shy in the corner beside a bookshelf. Cheddar bunnies and teething rings and laundry were strewn about, the smell of spit-up and Tucks wipes in the air. I steadied myself. When Joy was born, I'd texted. For their second, Eva, I'd bought but never mailed a twenty-four-month Beastie Boys onesie. Childless-person fuckery I planned to make up for now, kissing Joy and Eva and playing horsie with them. I took a photo of the new one sleeping on Ivy's chest, sent it to Theo, then posted up at the sink to pry apart plates cemented with oatmeal and cashew cheese.

"Do you believe that objects can bring you happiness?" Ivy called. "If you do, try our paper towel dispenser." I did, feeling the gentlest ticking as the paper product unfurled, a sound if not of forgiveness then at least of moral support. I went around the house collecting discarded nipple pads, wadded tissues, wipes and dirty diaper dumplings. Rust's game seemed to be petering out. Ivy fed Gwenny, as they were calling her, and I folded laundry.

Somber little Joy offered Ty a sip of her pretend tea. "Uh-oh," she said after he slurped of it, "that was poison."

"Oh no," he said. "What do I do?"

"You *die*!" she chirped.

Ty did die, was resurrected by antidote only to be poisoned again. Eva disappeared, then staggered in from the hall munching a crayon.

"Her poops are the most amazing colors," Ivy said to her own bare breasts.

"I don't know how you're doing this," I whispered.

Rust said, "It's all good." I could see why he was so serene. He hadn't lifted a finger since I got here except to tap his controller. But the scene worked, apparently, for Rust and Ivy—I'd never seen them moonier.

Ty read a story to Joy and Eva and I watched as little Gwenny set to suckling again on Ivy, my own milk portending descent. I regarded my pumping rig wearily from across the room. We watched the video game, some war with zombies and cars, so many cars, in the future. Ivy smiled down at us from the stratosphere, all doped up on oxytocin. She told me her latest birth story and simple words—*home, water*— made my teeth throb.

When Ty interrupted to ask Ivy whether she and Rust ever incorporated breastfeeding into their lovemaking, I said, "Don't be disgusting."

Ty was aghast. "People in Boulder do it all the time!"

I told Ty it seemed to me that Boulder had nearly ruined him.

"She's right," said Rust, finally interested enough to remove his headset. "If you had lived in Boulder for one more week I wouldn't have wanted to be your friend anymore."

"You know what he said to me in the car?" I offered, hungry for Rust's attention. "He said 'Reno's so rough.'"

"It *is* rough!" Ty said. "Boulder has bike paths and—"

"Boulder! Boulder! Boulder!" Rust shouted merrily. "It's all I hear about! It's making me want to fucking autoerotically asphyxiate myself."

"Language, my love," Ivy cooed.

I turned to her. "Ty told me on the freeway that he only eats mushrooms for 'spiritual exploration.'"

"'Consciousness expansion,'" Ty corrected.

"He said, I would never do it to 'have fun.'"

"I didn't do that, those bunny ears. That's *you*! You're like"—he clamped and unclamped air quotes and began to sing—"little bunny Foo Foo hopping through the forest . . ."

Ivy gently touched my neck. "You *are* wearing turquoise."

"It's lapis," I said, finding my pendant. "It's a power stone."

"You look like one of those Santa Fe ladies. What's with this bracelet?"

I gripped it. Sterling silver, mailed to my campus office by my biologist. "It was gifted me at a conference."

Ivy stroked her little chunk's fontanel. "I don't understand a thing you are saying."

I missed Ivy so bad, sitting beside her. I prayed for the two of us to go outside and smoke a bowl, though Ivy didn't smoke. She and I loved but no longer understood each other. Motherhood had wrenched us into separate spheres—she the attachment parent, me the detached mother. I had hoped she might be the first person I told about my teeth. But she'd been breastfeeding for four years straight. She'd slept in the same bed with her children every single night of their lives. I was trying not to judge her, but the Madonna radiance rolling off her scared the hell out of me. She'd been at home, unschooling her free-range babies since we last saw each other. I dropped mine at daycare forty hours a week, hours I spent at yoga, fucking around with various Innocents, or smoking weed in my hammock, crying and wondering what my baby thought of me. No, I didn't have to wonder—I knew.

My bitch mama left me with a stranger named Miss Moonbeam. A lying stranger baby wearer when what I need is to be free, naked as the day I was born, not so long ago. I like dancing and clapping and being startled. I like the yays at the ends of songs. I hate my lovie. I hate naps. I like putting little rocks into my mouth, and coins and beads, too. I like to find the buffed shiny islands of gum in the carpet at the library. I like to make things go all gone. *Miss Moonbeam taught me to say* all done *and* more *and* milk *and* eat *with my hands but she did not teach me to ask for anything I actually want like iPad or latte or make these teeth stop. Miss Moonbeam says the earth is our mother and I wish she was right that way she'd never leave and always be holding me. My bitch mama hardly holds me, only 90 percent of the time I'm awake and 15 percent of the time I'm asleep. Miss Moonbeam says to share but my bitch mama does selfish things like take a shower and try to finish a meal in peace. My bitch mama says she had a life before me and with my hands I say,* all done. *Miss Moonbeam says we don't bite and with my mouth I say, oh yes we do. Miss Moonbeam says we don't hit our friends and I say, Augie is not my friend; Kayden is not my friend; River is not my friend. My bitch mama signed the barefoot waiver. My bitch mama put me in tumbling class. My bitch mama wants me bilingual. I want to inchworm under the couch for some alone time. I want to lick lint.*

I want to jab a stick into the roof of my mouth. I want my body to listen to me, want my fingernails to stop growing, want to hoard my snot. My bitch mama doesn't understand me. She doesn't know what I want. She says this all the time. I don't know what you want from me. *Listen. I want your teeth in my hurting head. I want all the milk you can make and more. I want your whaley heartbeats. I want to rip your earrings out and your nose ring too, so that there is nothing shining in my way, nothing glinting between your eyes and mine mine mine.*

1975

Dear Denise,

It's been so long since I've written that I don't know where to begin. Work has been good and getting better, in fact that's where I am right now, in the darkroom at Cashman Photo. We are in the between-show lull, so I wanted to write you.

Three days ago I got a splinter in my eye and now have to wear a patch. I also encountered the flu, so I'm in great shape. Then I got caught by Morgan Cashman himself making off with pictures I made myself (very much against the rules), and there was a big scene in which I almost got fired. I was pretty worked up when I got off, so I went with some people after work and got drunk down at the bar here.

I've had two offers from other photography studios to go work for them. So far, I haven't acted on either, but I'm seriously considering going to Alan Photography. The cat from Alan came right into the lab looking for me. Alan is Cashman's arch enemy—they have a lab in the basement of Caesar's and do tremendous volume (I could handle it). I don't know how these people heard about me, but what they heard must've been good.

I have gone out with so many people since we last spoke, but mostly two cats—one named Brian (with the cabin—did I tell you about him?) and another named Jerry. Brian is nineteen and my favorite. He is really cute, looks a lot like Keith, but innocent. Jerry is (brace yourself) forty years old. He's into meditation and a vegetarian. Really a super nice cat, but a little too together for me, if you know what I mean.

Desperately need to talk to you. Short version: I'm flunking out of school. Haven't gone in two weeks. Was on "Intervention" at UnLove (my GPA got too bad) and then they kicked me out. I'm short one credit at Western, which will stop me from graduating. It's really a drag. I'll have to go to summer school to get that old piece of paper.

Sorry it took so long to write. I've got a million things to say, but work calls . . .

Dearest Nese,

I'm here in summer school, which started an hour late because of the flood. Did you hear about it? It was bad. I was at Caesar's when it hit, trying to get in to open up the lab and there was this river flowing through the middle of the parking lot. And this was no meager trickle. There were like 200 cars being washed into each other and down into the wash that runs water under the Strip. Then I heard the loudest crack: the bridge. When the bridge went, the river jumped over the Strip and completely flooded the Flamingo. Cars (with people in them) were washed away from the MGM and more from the Marina. Caesar's was literally an island, no way to get in or out without going through rushing water and mud and debris knee-deep at the shallowest point. I rolled up my pants and found a way. When I finally got in, I was covered with mud and panicked because I'd seen my mom's car go under the bridge. Totally destroyed. I found out later she wasn't in it.

The big fountain at Caesar's was completely drowned. The water ran all the way around the hotel and inside it. People crowded on the steps and waded around in the muck. I'm taking pictures the whole time. In a way it was like I'd wished it ...

Death toll is four. Blacks in North L.V. were stranded on their roofs for a day, some more. The gas tanks at Valor broke and power lines are still down on the north side. The Huntridge flooded up to the stage. Many, many accidents, cars stalled all over town. Our living room flooded. I've never seen Las Vegas in such a state, and old timers say they haven't either.

Hey-O Nese,

As you've probably heard, I flunked out of school. For good. Fucked off on summer school royally and that's it, I'm told. Oh well. Don't you love these cheery letters? I don't have a soul here I can talk to. Jack and Monica moved out and it's just Mom and me now. She's gone by the time I get home. Mom is alone all the time except for when Mark decides to come by. The only thing worse than when he doesn't come around is when he does. Is it better to be completely alone or be married to some-one you don't like? Are these the only options? I just don't want my only companion to be the T.V. Denise, where will we be? Left alone, like my mom? Or living with some adult baby, cooking and cleaning for him, feeding him, smelling his farts?

Strange things have been going down in my people relationships. The day after the flood I got a card from Keith. I haven't heard from him in almost a year. We were very close, but he never loved me. He was my element. But things change. They changed big time when I told him about the pregnancy. He said we'd "take care of it" together and then I heard nothing from him for months. I finally made the arrangements myself (Terri came with) and called him and told him. Suddenly he offered all kinds of help. I told him he was a bit late. That was the last time I'd talked to him.

Anyway, in his card Keith said he missed me, wanted to see me blah, blah, blah. I sat on it for a week or so, then called him. I went over to his apartment wanting to talk about this thing in me. I have been harboring ugly feelings for him for so long and I wanted them out. So, I let them out. I really let it rip. He told me to leave but then called me back and said I had a right to feel those things. He cried (!!!) and told me he had loved me, but was afraid. I saw that he was more right than he knew—he was afraid way, way down. And I saw that I'm not afraid. At least not in that deep down way. I said it was too late, that it couldn't be like that.

Haven't got much time, so I'll just cram the rest in: (1) finally went to Zion—holy shit! (2) finished my course in meditation—the change is massive and I hope to continue meditating for the rest of my life (3) haven't done any hard drugs or blacked out in three weeks. More to come on this, I hope.

Sending you a copy of the paper with my photo on the FRONT PAGE. Ok, must work now. Everyone is ok.

I love you,
Martha Claire

The Scene at the Arb

Dusk fell on Rust and Ivy's backyard, a quarter acre of wild sagebrush backed up to Peavine Peak. A slab of patio ringed by pea gravel and dandelions, ice plant from the previous owner, a wall of tumbleweeds blown against the fence, bamboo leaning over from the neighbor's yard. Out in the sagebrush, Joy and Eva scaled a play structure gifted by one set of grandparents and assembled by the other. Ty and I sat in lawn chairs on the slab, and Rust squatted on a cooler. Ivy reclined on a lounger with the new one. We couldn't see the sunset, but the hour was as golden as the dead bighorn at the airport had promised, the sky over the Sierras certainly aflame.

"How's Theo?" Ivy asked.

"Theo's fine," I said, all but wincing.

Ivy said, "Are you two still having a hard time?"

"We're not 'having a hard time.' We just don't know if we want to be married anymore."

"Because you slept with that student?" Ty, as if inquiring which font I used on my vita.

"Spooned with a graduate student," I replied. "And she wasn't my student. She's a theory person. Anyway, no, Theo doesn't care about that. That's just the administration that cares."

Ivy asked, her gentleness soft as a bosom and unbearable, "Then why aren't you sure if you want to be married anymore?"

"Because," I said, my biologist's most recent invitation to erotic rendezvous hot in my phone, "because of other things."

"What other things?" Ty wanted to know.

"Things like our espresso maker." I recalled for the assembled friends a time early in Theo's and my courtship—our marriage counselor encouraged such reveries—when Theo had risen an hour earlier than me, read the paper, then dressed and walked out into the snow. Each morning he came back, red-cheeked and smiling, and set a latte on my desk just as I sat down to write.

"An assistant could do that," was his opinion now. Now, we had an espresso maker. Now, we had a baby. And wasn't that wonderful? For hadn't I dreamt while Theo was gone, while sleeping alone in my bed reclaimed, of our baby? And hadn't Theo wished, while trudging through the snow, for an espresso maker?

My problem was I'd never learned to use the espresso maker, preferred the farm stand slash coffee shop around the corner. I'd get a latte, change the baby's diaper in the potty, torture myself by watching my favorite baristo flirt with some nymph in a romper.

The farm stand slash coffee shop had three teeny tiny tables scrunched in close. Once, Anne Carson met a former student at a table beside mine. These sorts of visitations do occur in Ann Arbor. Anne Carson sits diagonally from me, talking to her former student beside me, doling out affirmation and advice. I am eavesdropping slyly when Anne Carson looks right at me. She says, *I think the universe is tired of waiting for you to get the message.*

I said, "What, Anne Carson?"

Anne Carson was not talking to me. But also, she *was.*

I found the baristo on one of the apps. A long-limbed crust punk with sulky eyebrows and deep lines around his eyes from laughing so much, I imagined. I also imagined he had a nice long dick, and whacked off to this potentiality while awaiting his response.

Another Innocent, my baristo. The public Ivies are full of Innocents. None of them got their hands dirty. The last time I'd seen the baristo—in his bed, a mattress on the floor of course—he was moody, wondering why anyone would bring a child into this world. I knew why but didn't tell him. Because otherwise we'd have no excuse to get together and fuck.

I'd had my Innocents and Theo had Viv. Theo's best friends were, in this order: our daughter, then Viv, then me. Viv was a dancer. She lived somewhere in Europe on some residency or whatever. She and Theo met in Cuba, watching Alicia Alonso at the National Ballet. He had a whole romantic story about it: they had never touched, didn't need to, which was so much worse than some cliché mattress on a floor or one night of spooning reported to the Office of Institutional Equity or various other consensual walkabouts with various other adults. Viv traveled the world alone, sent all kinds of wacky currency to my daughter. Viv remembered everyone's birthdays, sent cards, gifts, long letters to which Theo wrote back immediately. It was all very *Age of Innocence.* I mostly boinked millennial preparers of beverages and schlepped to book festivals to hook up with whatever adequate rando lurked at the end of my signing line. This was what our open marriage looked like.

I asked Rust if he still had that weed left over from Burning Man, and could we bring it to the reading?

"She needs to be high before she goes onstage," Ty said. "She's a low-key drug addict."

"I've got to stop spectating," I said. "I'm hovering somewhere up there." We all looked up to the purpling sky, to the cottonwoods where Larry still dangled. Fun fact about cottonwoods is they have a life span of about a hundred years and most of the cottonwoods throughout the American West, the ones lining almost every river and stream from the bosque to the palouse are about a hundred years old. There aren't any new cottonwoods because for about a hundred years now there hasn't been enough water for babies.

"I see you!" said Rust. "You're in a hot air balloon."

"Dad," Ivy called up to the cottonwoods, "say hi to Claire for us!"

Larry said nothing, either did not hear us or did not care to respond.

I was in full-on mope mode. "And now apparently I'm supposed to talk to five hundred high schoolers tomorrow! I have no idea what I'm gonna say!"

"You're an artist!" Rust said. "Just have them lie on the floor and listen to *Pet Sounds*!"

I'm not an artist, but Rust is. For his senior thesis he got a grant to travel to Minneapolis, where, over a period of three weeks and with the aid of an ornithology post-doc he was cockteasing, he clandestinely released dozens of color-bred canaries throughout the employee mall of the 3M corporation, which you may know as manufacturer of the Post-it, which has trademarked the color canary yellow.

"How come you didn't prepare?" Ty asked.

"They *just* told me about it," I said, meaning I'd just read the email where they told me about it. "Two hours I have with these kids at some ungodly hour tomorrow morning. Then someone's taking me to the airport."

"Cancel it," Ivy said.

I couldn't cancel. I'd spent the honorarium. "They're children," I said. "Underserved."

Rust nodded. "That's it. Do your poor girl from the rurals bootstraps routine. For the encore do 'Art Saves.'"

"I'd love to, believe me," I said. "But I promised my therapist I'd stop doing things that make me feel like a fraud."

"You're not a fraud," said Ivy supportively. "Just a slacker."

"A slacker," Ty put his hand on my shoulder as if he'd read it somewhere in a manual, "and a bit of a coward."

"Actually," I said, "I've been described as 'searingly brave.'"

"By who?"

"*N+1.*"

"What is that?"

"My therapist also said so."

"The one who says you're a fraud?"

"The other one."

"That you're *searingly brave*?"

"Not 'searingly' but—"

"What for?"

"Having a baby before tenure."

They all looked at me. After a time, Rust said, "That's typical Oregon Trail Generation."

Ty nodded. "Concentrating on the homestead."

"What's the Oregon Trail Generation?" I asked.

"It's a think piece we all read," said Ivy, not bothering to hide her accusation. "I posted it on my Tumblr." I did not even know she had a Tumblr. I thought we were too old for Tumblr.

"The Oregon Trail Generation is us!" said Ty. "The generation that came of age along with the internet. Born in the eighties. Last of the analog natives. We had landlines and grew up to be digitally fluent. We played the Oregon Trail on Mac IIs in grade school and had cybersex on home PCs in middle school. Dial-up in high school, ethernet in college."

"Generational identity theory," Rust said. "Classic scam. Generations were invented by advertising executives. But this one is kinda neat! The idea is that technology changed so rapidly that it . . . isolated us from the generations we might have otherwise related to, Gen X on one side, Millennials on the other."

"We are *not* old Millennials!" said Ty. "We're a *microgeneration*."

I considered this for some time. It felt right.

Then Ty said, "Hey, can I ask you a writing question?"

Reluctantly, I said he could.

"What did that one review mean by 'sophomore slump'?"

Ivy shushed him.

"It's fine," I said. "In the *Times*, you mean? Basically, the critical consensus on my second book is that people really liked my first book."

"And 'overwrought.' What does that mean? Too long?"

"Bossy word choice," Rust said. "I warned you about that. You should try to stay as far away from your work as you can. Unless you really want to go up your own asshole, as Vonnegut said."

I told Rust that Vonnegut also said, *All this really happened, more or less,* but he went on.

"And now *this*? You're writing about this, this"—he flung his arms up to encompass everything around him, his homestead, his women—"this inanity!"

To Ty I said, "It means overwriting."

"*Over*writing," Ty exclaimed, "that's exactly the right word for it. I can see what makes you such a good teacher."

Ivy could not resist. "That, plus the cuddleslutting."

WHAT I DID NOT TELL my friends was I'd broken a rule, an unsaid one. Do I have to say it now?

"To be fair, it feels like I loved this person first," I'd told Theo. "Years ago." By *first* I meant something like *in a past life.* "Loved them, then you. Now them again."

Theo said, "'Fair'?"

I said my plan was to wait for it to come back around to him. Love, I guess I meant. My adoration. I said I was trying to stay put. I said this while packing my bag.

He said, "Are you ever going to put these clothes away or are you just going to high-grade them until I do laundry again?"

I said, "I can't find a trace of me in this house!"

He said, "This is not about the house."

"The house is haunted," I said. "Mildly. Admit that."

"I'm not denying it."

"You're not affirming it."

"I'm commiserating with you."

"Well, I'm not miserating," I said, "so maybe you're just a complainer."

"Oh, you're miserating."

"I'm honestly not, I just know this house has some bad juju, a little malevolence. The whole region does! It's making us fight."

"The house or the upper Midwest?"

"I have to get out of here."

"I'm sympathizing," Theo said. "I'm trying to. But if anyone's haunted, it's you."

I said maybe if I could get outside more . . .

If I had to say, absolutely had to right at this moment, I would have to admit that I am in love with various Innocents, my biologist and some others too, but not Theo, not my husband, not right now. I don't want to get into the weeds here. The point is as soon as the ground thawed, I started sleeping in a tent in our backyard. It was cold, and sometimes widow-makers swooped down from the black walnut, but it was quiet and I felt free out there, so free that one day I said, "I'm thinking of moving out, Theo."

"You already moved out."

"I mean out of the yard. My own place."

He said, "Where?"

"The Arb, probably," meaning the Arboretum. "I need to get a feel for the scene over there first."

Theo said, "You say you don't love me anymore but I don't believe you."

I said, "At yoga they say the only constant is change."

"Who says that? The yogi?"

"The chalkboard in the bathroom," I admitted. "But it speaks to me."

Theo was quiet awhile. Thinking of the mistakes he'd made, I assumed. Eventually he said, "What others?"

A question they all liked.

I CASED THE ARB at dusk in disguise as somebody's mother. L.L. Bean boots, Patagonia jacket, lined REI leggings, the baby in the UPPA. O, the trespassing a suburban white woman can get away with pushing a six-hundred-dollar stroller!

Theo didn't feel entirely comfortable with this.

"Relax," I said. "The Arb is public property."

"It's not. It's university property."

"A *public* university! Or has everyone forgotten that? And I'm an employee! They'd let me sleep in my office, wouldn't they? How many male professors going through divorces have slept in those offices over the years? They'd at least look the other way! The Arb is just an extension of my office."

"So sleep in your office then if we're going through a divorce."

"It's too depressing in there."

It wasn't even my office. It was Joyce Carol Oates's office. She was on perpetual leave so I was permitted to use it. But I didn't dare move her things, didn't make room on the wall of memorabilia opposite the desk: decades of JCO swag including first editions of her countless books, framed posters from gigs at the 92nd Street Y, and a portrait signed flirtily to her by Muhammad Ali. At office hours, students took in the JCO wall reverently. My favorite, the theoretician, said, "I guess you really like Joyce Carol Oates."

I told Theo, "I'll be fine at the Arb. I come from a long line of squatters." He seemed sad at me. I touched his arm. "You knew I was moving out, Theo. I technically already have."

"It's not that," he said. "I'm actually relieved you're moving out. Moved out. And I think it's cool you're following your . . . heart, or . . . whatever . . . is happening . . . out there"—he wagged his hand northward—"at the Arb. It's just . . . I'd gotten excited about you taking the baby out more."

"Oh, Theo."

"I thought you were starting to like spending time with her."

I agreed not to implicate the baby. I didn't need her anymore anyway. I procured various tools from Theo with little more resistance than a weary request for me to please put them back on their proper pegs in the shed when I was done (which just now I realized I forgot to do). I wrapped the tools in baby blankets and ferried them in the UPPA to the cemetery adjacent the Arb. I opened up a seam in a secluded segment of the fence, bent the new sharp prongs back and passed through.

A tent would be a tell. Tents practically screamed *hobo!* Whereas my hammock said *student*, said *white*, said *money*, soon said nothing at all, for as I got bolder and the trees leafed out, I cinched my straps higher and higher, so that by June I could smoke weed and read way up in canopy seclusion. When it got dark, if I had enough juice, I called Theo.

"Are you still glad I moved out?" I asked him.

"Yeah. But I'm sad, too."

We could have sex with other people or fall in love with other people, but not both. *Not both in the same person.* That was the rule I broke. His word, "rule." I felt it was more of a guideline. "An aspirational value," I said. We were describing human beings after all, flawed and confused, ever lost and imperfect. "In the best of times," I may have said.

Couldn't we be decent and loyal and at the same time completely free? Maybe things like "loyal" and "free" look different to different people, and did that make someone with a different "loyalty" or "freedom" wrong or bad? I sent him some links. Isn't the best kind of life one where all kinds of things happen? Theo did not see it this way. I could not apologize and come home because I was not sorry. I did not feel love was ever a bad thing. Days Theo was at the hospital and the baby was at Miss Moonbeam's I let myself into the house to shower and smell her things.

This was the scene at the Arb.

Disambiguation

The Oregon Trail was a historic migration route across the western United States. It is a physical depression in the ground in parts of Missouri, Kansas, Nebraska, Wyoming, Idaho and Oregon.

Oregon Trail may also refer to:

The Oregon Trail: Sketches of Prairie and Mountain Life (1849), a history of the Oregon Trail by
Oregon Trail (1923), an American film serial starring
The Old Oregon Trail (1928), an American western starring
The Oregon Trail (1936), an American film starring
The Oregon Trail (1939), an American serial starring
Oregon Trail (1945), a Sunset Carson western starring
The Oregon Trail (1959), an American film starring

The Oregon Trail (1971), an educational computer game by MECC

The Oregon Trail (1976), a television movie starring

The Oregon Trail (1977), an American television series starring

The Oregon Trail (2011), the 2011 version of a 1971 video game

The Oregon Trail, a card game by Pressman Toy Corporation based on the video game of the same name

Oregon Trail Middle School, a middle school in Kansas

"Generation Oregon Trail," Anna Garvey's theory of a microgeneration between Generation X and Millennials

The Oregon Trail Scenic Byway

IN THE ALLEY behind the bookstore Rust insisted we use a hemp wick instead of a lighter to smoke the Burning Man weed. "More organic that way."

"Best practices," Ty confirmed.

"Fine by me. I don't fuck with vapes. I'm a flower purist, like Willie Nelson. No popcorn lung for me!"

Ty told us about his work with a shaman on lucid dreaming. "Trying for a DILD," he said, "dream-induced lucid dream." He pushed his index finger into his palm, to test whether this was a dream or not. The trick, he said, was to do an impossible thing in your waking life so much that you'd do it in your dream life, only in the dream life he *would* push his finger through his hand and that's how he'd know he was dreaming and from there he could do anything.

Rust said, "What's the last thing you want to hear when you're going down on Willie Nelson?"

What? we asked.

"'I'm not Willie Nelson.'"

I said, "My grandma would go down on Willie Nelson. She has a rhinestone Willie Nelson pin on her cowboy hat. We had to listen to him anytime we went through Utah—"

Ty preempted my rendition of "On the Road Again." "Do we have time to go to the ATM machine?"

"No," I said. "And the M in 'ATM' stands for machine. You don't need the second 'machine.' You wouldn't say 'Automatic Teller Machine machine.' 'MLB baseball!' Why do people have trust issues with acronyms?"

The boys gaped at me, hemp wick flickering between them.

"You're right," I said. "I hear it. I've become a pedant. The tenure track has ruined me. The other day I told Theo that I found the grocery store's displaying its LaCroix in the foyer 'problematic.' It's only been five years and I've become completely insufferable."

Ty took a toke. "And you said nothing ever got done in academia."

He passed to Rust and Rust said, "Academia is death."

I said, "Let's tell college stories!"

Rust asked, "Are you a representative of the alumni association?"

I accepted the joint and the wick and asked Rust why he wasn't making art anymore.

"There's no 'making art' and not making art," he said. "There's just living. Art is just practice for being alive."

Ty said, "Show her your driver's license."

Rust looked bored but handed me his wallet. The license looked like a license. Stats, organ donor, unflattering photo, bighorn sheep on the header.

"I don't get it," I said.

Rust said, "There's nothing to 'get,'" and at the same time Ty said, "It's a mask."

"What?"

"He's wearing a mask of his own face."

"A prosthetic," Rust corrected.

"He made it," said Ty. "It took him like nine months."

"Well, a lot of that was experimenting with materials, setting up the lab in the garage, the classes."

"You took a class?"

"The Tahoe Shakespeare Fest does stagecraft workshops. I took a few."

I could see it now, barely. A rubbery quality about his jowls, a slight matte swell at the cheekbones. It looked more like him than him. "You made a mask of your own face for your driver's license photo."

"This was a few years ago," he scoffed. "I'm not really interested in that pranky stuff anymore."

"What are you into, then?" I asked.

"Living my life, being a father. There's nothing more radical, nothing more creative. You know Ivy had an orgasm when Gwenny was crowning? *That's* art."

I let this go, considered Theo's theory that Rust was now engaged in a super long-term performance art project. It was the only way to explain his recent phase of breeder orthodoxy. He sent us Sears Christmas cards with him and Ivy and the girls spit-shined in matching white shirts looking like a bunch of Mormons, Valentine's cards with conversation hearts taped inside. They went to Disneyland, shopped at Kohl's, had an actual white picket fence. Theo thought Rust was a genius. I thought he was just getting old. Old and boring and numb like the rest of us, graced rarely with brief, intense bursts of aliveness that feel dreamt in the morning. Tonight, I could already tell, would be one of these bursts.

Ty paused with the cashed bowl and asked, "What are you on a scale of one to ten, zero being not at all high and ten being the highest you've ever been personally?"

I evaluated myself a two-point-five.

"Where do you need to be to enjoy this reading?" he asked.

I said, "*Enjoy* is a specific word."

Ty said, "Survive, how about?"

I said a four would be nice.

"Then onward!" Ty blew out the cashed bowl and began to re-pack it.

Rust turned to me, his eyes tiny and flooded with blood. "For real," he said, "how's the homestead?"

The homestead was a place I visited. It was a place where the consensus was I was not by nature a very considerate person. A place where I had trouble thinking of things from another's point of view. Did it make it worse to be publicly celebrated for a capacity that the homestead knew to be stunted in me? The checks cashed, but I was beginning to suspect there was something dishonest in fashioning myself a master at transporting myself into others' points of view. There was maybe even something dangerous in not admitting that when we say we have endless empathy for and interest in other people what we in fact mean is that we exercise, ideally daily, empathy for and interest in ourselves, albeit all our various selves. These were not new thoughts, but recently they had led me to announce and demand commendation for the smallest acts of kindness.

"I opened your office door," I'd announce to Theo, "so it wouldn't be cold in there in the morning."

"I unloaded the dishwasher some!"

I couldn't help it. I had some loud little clock in my brain that kept track of exactly how long I was solely responsible for the baby, and every second more than my fair share had to be properly appreciated. I was not very good at being alone with her. She bit me, and I got too mad at her for it. I always had bruise rings on my forearms the exact size of her small mouth opened wide. I'd press the bruises when I wanted to feel something. I pressed one now.

Theo liked to tell how back in our courtship I wouldn't let him hold my hair when I threw up. Too cliché, I reasoned with puke in my hair. It took me a long time to let him be nice to me, to let him do nice things for me. After I had the baby, I couldn't stop. Visiting friends and family invariably noted how hyper-helpful Theo was, while delicately eliding the fact that I was hyper-needy. We never slept but Theo always had energy, had some engine inside him, chugging along. It was mostly love, but love shot through with fear, chivalry and surveillance. We watched each other like two big cats circling a room. He got up with me for night feedings, talked me through them. He made all the meals and changed all the diapers and rubbed my feet while I breastfed. When I finished, he took the baby from the pillow—I didn't even have to lift her—and rocked her, put her to sleep with the whitewater womb sound he made. They were best friends. I avoided them both between feedings by volunteering to do errands or yard work and executing these slowly and with backbreaking meticulousness. It took me an hour and a half to shovel and salt our sidewalk. Over the course of an afternoon I ripped every single weed from a flower bed by the root with my bare hands, pausing to rescue and relocate each displaced earthworm.

I'd been told many times by various constituencies that all this was perfectly common, avoiding parenting when you feel you're not particularly good at it, retreating into things you maybe are good at—be it worm rescue, snow shoveling or sex. Promiscuity, maternal ambivalence, wifely rage—many felt it, or even if not, considered such feelings *normal*. They stressed this. But what did I care that it was *normal*? My team of mental health professionals in particular didn't seem to understand that I wasn't comforted by being normal, that I took normal as an insult, that knowing these troubles were widely felt didn't ease them, only meant that on top of my avoidance and guilt and shame and numbness I now felt boring, a kind of death. Knowing all this was normal put me somewhere on the scale of pathetic to suicidal. I thought, *If this is normal, count me out.*

Ty passed me greens.

"Homestead's good," I said stonedly.

AT THE BOOKSTORE I put my copy of my book, the one with my annotations for dramatic pause or emphasis, my humble thankses and charming patter, onto a table, introduced myself to the booksellers and returned to find my copy gone. Shelved, sold, it didn't matter. It was lost and I would have to do my best with a blank store copy—never ideal. But I was feeling fine—four, four and a half, five fine. No worries, I said to myself. I kind of like giving bad readings because people leave me alone after.

Unfortunately, these were my people. They got me. While I Mr. Magooed my way through what I remembered of my opening patter, they laughed as only a hometown crowd could. Once I managed to find my excerpt and begin, they nodded, grunted and groaned in all the right places. They laughed at lines only Reno knew were funny. Their enthusiasm and generosity made me cast off my canned answers come Q&A, discard all my pro forma insights on the writing process and where my ideas came from. I would not, I resolved, answer the question I wished they'd asked, or turn their shitty not a question but more of a statement into an illuminating observation, as I'd learned to do on tour. Instead, I would give the people of Reno the dignity of deeply considering their true questions in all their existential incoherence.

The microphone began an aggressive, low-frequency *tsk* that no one else seemed to hear. I was up in the hot air balloon watching as I said, in closing and without prompting, context or attribution to Auden, "No poem ever saved a Jew from the oven."

After my mercifully short signing line, I signed stock, then found Ty and Rust at the reception at the bar across the street.

Rust hugged me. "That was exactly what this town needs!"

Ty said, "That was *actually* pretty good. I didn't understand a lot of it? Which I think was the point. So maybe I loved it?"

I said, "Can we not talk about it?"

Ty suggested I read from the first book next time. "But I liked the character based on me."

"She made you into a buffoon!" Rust said.

Ty shrugged. "I liked the line about my hair."

Rust said, "I loved when that girl in the front asked you about loneliness and 'the West' or whatever and you said, I feel lonelier now than I ever did in Nevada."

Lonely was not the right word, but before I could clarify, Rust and Ty were arguing whether I had portrayed Ty as a buffoon. I turned away before they could ask me to arbitrate (I had) and was immediately cornered by a local adjunct who'd gone to undergrad where I'd gone to grad school. She wanted to know: Was I down to reminisce? I allowed it, moved by her ardor for what had once been the Big Ten.

"We lived in the forty-dollar block but we charged fans of the other team fifty. Once, this truck of old guys parked on our lawn and paid and then, just as they were headed off to the stadium, they saw my roommate upstairs on the balcony with a beer bong. They like, called up! Like, Can I hit that? I'll give you beer money. My roommate's like, For sure! Starts like to come downstairs right? Old guy's like, No. 'Stay where you are.' He wanted to do a two-story beer bong. And he fucking did! Only, as my roommate's pouring and this guy is chugging, one of those huge bees, the slow drowsy-looking ones—"

"Carpenter bees."

"Sure. Floats over to the funnel. We all saw it. We were like, 'No!'—But also like, *'Yes!'*

"Then *zip*—bee flies right into the funnel! Sucked down the tube. Bro, we all watched it go down the pipe. The old-timer did too—but he didn't stop."

"He bonged the bee?"

"He bonged the bee! He paid us a hundred dollars for a parking spot and a bee bong!"

Rust had joined, asked, "Is any of this making sense to you? Are you an insider in her culture?"

I had to admit that I was. I asked who won the game.

The adjunct shrugged. "They did. And after the game the same guy crashed his truck into our side porch, but we didn't even care because we felt so grateful to have witnessed the bee bong, like, to have lived in its *same historical moment.* Plus we were renting."

I said, "Renting is *amazing.*"

She asked if I had a house.

I said, "We do."

The first person plural aroused her. "You're *married*?"

I nodded. "With a kid."

This sent her over. *"Eeeee!"* she squealed. "You have a little *baby*?"

I said, "Don't do that."

"Do what?"

"I know what you're doing and stop it. That's not why the fore-mothers marched."

"Stop what?" said the adjunct.

"Listen: I am a messenger from the future. I am you in ten years. Pay attention! Don't fetishize marriage and babies. Don't succumb to the axial tilt of monogamy! I don't pretend to know the details of your . . . situation, but I guarantee you, you're as free as you'll ever be. Have sex with anyone you want. Enjoy the fact that it might happen any minute. You could have sex with a man, a woman, both—tonight! You could have sex with someone twenty years older than you. You could have sex with someone from the other side of the planet. Better yet, be alone! Enjoy your body, come every day, worship at the altar of the divine goddess. Travel! Travel everywhere, especially short distances. Travel around your kitchen. Travel up some stairs and down again. Pick up and go. Enjoy all the holidays you won't get anymore— New Year's Eve, Halloween. Go to the lake, go camping, go on a boat. Go to Vegas for all I care. Even shitty, shitty St. Patrick's Day in Vegas is better than the best day at home with an infant."

A friend of the adjunct had joined us, waifish in a sparkly halter top and visibly concerned. "What's she talking about?"

The adjunct said, "Political lesbianism, maybe?"

I said, "I am delivering a message from the future."

"Like the Terminator," Rust helped.

"Yes!" I said, pointing vigorously at him, though in truth I have never seen those movies. "I'm like the Terminator! The reverse Termi-nator! I want you to *live*. I want you to flourish. I want you to *thrive*!"

"The Germinator," the adjunct said.

I said, "Exactly!" and we *cheers*ed.

A long and important pause.

"So . . ." said the sparkly friend, embarking on a new topic. I saw it coming at me like a malicious wave rolling up from a black and briny sea. I heard its roar in the back of her throat, saw my devastation in her shellacked eyes. I looked desperately around the bar for my friends, but they had forsaken me. I pleaded silently for the adjunct to inter-vene but knew she would not. My glass was empty and here it came, ruin, pain, destruction, death. She batted her eyelashes. ". . . what are you working on now?"

Why not tell them, these luminous childless women of Reno, why not tell them everything? That I was coming of age at an alarming rate. That I'd gained so much weight that my dean had stopped ask-ing me my major. That I did not appreciate the distinction between a symposium and a colloquium. That my chair had called me kiddo, both of us a little drunk at a daytime reception. That I liked it, that having-a-dad feeling. That for weeks into every term I forgot which classroom was mine, what time it was mine, my students' names. I forgot why the names on the buildings were on the buildings. Moth-erhood had cracked me in half. My self as a mother and my self as not were two different people, distinct. The woman they admired, who'd written the books they liked or at least had heard of, if only today, was on the other side of a canyon. Someone else had written them, elves-and-shoemaker style. A curtain fell across me each evening, after the baby was asleep, when I was supposed to be resting, supposed to be happy. Happiness is a scam, I know that, but was it so dumb to want something other than the blackout curtain I remembered from casino motel rooms, plastic-lined, unbreathable, which came on, over, upon me every evening? On the radio a whale was trapped in a man-made sound. *There are so few of these whales and the ocean is so vast and more importantly so noisy now that they can't hear each other, can't find each other, can't meet and make babies,* some voice said. That's why they'll go extinct, confirmed my biologist.

I asked my therapists when we would stop calling it post-partum depression and start calling it regular depression. One said, "A few years." The other said, cheerfully, "Right now, if you like!" For insurance purposes she read aloud the regular depression diagnosis in the *DSM*. I was seven for seven, ever the overachieving first-born Aries. Mostly I was a frame or two outside my body, a blur in a tintype at home or at work, driving or biking, pretending to listen to a supposed friend, our hands curled around small glasses of small-batch bourbon, to a student in Joyce's office, careful not to smudge the crescents of dried red wine dotting the laminate desk.

I drank. I smoked. I spectated. I sculpted reality as I moved through it. The only people I liked were the ones who gave me something for the page, yet I never wrote. I had more or less given up on the bullshit I flung to my students about stories bridging what divides us, about fiction's power to save the world. It was not even my own bullshit to begin with. It was not even my own pitchfork doing the flinging! I wanted to heave myself from the fetid hot tub of the human condition, so sick was I of everyone splashing around in there together. Narrative was failing me left and right. All it was was fallible. I checked various copyright pages and confirmed these to be unforgivably dated observations.

Yet the magic facts remained: On the first day of fall a woman woke up another woman. She didn't notice it at first. She had only been sleeping for two minutes after all, a morphine-induced micronap in a hospital suite. She woke, pushed and pushed for hours for nothing, then was wheeled to a freezing cold operating theater—a blustering plastic bodysuit was fitted to her and hot air blown inside it. While she heard only the whir of an industrial fan inside the world's most expensive blanket, a baby was cut out of her. She was sewn up and then, after she reminded the staff that she was there—they were comparing dashed plans, for it was a holiday weekend and they'd been called in—and wanted, very badly, her baby, wanted her right now, the two were wheeled from the operating room back to their suite, where the light suggested dawn though it was midday. Outside, it was raining biblically. She looked out the window then at the baby and back out the window and the overflow culvert below was completely and suddenly filled, the parking lot flooded. Cars floated down the hill. Certain wings of the hospital became barges, bobbing in the sea.

Yet through all this, she did not realize that she had become another woman. She did not realize this until well after the water receded and the baby turned from bruise purple to yellow to pink, until blood was squeezed from her heel and she slept three nights wrapped in a glowworm blanket. Until well after they scanned the baby's bar code and her bar code too, snipped their tags off and released them. Through all this she mistakenly believed she was still herself. Then she took the baby home.

The smells in her supposed house were foreign, the foods someone had packed into the freezer gray and unappetizing with ice. She found the books all around impenetrable, the furniture pointy and hazardously arranged. Shockingly violent films arrived in the mail, ordered by some psycho with her Netflix login. Her clothes and shoes did not fit. It had been summer when they set out for the hospital, only a few days ago. It had been early morning and late summer, mists hovering over shorn cornfields, humid. But it was cold now. The handwriting on the family message board was illegible to her. She was a new person now, which so many American women aspired to be—remade! She herself had often wished it. But now that she had been made anew she found it frightening. She did not know anything about this new person who was her. What were her interests? Who did she love? Was she also a writer? So far, no. The new woman was a mystery and a blank— she didn't seem to think much. She had trouble completing her sentences. People hit in the head had symptoms like these, she thought she remembered. She asked her husband whether she'd fallen in labor. She was maybe on the back end of a spell of amnesia, for some evidence could trigger memories of the woman she once was, such as this key ring on this hook, with its gym fob, library fob, shopper's club fob, three brass keys with imprints that read now like the names of isotopes: PH-007, LCA-3201, PH-111. So she had a job, somewhere, this woman I was, but I did not investigate further. Eventually, by some somnambulist logic, the new woman went on fulfilling the public and private obligations of the old, kept promises she herself had not made. People sprouted wings every day.

I FOUND RUST AND TY and told them it was time to go. Rust asked one of those questions they all like. "What's your problem?"

In couples therapy recently I'd told Theo, "My problem is I have trouble thinking of you as a person. I just forget to wonder what you'd want."

I'd taken the professor job without consulting him. The chair had called and said, "We'd like to offer you the job here," and I said, "Sure. Sounds good."

"You don't have to answer right now," he said. "Take some time to think it over—"

"I don't need to," I said.

"—consult your family," he continued. "Talk to your husband?"

"No thanks," I said, Theo beside me. "I'm good."

My problem is I can't figure out how sorry to be for the way I've been. I'm either a little sorry, very sorry, or not at all sorry.

My problem is some nights I come in late and forget to lock the door behind me. Some nights I leave the porch light on. Some nights I have been touching my knee to another's beneath a table.

My problem is I have too much space and spend a great deal of my time curating warm, inviting work tableaus that I do not then use. I am always moving my desk from one room to another, always rearranging the furniture then walking into it in the night, always taking over the kitchen table.

My problem is I get an email re: moment of silence but get it too late and the moment has passed and the moment was silent—I can recall it, only a half hour or so earlier—but while the moment was silent, in that I was alone, working, and silent, I did not, I don't think, use the moment to consider those we've lost, their sacrifices, nor the losses and sacrifices of their families, as the email urged. My problem is I have my own moment of silence and think not of victims, their families, but of the perpetrators, and the wrong ones, the early ones, their trench coats, their swastikas.

My problem is I can't find my phone, keys, wallet, sunglasses, regular glasses, shoes, purse, book, pen, lipstick, earrings, watch, mug of cold coffee and suspect these things are all hanging out somewhere without me.

My problem is I don't miss you.

My problem is I cannot grasp how final death is.

My problem is I have the job she never got to have and the education she never got to have and I'm intimidating and not as nurturing as anyone thought I'd be. My problem is I didn't convert. My problem is I'm all set.

My problem was born in Las Vegas at University Medical Center on April 28, 1957. My problem was almost fifty. My problem taught me to drive stick shift, to buy two boxes of hair dye, for we had the same thick hair. My problem taught me the names of all my body parts and that I decided who could and could not touch them. My problem is I never got to say goodbye, or I was always saying goodbye, goodbye, goodbye, goodbye, goodbye, goodbye, goodbye so the meaning absconded, as meaning does.

My problem is I grew up poor. My problem is I'm derivative, a copy of a copy, all faded. My problem is I have the thing where the wires in my brain are crossed and everything that's supposed to be joyous is frightening and vice versa. My problem is we married other people. My problem is I am hardly ever putting one foot in front of the other. I have a rock collection of rocks whose names I do not know and do not pretend to know. My problem is I am only a little bothered by all of this and want to change not at all.

DOWNTOWN RENO GOES pawnshop, wedding chapel, dispensary, cowboy bar, biker bar, tourist bar. Tattoo parlors with neon blazing and pictures of flesh taped against the windows. Karaoke bars and sports bars and a piano bar for bachelorettes. Antique store, liquor store, bail bondsman, strip club where you can get a blow job, strip club where you can get a steak. Chocolate bar, wine bar, a fight in the street outside Eighties Night. Motor lodges for the otherwise un-housed. Casinos turned condos, the Tongan church, the Catholic church, the Straight Edge coffee shop, generic new bistros and gastro-pubs by the river. Coach's was now a Segway store, the Satellite a yoga studio. We got a drink at the wedding chapel where Raymond Carver got married, now a self-described eatery. From there we walked to a dusty pizza parlor on the ground floor of an hourly motel, a suitably haunted place with TVs everywhere. On one TV was Wicker Man, a ghost who carried a picnic basket full of severed heads around west-ern Mass. But how many human heads could really fit in one picnic basket? Three at most. Perhaps he had upset the Puritans, this ghost, but post–Sandy Hook, Wicker Man was quaint.

On another TV a single mom had found a way to monetize her mania. She took a sledgehammer to drywall. She yanked non-period light fixtures off the walls and peeled back brittle ribbons of lino-leum with her bare hands. Rust said, "I love this woman."

On another TV an Illinois woman stopped an intruder with a medieval sword given to her as collateral for the loan of a horse, which was never returned to her because "it excaped." She used the sword, the reporter said, because at the time of the intrusion she could not locate her handgun. "I did not have to do it," she boasted. "No, I did not."

I said, "Do you think it's a bad sign that the touchstone of our gen-eration is a genocidal, ecocidal video game?"

Rust pointed out the scummy window. "Is that Stevie?"

"Where?" I said, aghast. Stevie was the last person I wanted to see.

"Across the street. The hesher on the skateboard."

Stevie had been in a thrash metal band called Slasher with my dead ex-boyfriend, the one who'd lived with Ty and Rust and Ivy and me. The apex of Slasher's career was without a doubt their brief sponsorship by Steel Reserve, who kept the malt liquor flowing in the basements of northern Nevada and southern Idaho where if Slasher took the stage at all it was with one or more band members having vomited or bleeding.

"He works in the vitamin aisle at Whole Foods now," Rust said. "I see him all the time."

Ty said, "The last time I saw him was that New Year's at the lake with Jesse."

Disambiguation: Jesse. Hebrew meaning "king" or "God exists," father of David, king of the Israelites. I hadn't heard his name in a long time. I learned he was dead from Lise, who found out on Myspace, very Oregon Trail.

I seethed at Stevie where he waxed a curb outside a pawnshop specializing in wedding rings and sterling silver. "Fucking Stevie. You know I missed my grad school orientation mixer because I was having Jesse's abortion? It really put me at a disadvantage socially."

"That wasn't Stevie's fault."

"No, it was Jesse's fault and my fault and I can't take any more punishment and Jesse is dead."

Rust flinched. "You don't have to say it like that." After Jesse died, Rust painted a mural of him high on the wall of the Hacienda, the flophouse where all the Polish teenagers who worked the casinos in summer stayed. The mural was painted over when the Hacienda was turned into condos, but for years Jesse had watched over the city, or Rust had. I'd been in Ohio with no one watching over me.

"I'm going to say something to him." I got up, feeling righteous. I always do something stupid when I'm feeling righteous. I marched out of the restaurant and across the street. When he realized who I was, Stevie said, "Oh, shit," and hugged me. I let him. He smelled good, yeasty from skating, and my wires were all crossed.

"Rust said you were over here," I said, gesturing to the window of the pizza shop where he and Ty watched us. Stevie wagged a hang ten at them and they waved.

"I heard that guy is hella rich now," he said, meaning Ty.

"That's Tesla propaganda," I said. "You know they don't pay taxes? We pay their taxes. Not me, but—Did you know the gigafactory has no windows? Are you aware of the impact of lithium mining in the Great Basin, these mining companies poisoning the water and extincting snails and bulldozing old-growth sage forests and shit!" Buzzing quiet. "We were just talking about Jesse."

"Oh, bro," said Stevie, shaking his head. "I think about Jesse every day."

"So do I," I said, though this was not remotely true. "I guess you didn't do much to help him."

Stevie looked down to where he gripped the nose of his board. "Those were crazy times."

I said, "Did you even, like, *care* about him?"

"I loved him like a brother," said Stevie, plainly hurt. "I tried to. But you can't love when you're . . . that way. You can't think of anyone 'sides yourself. *Not even* yourself, yeah?"

"Yeah," I admitted. I knew the words to this song but couldn't sing along.

"Jesse wasn't like that though," Stevie said, "even at his worst he wasn't an *addict*. He was the most giving person I ever knew."

"Me too," I said and meant. "But I still hate him."

Again we stood in silence for a while, then Stevie followed me into the restaurant to say hi to Rust and Ty. He and Rust talked about colloidal silver for a really long time. Apparently, Steve was also growing his own mushrooms now, because when our slices came he offered to sprinkle some on top, an offer I accepted on behalf of all of us. There were ghosts and omens all around and we needed all the interpretive help we could get.

AFTER EATING, Ty and Rust and I heard drumming on the street and drifted toward it, giggling and waiting for the shrooms to kick in. From the Sierra Street bridge we saw whirling wheels of flames spinning across the courtyard of the Pioneer Theater and went to them like moths. It was Controlled Burn, a local fire-dancing troupe who performed at Burning Man, decompression parties, proms and casino openings, I learned from a business card someone handed me. The Pioneer seemed to me a little upscale for Controlled Burn. It was the only non-smoking venue in town, usually had the Reno Phil or a play going on under its gleaming gold geodesic dome. Late at night Jesse and I used to climb atop it to look at the stars, though we knew they'd be annihilated by the city.

Dancers flung fireballs on chains, twirled flaming staffs and batons. We tried to stay upwind, for Ty had a time trial in two weeks and felt the butane fumes would compromise his lung capacity. The crowd was upper-crust Burner: white men with dreads in tuxedos, women with septum piercings in evening gowns. Rust sent some texts and soon said, "My buddy's working the door."

The buddy let us into the Pioneer, its lobby decorated with

sculptures and photos of art cars. Some sculptures were for sale. The theater was set in rounds for dinner, chandeliers and centerpieces, wedge salads splayed on small plates, ice water sweating. A fundraiser, Rust's doorman buddy informed us.

We perused the works in the lobby, ignoring sniffs from the paying patrons. The sculptures—bike parts, wire, rocks, driftwood and plaster—began to shimmer a little. I looked to Rust to confirm that we hated them, but he'd disappeared and once again where Rust had been a sparkly thing approached.

"Excuse me, Germinator?" She was talking to me. "Remember me? You gave my friend some advice for the present?"

Ty joined, beaming at the woman's breasts heaving beneath a thousand little disks of metallic plastic. "Can I touch your shirt?"

"No thanks," she said, raising a stop sign hand. "I'm all set."

Ty pointed at her hand. "That is awesome. I really, *really* respect that you said that," and he left.

She turned back to me conspiratorially, a bit sheepish even. I could tell she was about to say something that was difficult for her and resolved to honor it, whatever it was. She took in extra air and said, "I was wondering if you could tell me about the future. About marriage and motherhood. Is it as bad as you say? Can you really not be an artist? Are *all* the holidays ruined?"

I thought about it. "Some get better, actually. Christmas. Halloween. All you need on the Fourth of July is a box of sparklers. Pregnancy makes you appreciate your body kind of. And living with another person is . . . nice. Things appear, get bought even though you didn't buy them, get cleaned even though you didn't clean them. They get fucked up too, by the kid, but even that's kind of magic. You turn around and something's in shards—something you were given, something you thought you liked but see now that maybe you never liked, this thing you maybe even asked for but it made you feel like shit without you even knowing. Knowing it up top, I mean. In the deep, you always knew. Your body knows. Things you thought were important to you suddenly aren't. You have an excuse to get out of anything you want. You can work on your, what do the blogs call them? Found family—and give up on your real family. That's my favorite part."

She blinked slowly. Her eyeshadow had run into her lid creases and I ached to wipe them. "That sounds amazing," she said. "My real family has been such a disappointment. Not my brother. Well," she revised, eyes down, those shining lines of whale fat and rock dust, "him, too."

I went on. I said one nice thing about the future is you can admit what you've given up on, admit it to yourself I mean. "Not to your person. That's something else," I said. I said there was much about these thresholds that was impossible to describe from the other side, especially when everyone's mind was stuffed full with so much Disney garbage and other costly distractions, but that basically I found it to be a demolishing, a taking down to the studs at least, and that I believed that while it rarely happened—most people went *back*, wanted their bodies *back*, their old self *back*—on some occasions it did make you new.

"No one knows what's going to happen," I said, realizing it. "So that's a neat part about the future."

She nodded, thanked me, and I departed feeling like an angel. Together Ty and I found Rust in the ballroom beside a catering cart stocked with desserts, an invitation in his hand. Two hundred and fifty dollars per plate, he showed us. The after-party another hundred. Pretty cheap by fundraiser standards, downright laughable in some of the rooms I'd been in, but Ty did a triple-take. "I thought they were supposed to burn their art!"

"You're such a rube," I said.

"He's *not* a rube," Rust snapped. "They *are* supposed to burn their art. They're supposed to destroy everything! That's what the burn's about. It's about annihilating the ego. It's not about . . ." He struggled, gesturing finally to the dessert cart before him, the elegantly adorned treats varnished in egg wash, ganached to velvet, whipped and pinwheeled into edible cups and cubes of pastel fondant.

Rust was right. Ty was not the rube. "Come on," I said. "Burning Man has an airport for private jets."

"The Valley people bring their own bathrooms," Ty said, too impressed.

"And air-conditioned yurts and gourmet chefs," I confirmed.

"Oh really?" Rust asked. "Where did you read that, in *The New York Times*?"

"Yes actually."

Ty said, "Elon's camp has Sherpas. That sounds really nice."

"Elon," said Rust, his face pleated in frustration, sorrow even, his hands curled around the handle of the catering cart. It occurred to me that he might flip it. He looked beautiful, but scary. Possibly this was the mushrooms. I wished we were outside and then—*voilà!*—we were.

We exploded out the back doors of the theater, Rust pushing the cart up the handicap ramp. I suggested we take the desserts to my hotel—I still hadn't checked in, had left my breast pump in Ty's car parked by the bookstore—but as we pushed the rattling cart along the river Rust had a better idea.

He led us to the Arlington Avenue bridge and beneath it, to the place where Wingfield Island parts the black waters of the Truckee, a place known locally as the Juggalo bathtub, where we distributed the desserts to the Juggalos and their Juggalo dogs. Someone wondered lamely if that was a good idea, for the dogs. Someone said cave dogs ate carob.

In gratitude the Juggalos offered us swigs from their forties and a trash bag of old popcorn they'd pulled from the dumpster behind the movie theater. We took the trash bag of popcorn across the bridge to the island, beyond the amphitheater and the Port-a-Johns with needles all around. We picnicked at the spot from which we'd once watched a white-water rafting competition, kayakers flipping in the man-made rapids. Sometimes it took them a long time to come up, the kayakers. I reminded Rust and Ty of that day—neither of them remembered the kayaks flipping into the air, the awful, jerky, electrifying bob of them overturned.

My breasts were hard, begging. My teeth seemed serene. In my tote bag I found my iPod. What a wonder this device was! How heavy! How unattached! It accomplished next to nothing—perfect fetish object of the Oregon Trail Generation. Ty and Rust coveted it, then went back to staring at the sky in silence. Receiving messages, I hoped.

The iPod felt amazing, the gummy wheel right where I left it. The tendons of my hand and arm had memorized the faintest ticks of its rotation, and these were still there, a musculoskeletal time capsule. A sonic time capsule too, for I remembered now that the iPod's offerings dated from the era between another now-lost iPod and one stolen computer, containing not all the music I'd ever owned, as the iPod had come to in my imagination, but in fact only the music from a very narrow era, a microgeneration comprising approximately my last year in Reno.

I decided to do some hardcore time travel.

I wheeled to the Ps. There, between Paul Simon and the Pixies, I found my father, a recording of him ripped from a CD I'd bought that year from a more innocent internet. Its title is "Paul Watkins Reflects, June 1988."

I put my feet in the river. Maybe this is where he would have ended up anyway, my father, if he'd stayed at home in Sherman Oaks, kept singing and playing music. On my iPod. He could have had a record deal, my mother always bragged, if not for the fire.

June, 1988, says his sandstone voice from Tecopa. My father is making a tape for someone who's made one for him, some Nick. In my headphones he says, *Hello, Nick. This is Paul, Paul Watkins.*

June 1988. He has twenty-five months to live. He thanks Nick for his concern and assures him that his cancer is not an uncomfortable topic because he's *got a good remission going.* He is *in a victorious position.*

This turned out to have a really happy ending, he assures this Nick. *I have this old homestead in the desert, with water, trees. I have two wonderful children, little girls, three and four. Claire and Lise. Claire is the four-year-old. Lise is the three-year-old. They're just delightful. I have a wonderful wife I'm very much in love with, Martha. That's truly a blessing. It's truly wonderful. Not that it's all, how would you say? Daisies and sunbeams, or whatever. But it is, pretty much, much of the time. And getting better all the time.*

He says, *I have a really good chance of having a really wonderful life.* In two years he'll be in Malibu. But for now he is in the past tense. *Cancer served me very well. It was as though I got grabbed ahold of* by the neck, like God grabbed me by the neck and said, "You want to look at your life and, uh, get it back in the productive mode? You want to really live it, or do you want to continue to rape, pillage and plunder?"

He breathes. I breathe.

Not that I was out raping, pillaging and plundering. But in a sense, yes, there is that element there, the element of subjugating the women in my life, there's the element of not being able to be happy, of not being able to be happy having children.

I'm reminded that my mother called me once, my last year in Reno, the year of our Lord iPod. She'd just slit her wrists with a steak knife. "I want to say goodbye," she said. Then, confoundingly, "I miss your dad."

"Well, you're not going to join him," I said. "I mean, if you kill yourself you're going to hell, right?" We were tired, falling back on a cosmology neither of us believed in.

"Then I'll see him there," she said.

"You think Dad's in hell?"

She laughed. "Sweetheart, he was Charles Manson's number one procurer of young girls."

Downstream, two buildings rose on either bank of the Truckee, a parking garage on one side, the courthouse on the other. Maybe six stories each. Somewhere in the parking garage there was a spot where a man once stood and aimed and shot across the river into the courthouse, into the office of the judge who had presided over his divorce. Needless to say, the ex-wife was already dead. All these ghosts were headed to the basin from which no water escapes. That did not seem so bad, the current holding me in its strong arms.

My father said, to this Nick, whoever the fuck he was, *There definitely is mystery and magic, and this is a matter of fact. . . . Life is in fact a wonderful and wide, wide thing. I am an avid lover of life. I suppose that's what's gotten me into so much trouble.*

Rust appeared beside me. I was somehow in water up to my chest, holding the iPod high overhead like the very saddest person. From across the tugging black water a Juggalo called out, "Be careful, you psycho bitch!" I remember slipping on a rock, dropping the iPod, my father saying, *There's nothing wrong with not knowing who you are.* Rust grasped my wrist and reached back for Ty, stretched toward us from a high rock. "Get off me," I guess I said, though I didn't pull back or hit anyone, as I remember wanting to.

After the iPod fiasco, we walked wet and shivering to a bench. We sat for some time until the free tourist bus called the Spirit picked us up. We were silent, lulled by the bus's vibrations. I watched my face in the greasy window and dozed off, the Spirit circuiting the city who knows how many times until Rust nudged me at our stop downtown, at the mouth of the valet loop at one of the big casinos. Mine, I realized, though I'd never checked in. We sat on one of the brass luggage carts parked near the door. The sun was coming up. I was wet and cold but everything felt new. I swelled with love for this grotesque crossing where everything was always open. In Reno there was no emotional last call. A person could completely avoid the black wave at bedtime. Just stay up until you collapse. I missed that. I missed how you were always wanted here, how you never missed anything, how the party didn't start until you got here. But Reno also felt, for the first time—and possibly this was the drugs—over.

I looked at my old friends, sitting beside me on the shiny luggage cart smudged with fingerprints. I told them, "I'm probably not going to go home."

Ty spoke first. "But all your stuff is there."

"I don't need it," I said. "I'm burning my life out from the inside like a canoe."

Ty began, "What about Theo and—"

"I'm unhappy," I said. "I know happiness is a scam, but . . . unhappiness is real."

"She's Gatsbying," Rust explained. "You're trying to Gatsby."

"You're supposed to get rid of everything that doesn't spark joy." I'd read this in a women's magazine in the waiting room of the pediatric dentist and it had had a profound impact on me.

"Joy?" Ty asked, as if reminded of a charming, antique sentiment he had not thought about for years.

Rust shrugged. "My paper towel dispenser brings me joy."

"You do have a really great paper towel dispenser," I said. "I'll grant you that. But I'm talking about *real* joy. Elation. I'm talking about uncontrollable laughter of the soul."

"You don't feel that?" Ty said.

Against my better judgment I said, "You *do*?" I pressed the bite bruise on my forearm, liking the pain. "I don't feel anything. I'm just . . . floating. Like they're all I have connecting me to land. There's a lot of pressure on one spit of sand. What with the sea levels rising. Is this making sense? I haven't laughed in like, a year."

A valet ambled over from the valet kiosk. "You can't sit there," he said. We stood.

"I get it," said Rust.

"What I get," said Ty, "is that you're turning out to be a dirtbag."

The thought had occurred to me. I said, "I guess I am."

"She's not a dirtbag," said Rust, who's always known what everyone is and isn't. "That's the problem. She's not a dirtbag, but she wants to be."

I said I wanted to behave like a man, a slightly bad one.

Ty said I was certainly doing that. Rust said maybe I should get some rest.

"Okay, yeah, see you," I said, not hugging or touching either of them, heading toward the casino.

"That's very Oregon Trail," called Ty. "Not good at goodbyes."

I turned back, considered trying, but was distracted by a Tesla pulling into the valet rotunda with *Morning Edition* cranked. A Rotary luncheon type in a peach blazer and a pristine cowboy hat with a seed-bead hatband popped out of the Tesla and said my name.

"You're being recognized," said Rust.

"You're famous," said Ty, impressed at last.

The Rotarian said, "They told me you were punctual, but wow!" She shook my hand. "And you're wet!" she said, as if this was some sort of bonus.

This was Wendy, a volunteer with the Nevada Arts and Humanities Council, a daisy chain of words vaguely familiar to me. Wendy was to be my author escort this morning. "We're headed to Hug High, isn't that right?" She opened the passenger side door. "Will your friends be joining us?" Without awaiting an answer she said, "That's wonderful, just wonderful!"

Ty rode shotgun and flirted with Wendy by complimenting her bumper stickers (GRAVITY: JUST A THEORY and GRAVITY: IT'S THE LAW!) while Rust and I got carsick in the backseat. It no longer surprised me when the person elected to drive me around was a terrible driver. Maybe the pressure of escort service warps an otherwise decent driver into a bad one. Case in point: Wendy, confused, tentative, apologetic, fearful, and hyper-yielding, insisting others take her turn at four-ways, coming to full stops in scenarios requiring a merge, perversely obliged to make conversation all the while. She explained that she had never been to Hug High—"It's pretty rough, isn't it?" Funnily enough she actually had no idea where the school was!

Wendy fiddled with her GPS, refusing Ty's help with navigation. She had every last little thing under control. We three should sit back and relax, she said, running a red light. I fantasized that we might never make it to Hug, as I had prepared nothing, did not even have a copy of my book on me. Turning in to the high school at last, Wendy became trapped in the bus lane. She would rather not let us disembark and walk to the office, though we could all see clearly from the car the locked front door marked *Visitors*—she was the escort, after all. She circled the campus three times before accruing the courage to enter the faculty parking lot, where a nervous assistant principal waited. The assistant principal looked me up and down, clearly considering hosting a writer at his school a tremendous favor to the Council, personified in Wendy, who in turn clearly believed the benevolence belonged to the Council for spreading the creative spirit to this underserved school. Meanwhile I of course felt it was I—coming down and still quite damp—who was truly altruistic, despite the fact that I had, as I've said, prepared nothing and been paid for that nothing long ago, an honorarium I'd spent on edibles and a cashmere sweater.

The assistant principal noted that I had not responded to any of his secretary's emails inquiring whether my presentation required audio/visual components.

"Of course it does," said Ty.

Rust said, "The professor's presentation is extremely audio/visual."

"For different learning styles," I explained, and everyone nodded solemnly.

The assistant principal sat us in front of the guidance office in a row of metal chairs welded together. A counselor came out of her office and said, "The students are *so* looking forward to your presentation, Professor." I asked her how many students were expected to attend the assembly. "All of them!" she chirruped. "Though the sophomores have ASVAB today so they will have to miss." She made a pouty face—for all those black and brown and poor sophomores tossed by the Armed Services Vocational Aptitude Battery into the chum bucket of war, I could only assume. I made a pouty face back. When the guidance counselor returned to her office, I asked my friends in a desperate whisper-scream what the fuck I was going to do.

Ty shrugged. "Do your thing you do when you teach."

"I teach pass-fail *electives* at a flagship institution! That's ten to twelve of our best and brightest who semi want to be there. These kids are gen pop!"

Rust said, "How about that game they play at camp where you make a story together and everyone says a word?"

"Exquisite Corpse," I said. "That's what it's called."

"See, you're such a pro!" said Ty.

"Let's practice!" Rust clasped his hands together like a youth pastor, excited to see me get some purchase on my rumored expertise. I said, "We'll each say a word . . ."

"I'll start!" said Rust. "'Once upon.' Fuck! Harder than it looks. 'Once.'"

"Upon," I said.

"A," Ty said.

"Time."

"There."

"Was."

"A."

"Tall."

"Lusty."

"Dild."

I put my face in my hands. "I can't do this! With adolescents? In a *public school*? Fuck. I'm fucked." I stood up, thought about running but my butthole winked. I blew it out in the girls' bathroom, washed my hands and got some water from a drinking fountain. Stu-co painted homecoming posters hung overhead with masking tape. I felt the paper crinkle and it made me feel a little better, as did Rust, who had begged a pack of Post-its and a pen from a pretty secretary and used these to write tiny notes of encouragement and ardor that he was now sliding into the vents of random lockers. *This is not a mistake. The cut worm forgives the plow.* That sort of thing. He gave me one.

You are not a fuckup.

Just then a tone sounded and the halls coagulated with teens. Lockers slammed. I felt as afraid as I had in my own high school, though it was a more diffuse fear, since it was difficult to discern the social strata that had been so painfully obvious to me as a kid and which I knew determined all life for the students here, so I felt afraid of nearly all of them, minus the ones who were so plainly at the bottom of the pecking order that they made me want to die—real "It gets better" types. I hoped Rust's notes would find them. The assistant principal reappeared and hustled us to the gymnasium. "Simply plug your device into the source cable on the podium," he said, showing me the stage. "Push audio mute to get sound, visual mute to get picture. If you want the screen lowered, push the down arrow."

With the student body minus the sophomores in the gym, the teachers set about silencing their segments of the bleachers. *Sit, sit, sit,* they said. The assistant principal went to the podium and read a list of small meaningless facts about me written by myself. The audience clapped as required. Ty nudged me and I stood, dizzy. I thought: I might pass out! What a deus ex machina that would be!

But I made it to the podium, the AV hookup waiting like a forked tongue. I shivved my hands into my damp pockets, half expecting the iPod. I found my phone instead, slight and omniscient.

"I want you to stand up," I said.

No one moved.

"Stand up, up," I tried. "Please."

The teachers looked around helplessly, hoping the assistant principal might intervene, but he did not.

"Come down off those bleachers," I said, gesturing to the wide plain of gymnasium floor between us.

The kids stared. Some shifted on the bleachers. Someone cackled, sending the heat of shame up my neck. I should have known children would see right through a sham like me. My hands began to tremble. My voice felt like some wet netting had been thrown over it. Again I said, "Please."

Then, down front, I glimpsed some movement. It was Ty, ever the obedient valedictorian, standing. Beside him Rust also stood, nodding emphatically.

"That's right," I said, clearing the webbing from my throat. "Up, up! Stand up and come down here to the floor." Ty and Rust came toward me, only them, all the scary teens watching. I loved them for it. Eventually, the teachers signaled for the students to obey me and they did.

"That's right," I said, over the thundering of them coming down the collapsible metal bleachers. "Now," I said, "lie down. We are going to do a creative writing exercise." I plugged my phone into the AV system, unpressed audio mute as I'd been instructed. I'd maybe never felt so professional, still damp from the river. "That's right, everyone find a space to lie down." I invited some of the kids up on the platform stage. I remembered from teaching that students would do whatever I said if only I said it many times:

"Come up, come up, come up, lie down, lie down, that's right, just lie down." Soon only the teachers and the assistant principal remained in the bleachers, most of them on their phones. On mine I found my music, the navigation clicking throughout the gym. Rust got up and killed the lights and the kids shrieked perfectly.

Hundreds of phones winked on, then were extinguished under the assistant principal's threat of confiscation. "Close your eyes," I said into the microphone. "Close your eyes. Close them and let your creativity flow."

I pressed play. Brian Wilson's somber, whaley song hummed up into the rafters of the gymnasium. His soothing coo lay over the giggling students, silenced the clomping of their humongous shoes against the basketball court, softened their sneezes and coughs, pillowed their wisecracks and gave cover to their heavy petting. We heard Brian's baleful plinking, his breathy begging. We swayed his dreamy sway.

My biologist's word, dreamy.

Pet Sounds always makes me think of my dad, of him and Charlie taking a little orgy contingent to Dennis Wilson's house *just to blow the minds of his "hip" guests.*

And then what, I wonder, once their minds were blown? Make all the love you can in all the ways you can and then what? Make art, maybe? I'd like to put it that way. I like to picture them all making music together in the afterglow. I hoped my dad got to jam with Brian. I hoped the girls sang.

And what a relief it was at last to honor the impulse I have every single time I stand at a podium! I lay down behind it, curled into the fetal position and closed my eyes, trying for a DILD.

1974

Denise,

Do you remember how when we were young it was just you and me? There were no Cyndis or Terris. No Harrys, Keiths, or Petes. No Nixons. It was just you and me.

Al, my editor, is the most far-out man. He's shorter than me and about 50 years old, but I'm amazed how vital he is. He calls me "kid" or "baby" and always helps me with my homework. He edited my government paper on war and wrote a preface for it and said it was good. He's showing a lot of interest in my work, too.

Everyone else at the paper is grade-A asshole. Last night, Al was off and I got in a hassle with the sports writer, Vince. He told me to take out some copy but it was after 11 o'clock. (I get off at 11.) I was studying for a test in the lobby, waiting for my mom to pick me up. He called me a "no good rotten little bitch." I went outside to wait for my mom. I was going to quit. Tonight, I told Al and he told me if something like that happens again to just leave and then come tell him and he'll get it straightened out right away. "But don't quit!"

Today I did not go to Government second period (Mr. Byrnes's class). He came looking for me fourth period in my Religions class. I thought my ass was up shit creek, but he said he just finished my term paper and wanted to tell me it was very good. That made me happy. He's running for City Commissioner in the next election and I'm going to work for him. I would cry for joy if he got into office. He's a good man.

We had our last speaker in Religions today. After having about 20 people speaking on all the different religions, this man was really refreshing. He was an atheist, owns the largest library in Nevada. Al says he's well-known among the elite and the newspapermen around town. He was completely overwhelming.

Al is the only one who takes the time to answer all the stupid questions I ask and he's the only one who really cares enough to take the time to help me learn to write. Anyway, he's not going to be editor anymore. I guess the boss doesn't like Al, so he gave him the City Hall beat and made Vince (the sports writer) editor. I'm tempted to quit. It's really going to be a drag working with this chauvinist. It's already a hassle. I missed a tape on a dumb sports thing and two of the writers and the new "editor" jumped on my ass.

I'm all typed out. It's time for me to go home, finally.

> Give everyone my love and take care,
> Martha

Denise,

I have been trying to get a hold of you by phone for the last two days. You must be an awful busy girl. You never seem to be home. I had to laugh at your experience with our noble public school system. I realize it was a bummer for you, but now at least you have some idea of how these fantastic, efficient, well-organized public schools work. What happened to you is so typical of things that happen every day simply because of the shape of the place. It is outrageously stupid, but people just don't want change. To most people, change is the most dreaded word in the English language.

Today was the strangest day. I skipped, spent the morning cleaning Harry's apartment, got home about noon. When I got there my brother Jack, Pete and Terri were there waiting for me. Jack was really mad, kept saying, "Where have you been all day? I've been waiting for you to come home." Then he gave me a lid. Just gave it to me. It was really weird. We just got high and talked. I was getting ready for work when Steve Sears came over (Steve with the van) loaded on his ass on downers. I was really pressed for time, but he just wouldn't take the hint. He asked if we could go back in my room and I said all right. We went back there and he started talking about all his problems and how he was just so heavily into dealing dope and how he didn't have anyone to talk to. I said I'd noticed. His parents are really on his back because he smokes pot. They think he's an addict, user, hippie, sick, pervert, blah blah. He's really hung up about it. Then he started ranting about how he could get me any dope I wanted. He took two downers out of his pocket and said he wanted me to have them so he wouldn't take them, but I told him I didn't like downers, so he popped both of them into his mouth. He must've taken some earlier because right away he was really in bad shape. Then he started talking about how sorry he was that he didn't "take" me back when I liked him (actually what happened is I went out with him a couple times and I liked him a little but it was really no big deal. He called me one day and told me he was hung up on Cyn and I said fine, whatever). I kept saying to Steve that I was going to be late for work and that I better go and finally he got up to leave (which itself took ten minutes) and as he was walking out the bedroom door he (of course) turned and kissed me. I said goodbye, Steve. End of tale.

Now I'm at work where the sports dept. is in the process of being moved into a larger room and everything is a mess plus the new set-up is going to make me walk about twice as much as I was before. Yet another bummer for those keeping score at home.

I have my classes for next semester. They are:

1. World Lit I
2. American Lit II
3. P.E.
4. World Lit IV—Shakespeare
5. Lunch
6. Quest (can't tell you what this is)
7. Arts and Crafts

Oh, yeah! Forgive me, but I wanted to tell you about the dream I had last night. I dreamt that I was out in front of the school and I was waiting for someone to pick me up. Someone yelled for me and I looked up. Both Keith and Harry were waiting for me. This reporter from work was waiting for me too, all of them expecting me to go with them. I didn't know what to do but left with Keith because he was sitting in his father's blue Mustang. I'm deep as a spoon. A slut with a decision-making complex, Cyn says.

I haven't seen Harry since last Friday. I haven't had a way over there and I have so much homework I just don't have time. He hasn't called me either, so I know he's not too worried about it. We are going to break up pretty soon, I fear. Or what I think will happen is that we will never break up, we'll just not see each other ever again and I'll never be free.

Altogether now,
Martha

Hey-O Nese,

Missed week of school screwed me up royally. The day I got back my World Lit teacher handed me twelve pages of notes and told me I have a test on them the next morning, so I made a big cheat sheet. My American Lit teacher told me to read a 50-page play overnight. I did. My Quest teacher told me I was going before the board in a week. Jeff (my Quest partner) didn't do a damn thing while I was gone, so we had virtually nothing to present. What made it even worse was the fact that another couple are doing the same thing and they have interviewed close to 20 assemblymen, while we have done three. Mr. Byrnes really came down on us with the old "if you can't handle it, get out" trip. We had two days before our seminar (or whatever) so I yelled at Jeff and he yelled at me and we both got down and did some work. Ok, really we didn't do all that much work, but I read the shit and decided that we would come out of the thing shining. And we did! After we answered a few questions (quite well, if I do say so myself) the panel stopped and asked us what grade we were in, greatly impressed that we were only juniors, made little notes in their books and shit. One of the people on the board was a writer for another newspaper, very jazzed when he found out I work for *The Sun*. When it was all over Mr. Byrnes came outside and shook our hands, grin ear to ear. He looked like he wanted to hug us. So, the heads did all right.

I bought "Clouds." I really like it but you can tell it's her early work. I haven't seen my mother since Wednesday of last week. I wonder how she is.

At the present time I am semi fucked up mentally. I think it's time for a change but I can't see the way. I'm tired of waiting. I wish I didn't have to sleep, could go from running one day to running the next. Then I wouldn't think or dream.

Work is piling up—a man shot himself, his lover, and her friend tonight. Steve (the crybaby with the van) is continually calling me and asking me to go out. I'm beginning to get very rude with him because I have a feeling that's what it's going to take. I wish he'd get the message. I don't even answer the phone anymore if anyone else is home.

Shit. Just poured Coke all over my leg.

Dear Denise,

Hey-o! Just sitting at work looking at stupid motherfucking Vince Lyndelle (the sports editor who replaced Al). I hate working with him so I hang out in the back shop all night. Congrats on seeing Joni, although I was a little bit jealous.

I got my income tax return ($140) and I have about $60 left. I have been buying a lot of clothes. So far I have two pants (dark Levi's and light blue cotton), four shirts: one is like a white muscle shirt with light, see-through flowers, one is a beige smock top, with yellow and brown flowers and puffy sleeves, one is dark blue with white flowers, sort of wraparound type, and a blue short-sleeve sweater like yours. Two pairs of shoes. I will probably go out and spend the rest of my money this weekend. It's insane how fun it is to be able to go out and buy anything I happen to want. I've bought other things too—plants, food, jewelry, some paint. But mainly I'm buying clothes. I just got sick of running around in Monica's holey Levi's all the time. Money is my new favorite drug.

Put on another scene today (from Shakespeare's *As You Like It*). It came off pretty okay. That class is getting to be fun. I'm not doing as badly as I thought I would.

We interviewed this Assemblyman the other day in my Quest class. It was a bit touchy. I got loaded at lunch before the interview because besides being an Assemblyman, the guy is a big, big Army cock, all decked out in uniform. You bet he was surprised when he saw me sitting there with my recorder. Being so loaded I told him what I thought about war. It turned out pretty interesting. I can't agree with the guy, but at least he knows what he believes in.

Do you remember that book I showed you? Buckminster Fuller? Fuller's going to be out at the university next Monday and I'm going to see him. It costs money to get into the lecture, but it's worth it. I don't know if you got into Fuller, Spaceship Earth and all that, but I know you read at least part of it and you have to admit the man has seen the future.

Who all went to Joni Mitchell? What are you going to do this summer? I'm probably going to work so I can have some money to boogie on down the road when the time comes. I'd like to catch the Shakespeare festival together.

Love,
Martha

Dear Cuz,

Tonight Monica was taking me to work and Pete came along for the ride. We got to talking about Munchie and his friends, a bunch of little rip-offs. Pete was bloviating about how Munchie and those guys had broken into a lady's car on Christmas Eve and stolen her purse and got $140. I was completely amazed by this. For some strange reason I don't think it's right to steal from our own fuckin' neighbor. I said something about how that was a pretty low thing to do and Pete said, "Shit, it's a good way to get money." I couldn't believe it. I started saying, "How do you feel when someone steals your money? Can't you put yourself in the other person's place?" etc. but then I just . . . let go. I thought: I used to know a guy named Pete Felix.

I've got to get out of here. I joined the credit union at work tonight. I told them to take $25 dollars out of my paycheck every week. I'm going to save up and get out of here as soon as possible. I can't stand it. Denise, please try your hardest to get a job. I want to find out what it's like out there.

Dear Denise,

Brace yourself, this is going to be a weird one. First of all—and this is very very confidential so please please don't tell anyone—I have been having doubts about telling even you:

I had a little episode with Keith. I don't know if you're interested, but I've got to tell someone. Keith has been going out with this chick Cecelia for months. He's probably going with her again now, but I'll get there. Anyway, Cece and Keith broke up and Keith started coming around my house again. I'm not home hell of a lot so I didn't see him much plus I was trying to avoid him because I still want him and I was afraid of what would happen if we were alone together. I don't know what it is about him! He's just got it and I can't stay away. So, the other night he came over after I got off work and we went shopping for my mother together. Then we came home and made some cookies. My sister had gone to bed and my mom had gone out with Mark, so it was just me and Keith. We sat and talked for hours. He and I agreed on just about everything—getting out of here especially. It helped to know that someone else had seen all this and I'm not going out of my mind. It got to be about 4 o'clock in the morning before he left. I regressed to where I was two years ago with Keith. It was really a lot of fun and honestly I enJOYed myself, but Monday morning I woke up to the reality that I couldn't even wonder about how he felt about me. I knew (and know) that he absolutely does not give a shit about me. Not that I didn't know that that night. He has told me that before in so many ways, but now I have accepted it. Since then I have seen Keith for maybe three minutes twice this week and at school and he's a real nice dude but that's all. A fun little epic.

I got called into the principal's office yesterday. I knew I couldn't be in trouble because the man does not deal with petty ditcher stoners who get good grades. So I went to him and asked, What's the problem? and he said no problem and proceeded to explain that this professor at the university called him looking for me and he wanted Miller (the principal) to get a hold of me for him. The professor didn't know anything about me except my name (which he spelled incorrectly) and the fact that I went to Western and that I asked a question at Buckminster Fuller. This prof left a number, but no one answered when I tried so I called the university but no one answered there either. I don't know what the hell is going on but I don't know how to reach this man, so I guess I'll wait. Miller wants me to ask the prof some questions and then come back to him with the answers. Like I said, I don't know what the hell's going on. I figure if they went through the hassle to get hold of me once they'll do it again if it's that important.

Epic the next: Vince, the editor/sportswriter, has been asking me out. He just got divorced and he has a little four-year-old boy. Tonight he showed me pictures. He's looking for a mother for his kid and boy he's looking in the wrong place. He's called me several times but I've kept it pretty cool and shall continue to do so.

I'm pretty high and it was just outrageously nice to hear from you. Don't worry about losing that letter–I really don't care what happens to it or who reads it. I'm not ashamed and don't regret my actions at all. Keith and I avoid each other pretty much. When we do meet, it's very tense. He wants to make it very clear that he doesn't love me and I want to make it very clear that I don't expect him to.

I did a crazy thing yesterday. I knew I shouldn't and that I would get in trouble, but I just wanted it so bad I did. I went out and adopted a kitten. Isn't that just what I need? It will probably turn out to be Harry's and mine (will explain later on down the page). It's black with bright blue eyes and doesn't have a name yet. He's (at least I got a male) so little I have to feed him out of a baby bottle. When I walk around he follows me everywhere, unless he's asleep. I love him so much.

Now about Harry. Yes, I got back with him and I've never been so happy (almost). We each had our little line of lovers while we were split up, but that's over. It is subject to ending again, but I really doubt it will, at least not for a while. I am keeping the kitten over at his apartment until it gets old enough to fend among the other cats at my mom's house.

Work has been totally far-out. I had three stories in the paper last week, which is a hell of a lot for a copy girl. I sure am still getting paid copy girl wages, which is a bitch, but when I leave this place to go to a good paper I can say that I started writing News at sixteen.

School has been a drag, but I HAVE FINALLY BEAT THE SYS-TEM!!! Did I tell you about the Dean's office? I got suspended for ditching so my mom came in and we made an agreement with the Dean that I can have a pass off-campus whenever I want. My mom wrote a note that they've put in my file and all I do is go into the office, tell them I want the pass and they give it to me. I don't even have to say where I'm going! The Dean is pushing for me to do a bridge year at UNLV next year. That means I'll get my first year out of the way while I finish high school. The institution (school) is a bunch of shit, but if I want a good job I have to go to college. I'm up to state senators on my list of interviews in Quest. This class has opened my eyes to how things are supposed to be run versus how they are run. I am supposed to write some bullshit, fact-finding type paper at the end of all this for the Dean, but I'm going to write a very radical thing, something that tells it like it is. I don't like how it is.

My sister is in the hospital. I went to see her today but she was really in pain and couldn't talk so I just gave her this plant I got her and left. She had something (a cyst or something) in her uterus. They had to cut her open. I hope she hurries up and gets better.

Good morning! Sitting here smoking a joint and getting very high so bear with me, please. Feeling very guilty. "What would He think if He saw me smoking a joint?" I think. Then: none of my beeswax what He thinks of me.

Surprise! Harry told me to make an appointment to get my contact lenses for my birthday. I'd like to change my eye color—how far can you go on shit brown? I don't know if I'll look any better, but it will be nice not to have eighteen pounds of glass and metal sitting on my nose.

I'm in Shakespeare class now. Just can't get into reading for some reason. It's only fourth period and I've already ditched two classes today. I'm blowing it, but don't care.

I have to go to the doctor today. I'm about four days late on my period and my breasts are swollen to a thirty-eight. Ridiculous! I can't even lay on my stomach because they hurt so much. The rest of my sex organs are fucking up too. I don't know what it all adds up to but I guess I'll find out today. I hope it's not—

I'm going to send this thing today! I know these bits are pretty incoherent, but I hope you understand them.

     Love you,
     Martha

Denise,

School's out. No one telling me what to do. Cyndi and Jack and Keith graduated two nights ago; I guess they are Adults. I went to a party on grad night at Keith's country club and have not yet risen from it. I got pretty drunk but not so anyone could tell. Keith strutted around with his fancy SOC friends who drive LTDs and wear formals and suits. A blonde chick hung on his arm. Keith introduced me to her as "Jack's sister," as if I had never been anything to him. Which I never have been. He lies to me without lying. He comes to my house and we talk for hours about love and the future and the changes and I understand him and he understands me, but to the blonde in the black dress with pearls around her neck I am Jack's sister. No one knows about how we were, so Keith doesn't have to worry about his reputation being soiled by the little pauper from Fairway and he glides off early with his rich bitch because she is taking him to a dinner show at the Hilton. What is having someone give you their whole self compared to a dinner show at the Hilton? And the kicker: before they go Keith mentions casually that they are going to Reno in the morning. To get married.

The next morning I got Yo-yo and drove the car to the mountains and walked for hours. I still felt degraded in the worst way but I could also feel the wind coming up, strong and cooling. I let it blow right through me until I felt clean.

At home I let Yo-yo in the house and he runs to Keith sitting at the kitchen table. I said, "I thought you went to Reno."

"No, I decided not to go. Would you like a fry?"

"No thank you," I say, and want to kick my own goddamn stupid asshole head for ever thinking Keith was what I thought he was. He is everything I thought he wasn't. But I don't hate him, I hate me for being so fucking dumb. Him at the table makes me want to scream, so I leave him there and walk out the back door into the desert.

At 5 A.M. I come home looking for a little peace. Keith's sleeping on the couch with his mouth open and I smile at him, thinking oh, God, leave me alone, and stumble into bed. When I wake up he's gone. Has not been seen since. I know I am sick in the mind to feel this for all these years no matter what he does. I don't know how to cure myself. I used to say I'd grow out of this thing, we'd both grow up and then it would be different and we wouldn't need each other anymore. But now I realize I've been saying that for years. When am I going to stop killing myself for his pleasure?

Not that I expect you to have the answer. I don't care if you understand this or if you approve of it or if you think I'm as crazy as I think I am. I love Keith. It's a ripping, hateful love. Why can't I outgrow it? How many years will he take from me?

Don't get bummed by this letter. Really, I feel better having written it and hope you can just take it for that.

> Your sinking but swimming cousin,
> Martha...

Dear Nese,

Harry and I are not going together anymore. He said he was tired of me, that I tried too hard to please him, and I was "no challenge to hold anymore," and that maybe he'd see me sometime.

This was in the library at UNLV. I had gone to class and Harry surprised me after and said he wanted to get loaded at some tiki bar and I said who wouldn't but I had to study and was going to the library. He followed me there acting huffy and when I got inside I told him we had to talk and whispered what the fuck was the problem? That's when he told me all that stuff. He also said I couldn't live without him. I told him, not whispering, to never get it into his head that I couldn't live without him because I damn well could. I said I lived through more than him every single day. He said "good" and left.

I am sort of glad the whole thing happened. There are tons of downers going around. I haven't taken any and never will after seeing everyone on them. A bunch of staggering, drunken slobs and Harry the biggest asshole of them all. But he's an asshole when he's straight.

School at the university is pretty mellow but there's a lot of work and I haven't gotten into it a lot because this thing with Harry has bummed me out and I don't have enough money to get all the books.

I got my senior pictures. They really aren't too bad. I'll send you one after we get them processed or whatever.

       Alive and well,
       Martha

Dear Denise,

This is your typewriter I'm typing this on. Remember the old one your mom gave Monica? Well, I fixed it and now I'm using it. I love it.

Everything else is going steadily downhill. I'll start with my current love affair. I can't say I'm enjoying it. I think I told you about Vince, my editor from *The Sun*? Well, I've been going out with him and it was pretty mellow but now he's beginning to cling and claw. He's been calling me every night and last night I told him I really didn't want to see him for a while and tonight he called and asked me to come over and I just flat out told him I did not want to. He got kind of hot and he'll without a doubt kill all my stories now, but after this thing with Harry and Keith still sniffing around I'm really not up to taking on another maniac. I'm also hanging with this cat Bob (19) and his two brothers (17, 16). Terri and I went to the mountains with them.

Pete had a major freak out on Friday the 13th and beat up Terri's brother, John. He also busted Terri's window and tore her parents' bedroom apart. He just blew a fuse for no apparent reason and went wild. Then he was all right for a week or so until last night when he almost killed Terri in my living room. They got in their hassle and Terri started screaming and my mom woke up and called the pigs. They never came.

UnLove (UNLV) is really getting to be a gas. I can do what I want when I want as long as I keep up on my high school classes too. The atmosphere at college is different. Less bullshit.

Speaking of bullshit, Keith brought his girlfriend over here last night and I almost murdered both of them. I still feel for him and he knows it. I wish he'd stay away so I never have to see his ugly face. She's really not a bad chick for an SOC. Keith foxy as ever, honestly.

Anyhow, write and let me know what you're doing. How's school going? I'm being pretty lazy but doing all right. Got to go wash my hair.

Miss you and love,
Martha

Ate some mushrooms last night and it was unbelievable. There was absolutely no acid paranoia. Ate them with Terri and we talked and laughed for about four hours straight. Terri is so beautiful. Her parents got down on us for making too much noise but even that didn't bum us out. Terri just told them sweetly not to bug us and we went and had a great time in the desert staying up all night even though there was no speed in the stuff. It didn't take all that much to get off, either. Approx a thousand times better than acid. If you ever get a chance to eat them, do it! You can do it anywhere and with anyone and there is no fear of the Big Freak Out.

Everything else is moving pretty much normal around here. I've gone out with Harry about four times since we broke up. I like it better this way.

It all started last night when Keith came over. As you know, I have had this thing going with Keith for quite some time. Well, he was paying special attention to Terri last night. Anyway, we all ended up drinking two bottles of whiskey then Kathy came over and Keith shifted his attention to her.

Let me tell you about Kathy. She's fourteen, very beautiful. She has long thick dark brown hair below her waist. She has very dark eyes and a nice face. Her body is perfect. She's rich and dresses beautifully and is very nice besides.

So, we all got very drunk and eventually Keith and Jack went to the movies. Terri, young Kathy and I sat in my room and talked. I wasn't saying much, just listening to them two talk. They started talking about Keith. Long story short, we found out that he was trying to make both of them. Well, they were pissed off enough at him for screwing them around but when I said, "Make that three," they almost died. I was in pretty bad shape myself, drunk and crying and shit.

Terri wants to go out with him still and I think Kathy does too, but neither of them want to cross me. I told both of them to go ahead, I even recommend it, but they insist on trying to please me. This trio trip is starting to bum me out.

I can't remember what happened after Terri and Kathy went home. I remember a phone ringing and this morning when I woke up I discovered a number of things: (1) my hand had been bleeding and my legs were all bruised up, dried blood all over my hand and in my bed, and (2) a note from Brian Dunbar on the floor saying he is "still wishing to go to the mountains. Please call me or I'll call you by 10" and (3) Brian's wallet and $25 laying the floor. Denise, I honestly have no idea where any of this came from. I must have hassled with someone or something, and no one seems to know.

That's my lost night.

Dear Denise,

Things have changed a lot around here. I left the paper and got a job at this place called Fun City Arcade. I sit in this booth and make sure people don't tear the place up. It is a truly shitty job, but I need the money. My boss is nice, about 22 and gets high so we can talk at least.

I spent the last two days in the mountains at Tim's cabin with Tim and Brian. We mostly partied and cleaned the cabin for winter. The first snow of the season fell when we were up there. It was a gas. Harry went to New York Tuesday. I spent two days with him before he left and I think that I understand the relationship a lot better now. He said I am "a lifelong thing" for him and that I was thinking about us in a very "limited perspective." He's going for a couple of months to visit his brothers and family and I can't say I blame him. I'd be gone in two minutes if I had the means. I think more than anything else I'm jealous of him because he gets to come and go and I don't. I really love him, but I don't need him to live. He gave me a ring. We understand each other and that's enough. He left all his stuff here, TV, stereo, books which I have made good use of.

In fact I am sending you one. It won't help you "escape." It's not a story to take your mind off what you are doing. It is to put your mind into what you are doing. To make you look at yourself. Whenever I get to feeling like you sound, I read this book. If you don't understand it, read it again. It's about how the pain comes from trying to get away from the pain.

One more garbage article before I close: I have sent an application to the University of Colorado at Boulder.

Dear Denise,

I'm glad the book made you think. If you really want a job, get one! You can't baby yourself forever. About the sex thing—don't worry. Everyone at one time or another questions their sexuality. I went to the school psychiatrist for exactly the same reason. He really didn't help me too much—said I sounded hysterical—so I have to work it out myself, but I know it is normal to have those feelings you describe because we have both male and female hormones. Don't worry about it. It's totally normal!

I have been having a good time, learning a lot at UnLove, seeing a lot of Keith but being independent. Of course, I know better than to make anything out of it. Keith is 99% imagination. I don't regret anything I've ever said or done with him, but I sort of wish I didn't love him because then I could be free.

Dear Denise,

Terri got put on restriction for a week because she got excessive absences in her first period. My mother couldn't believe that a parent would actually put a 17-year-old on restriction. She said it was the stupidest thing she's ever heard. Now Terri can't go skiing this week-end, and since she was my ride, neither can I. I've been trying to learn but I'm pretty cloddy on skis. I'm still working at that pinball arcade and it's still a drag, but I still need the money. Mark is trying to get me on at the El Cortez so I can make some bucks before I leave for school.

Harry is still in New York. I miss him. I called him the other day and he has no idea when he'll come back but he said he'd see me again.

Until four days ago I'd been having a fairly mellow relationship with Keith. He'd come over every day (sometimes twice a day) and we were getting pretty friendly, even in front of other people, and I was digging it. We'd spend hours and hours at night gossiping about the daily bullshit, hitting that vitamin G. Then, maybe four days ago, I ran out of things to say so I started listening. It's taken me a long time to realize it, but Keith and I have absolutely nothing in common. We basi-cally think different. He values things that have zero meaning to me. We don't even get along. For the longest time I thought I was in love with him when really we're on completely different wavelengths. Like, I love this person, but do I even *like* him? I've seen him both today and yesterday but I don't feel that bigness in my heart anymore. I feel numb, dead, and he's yammering on . . .

Hey Nese,

I'm here at Fun City (what fun) listening to the kids scream and the bells ring. Lights flashing, degenerates everywhere. In case it isn't ap-parent: I hate this place. My boss (big stoner asshole) left me here by myself so that I have to work for nine hours straight without a lunch break.

Anyway, I don't pretend Keith loves me because I know he doesn't, but he feels good, and that sure helps. I hope this doesn't blow your idea of me. That guy has an unbelievable power over me. I thought I'd grow out of all this, but I think it will be with me until the end of my days.

Got to go now. Place is busy.

Love,
Martha

Happy turkey day. I tried to call you but no one was home. I figure you could be a number of places. I'm feeling pretty strange these days. I feel time passing. My mom's house is so quiet I could die. Everybody's working. This chick I know turned me on to a bunch of pot and I've been smoking all morning and now it's like I'm trapped in my head. I'm beginning to realize what I think I see isn't necessarily what is there at all. I hope you have a very foodful day.

Gobble, gobble,

love,
Martha

I Love You but
I've Chosen Darkness

I spent the morning before I left for Reno on Myspace looking at pictures of my dead ex-boyfriend. The phrase *my dead ex-boyfriend* is syntactically ambiguous. You can't tell from it whether this boyfriend and I were together when he died. We were not. We'd been broken up for about two years. We were together for three then apart for two, then he died. He died in a car crash.

Myspace is still with us. You could dog-ear this page literally or figuratively, bookmark it, set aside this volume or swipe to a new screen new beginning and find my Myspace page or yours, assuming you were aged fifteen to say twenty-five in the early aughts. The reason Myspace failed isn't because it was populist or ugly or bought by News Corp but because it was hard to talk about: *my Myspace* is harder to say than *my Facebook*. The uncooperative cadence of the phrase *my Myspace page* perfectly encapsulates the awkwardness of the early aughts, when our story begins.

HIS NAME WAS JESSE but in the years between our breakup and his death he went by Jesse Ray, meaning his new friends and his new girlfriend called him Jesse Ray. I never called him Jesse Ray. No one from our old group ever called him that. A lot of us grew up together, don't speak of him much now, maybe because we don't know what to call him.

I remember his body best of all because it was covered in tattoos. Not covered, that's lazy. His body could not have been covered because in fact his tattoos were a secret from a few important people—his parents mainly and the people in their church. It's not that his parents didn't know him as I thought then but the him they knew was not the him I knew. There were at least three Jesses at the time of his death: Jesse, Jesse, and Jesse Ray. His parents knew one, I knew another, his new friends and new girlfriend knew a third. The only person who knew them all was probably his biological mom K, who lived in Elko and knew everything. Jesse and I once fucked in the sacred vestibule of the Mormon Church in Ruth, Nevada, while his grandfather's ninetieth birthday was taking place in the multipurpose room down the hall, and she knew about that, for example. K had been a waitress her whole working life. She was basically omniscient.

Clothed, Jesse was just a tall lean white guy. Long feminine fingers, goofy mop of glossy brown curls he was vain about, a stupid soul patch sometimes, sometimes a mustache, eyelashes of a fawn. I'm still attracted to men like him. But when he undressed he revealed torso, biceps and thighs crowded with ink: a scarecrow and graffiti he photographed in the Reno railyard and his own let's say underaccomplished drawings. His collarbones said *I love you but I've chosen darkness.* With a period, as in end of discussion. We'd been friends of friends in high school, where his stepmother was a health teacher who believed in immaculate conception. I'm being unfair. She was a lot of other things too, but her stern piety made her stepson's secret rebellion first-rate gossip. That and he'd had many of these tattoos done with an improvised apparatus built of a Bic pen.

Jesse was on the football team, wore eyeliner and sometimes other makeup with his jersey at home games, suit on away days. He dated evangelical girls who would only permit him anal sex, another secret from his parents. Theirs too, I assume. His father was a bearded giant, an HVAC repairman, taught karate, led a home church of his own strict and eccentric doctrine. Their study was based on a code he had developed for unlocking the secret meanings of the Bible, something about every seventh word or fourth word. Each in their small congregation had their own three-ring binder with highlighted decryption glyphs in plastic sheaths. Jesse's father had had a shipping container buried somewhere on their property, stocked with supplies to wait out the days between Y2K and the rapture. All this I gathered from Jesse, for though at that time *I* still possessed my anal virginity, I was never invited. This could be because my stepfather rocked very serious prison tattoos on every region of his corpus including his neck and hands, but was probably because my family didn't have a church.

I paid little attention to Jesse in high school because he was a rollerblader and I preferred skateboarders and suspected him gay. I was fourteen, fifteen, sixteen and didn't know how to spend time with a boy who didn't want to fuck me. Then all of a sudden it was August and all the swimming pools in town had gone mouth-warm so you didn't even want to swim until after sundown and Jesse was back from college and I was headed off to the same one in a few weeks. He was working a/c, wrung out from crawling under trailers in 120-degree weather in long sleeves so his dad wouldn't see his tattoos.

We were at our friend Seth's, whose father made us Budweiser with Clamato. We were eighteen, nineteen years old. By dusk Jesse and I were alone in Seth's parents' semi-aboveground pool. I gave him a shoulder massage—his shoulders pallid, his neck and face sun-leathered save for little white hyphens at his temples where the arms of his sunglasses rested. After the massage Jesse said, in the voice of an animated luchador from a web series we all watched then, "Maybe you want to take your top off?"

I was somewhere between willing and compliant. *Down* we called it, as in *she's down,* short for *down to fuck* or *DTF,* which is what it said beside my name on the wall in the football locker room, Jesse said. *Claire Watkins = DTF,* inked as an insult but I've never taken it as one. I was indeed down to fuck. I was curious, liked exploring other bodies. I also liked to be liked, who doesn't?

"This is why I have no respect for rapists," Jesse said, cupping the white triangles of my boobs and glancing into the house to see whether anyone was at the sliding glass door. We couldn't tell, didn't care. Seth's older brother was the hottest guy I'd seen IRL and it turned me on to think of him watching.

Jesse said, "Girls are really nice. Most of them will do whatever."

I told him that was because he looked like a white trash Ryan Phillippe.

He blushed, turned the color he would ask me to dust across his cheekbones some mornings in the bathroom of the one-bedroom we later rented behind a halfway house off I-80. "You just have to ask. That's all they want. All consent is is asking. If you can't even ask, you're a pussy."

"You're using that word wrong," I said, lifting myself topless to the edge of the swimming pool.

"What, 'pussy'?"

I pulled him close, worried about my stomach rolls. I had probably been reading my mother's copy of *Our Bodies Ourselves*. "You're using it as an insult meaning weak," I murmured into his neck. "The pussy—by which I assume you mean the vulva, clitoris, vagina and cervix—is extremely resilient. The uterus is the strongest muscle in any body. The clitoris has twice as many nerve endings as the penis."

Jesse had freed his from his board shorts. "No for real," he nodded, "pussies are tremendous."

"Also," I said, "it's a term that belongs to a community. Like the n-word. I can say it but you can't." I pulled the crotch of my swimsuit to the side and we kissed.

I said, "I can use it as an insult or in reference to my anatomy. I can say, 'Fuck my pussy, Jesse.' Or, 'Let's fuck, you pussy.'"

ALL THIS WAS MOSTLY FUN and erotic (though we rarely came) but it was also my survival strategy. You could question its efficacy since it made sweet boys afraid of me so that I always ended up with the crazies but in this manner I went from being raised by a pack of coyotes to a fellowship at Princeton where I sat next to John McPhee at a dinner and we talked about rocks and he wasn't at all afraid of me.

Anyway, I didn't like sweet boys. I liked filthy weirdos who scared me a little and I still do.

Someone eventually shooed us out of Seth's pool and Jesse and I drove out to BLM land and lit off fireworks and fucked a few times in the back of his little pickup where he said, "How do you like it?" and "No, I'm asking." Then we were boyfriend and girlfriend and then we lived together up in Reno working retail and fast food and taking night classes and Jesse quit drinking and proposed on Christmas and I reneged on New Year's and Jesse started snowboarding and going to shows and doing hard drugs and I started writing and Jesse fucked a girl in a tent up at Stampede Reservoir and another girl at the Straight Edge house and I fucked a kid whose dad had an amazing cabin at Tahoe and in this manner Jesse and I broke up a few dozen times and eventually tacked a curtain across our living room and that became my bedroom where I would occasionally find Jesse napping in my bed because he missed my smell or on my computer without my permission doing homework or jacking off.

Jesse lived like he knew he was dying, a saccharine nugget of pinspiration terrifying to actually behold. Take it from me, you do not want to room with anyone who actively lives like he's dying. His body was coiled with eros, anarchy and other dark sparkling energy. He looked for fights at shows or by wearing eyeliner and little boys' superhero shirts he bought at Walmart to strip clubs, waited for someone to call him a faggot and then beat their ass. He had been on the club boxing team before he dropped out, and tech bros in town for bachelor parties did not expect his long arms, nor his gigantic martial arts father. Afterward he went to Awful Awful for an Awful Awful or a buffet for prime rib.

He got gnarly nosebleeds all the time and our best talks happened with him in the tub letting the blood slide down his face and red the warm water. He was in the mug club at the tavern around the corner, an investment he called it, not because a mug club member received his beers in a personalized stein, though that was appreciated, but because members could purchase another pint for a friend for a dollar, which Jesse did often and then occasionally he smashed the pint on the floor to emphasize a punch line or one time into the side of a guy's head because the guy called Jesse's favorite milf waitress a cunt.

He liked to sing classic rock karaoke and uproot street signs and use them to smash too-nice cars parked in our bad neighborhood. He once shit his pants while rollerblading to work then worked his whole shift like that. He owned three pairs of rollerblades, two snowboards and about a dozen books in a crate beside his sleeping bag until he read *Walden* and announced, "I don't need this crate!" We had taco night at our apartment every Tuesday for all the runts and strays in our friend group and Jesse cooked the meat. He cut lilacs from the bushes on campus with his Leatherman and piled them on my unmade bed even though we were broken up because the previous spring we'd been walking together and I guess I'd stopped and smelled them. He stole a keg from behind a liquor store and I could not get his new friends to leave our apartment until it was tapped at which point Jesse rolled it back where he found it. He was very good at keeping secrets. Needless to say he became a junkie junked out on all sorts of things near the end but he was also very much alive.

One day I came home from my new job forging signatures for my butch Women's Studies professor at the subprime mortgage company she owned with her lover and Jesse was at my computer, a piece-of-shit

Dell I'd maxed out my credit card for. He must have gotten a nose-bleed during, because he was jacking off covered in blood. I let him finish, kissing him, then told him it was time to get the fuck out and he agreed he would after the World Cup because we'd gone halvsies on the cable.

There is no story—he was there then he was gone. I am a dumb lump scratching my head baffled by this most basic, ultimate fact: he was there then he was not.

I found out he'd died from my sister, who found out on Myspace. His current-now-suddenly-former girlfriend was in mourning: black hair black clothes black makeup, long all-caps passages of pure screaming grief. You want to know whether I hated her? I did.

People die on the internet now, really die. We can watch them die in real time, every gruesome frame if we like, and sometimes if we don't. In dorm rooms, in cars, off bridges, black and brown people executed by the state, unarmed fleeing autistic hands up, fathers mothers children sisters starring in snuff films screened in the airport.

Of Jesse I have only pictures—his body on Myspace. I like the selfies best, you can see his gaze in them, see what he thought was hardcore, what he thought was punk. The last he posted before he died are of some operation he had, his fingers folded in metal horns beside staples in a savage line from his sternum to his navel, a few inflamed sutures beneath the navel disrupting the outline of a new tattoo on his abdomen, one I don't recognize.

There was a car crash, someone was fucked up, probably everyone, though I don't know that for sure. I heard Jesse was flung through the windshield into the desert, on the way out to BLM land, the place we first made love. I'd like to put it that way.

He kept secrets, hated condoms. I watch his ex online for signs and symptoms. I check his Myspace and I know she does too since she is me is my own sister. We have the same thing living in our blood now. I am not doing a good job of this.

Jesse always let me be the good guy. He did not pay much attention to what I was doing and this is the version of freedom I have grown most accustomed to—most protective of. He saw I was a watcher and gave me something worth watching. He was not violent but he enjoyed violence. He was a vandal and a fighter but he was never mean, never tolerated meanness. He was the person I called when I was afraid. He walked me anywhere I asked him to though he admitted the only time he felt unsafe on the street was anytime he had a girl with him. He always let me be the better person even though I wasn't better than anyone. He wasn't cracked up but he let me be the steady hand, made me make myself feel safe. When I was with him I was always in control and this was true somehow even the night we drove to Berkeley to see Radiohead and after drove a little stoned across the bridge and slept at my sister's place in the Tenderloin, on the living room floor because we were twenty, twenty-one.

He was harmless there, the street was noisy, and the living room was lit orange from the soda streetlights and we collapsed into a hillock of sleeping bags and yoga mats and pillows and somewhere in there my sister's cat making my eyes itch. I woke up with Jesse rolled atop me wanting sex. I was tired, didn't want it he was not at all violent but also not relenting, his body unyielding, his long arms beefed up from snowboarding all winter and lifting boxes in the stockroom at work. He held me down.

I remember thinking in italics. *Is this when it happens?* And then I answered myself. *That's up to you.* I decided that it wasn't, it was simpler. I was determined to make it out of college unraped, an actual goal I had. Though before I even started college I met a kid in the shoe store where I worked who invited me to a party but the party was just playing cards and so I was playing poker, a tourist's game, with him and some other people and drinking a Corona, then I woke up and it was morning and I was on the bathroom floor sore with my pants around my ankles. I walked into the master bedroom looking for the kid who'd invited me, whose apartment it was, the only person I knew at this party. He was in bed asleep with an erection, no blankets, and another girl I didn't recognize naked, spread-eagled on the bed, her hands tied to the bedposts I think, but I could be wrong. I wrote my phone number on his bathroom mirror with what I am just realizing now must have been her lipstick.

What's your family church? Jesse's father asked me the one time in three years I had dinner at their house. We don't have one, I said, or maybe I said *work*. Work was our church, and laughter too. Laughter and work and words. Rocks and photographs and dogs and books and TV. Breaking into houses, viewing things at night. My sister my mother and me around the kitchen table bullshitting. The earth the body the sisterhood.

THEO HAS A DEAD LOVE TOO. We traded them on our first date, by my count the night we were the last two left at the bar, and we walked to the United Dairy Farmers on High Street for ice cream that we took to another, hipper bar open later, where we sat on stools playing footsie and drinking beer and eating sundaes with the ghosts and thereafter went home and dry humped without kissing in my bed, where eventually Theo slept with his jeans on. This was in Ohio.

Telling Theo about Jesse was as intimate with another person as I've ever been, was my way of telling him about my mother. Theo would not know her name for months.

Theo's love had been in grad school. She went on a research trip to South America, something with biomes, bacteria, got an infection but didn't know it. She came back to the States and died in her sleep. Her roommate found her in the morning, cold in her bed. She'd had bulimia some thought, and that might have compromised her immune system.

Theo never got to see her body. I never saw Jesse, never saw my mother. She was cremated while I finished my midterms. By the time I got home she was the ash we spread in the garden in Tecopa, where she had spread my father. I don't know where Jesse is now.

Jesse, I wish you were here. America is violent and queer as fuck. The snowbanks are rising and every morning I drive over a frozen river past a mosque an elementary school this week sent a letter threatening *a great time for patriotic Americans*. I pass a kid who looks like you walks like you, I pass a sculpture by Maya Lin called *Wave Field*, which is like a bunch of waves made of grass, covered in snow, so like a bunch of bumpy snow. I drive to a strip mall and smoke weed in my SUV and do rich-bitch yoga with these fierce old dykes and suburban sorority girls and other basic traitorous cunts, all of them my sisters, and for twenty dollars each we all come out an hour later looking like we just got fucked.

Maya Lin was selected to design the Vietnam Memorial when she was still an undergrad at Yale. Ross Perot called her an egg roll, remember? We were kids. Did you ever get to see the Vietnam Memorial? I don't think you did. I've seen most of the monuments in DC. I've been to Paris and The Hague and Antwerp for a night and London and Toronto and the Amalfi Coast in Italy and Wales twice. I've had coffee with Margaret Atwood, lunch with Justice Stephen Breyer, and a beer with one of the *Game of Thrones* bros. Once I was talking to Michael Chabon at a reception and Ira Glass interrupted Chabon to talk to *me* and then—then!—someone cut in to talk to Ira and it was Meryl Streep.

Sorry. There are only so many people I can talk to about these things.

Jesse, when Lise came to visit me she had this strange look on her face and I finally said what what tell me and she said do you realize that our parents could not have afforded the dollhouse version of this house? I spent the morning looking for you on Myspace and trying to untangle a mess of sad white cords made by slaves, and this too is America. We have electric cars sort of and the Tesla gigafactory outside Sparks is the largest building in the world. We have virtual reality headsets and as you predicted people use them mostly for porn. We have hd porn. My sister works with a woman in Vegas who was raped repeatedly by her husband, he liked to watch hd porn on his vr headset during. I can't shake that.

I can't shake the pictures you posted of your body, hundreds of them, on Myspace. In some you are Jesse, in some you are Jesse Ray alive but dying, actively dying, looking dead, choosing darkness. In none of them in an unnamed album you are finally and truly dead. You are a torso beneath a sheet in the desert. There is a shattered windshield, a cop car, an ambulance, a fire engine tilted on the soft shoulder of the highway, lights blazing. The sun is rising and the mountains are indigo above you. Someone has tucked you up so none of you is showing so we don't have to see the parts of you we don't want to.

You were here, then you were gone.

I love you. Am practicing saying that.

1973

Dear Denise,

Terri and I just hit upon a fantastic idea. We are going to start an underground paper at our school! I was sitting at my typewriter writing an editorial for the school newspaper about the defects of the school system, how it trains you to be a worker bee and how they let the pigs and the war machine prey on us. Terri called and I read it to her. She said it meant too much for them to print. She said it said something and they'd never print it. She was right. I said yeah and, "We should start our own paper." Then we both knew we would.

Keith came over and he explained the whole legal side of the thing. It's super complicated, but if we work our butts off, we can do it. And I will! It's going to take about $300 to start. We'll probably have to sell advertisements in it. It will take many more people than just me and Terri and you (you've already been recruited), but I think we can pull it off. So, if you run into anything you think might be interesting, write it up and send it fast. Try to get the views of people around your school and if anyone wants to help, give them my address. We welcome any help at all.

Keith is as smart as a son-of-a-bitch. He knew everything about starting a paper. He sat here for an hour and a half and explained it to me. He's considering being our business manager. He is quitting his job tomorrow because they want him to get his hair cut. Maybe he's not so straight after all? Sorry, I can't help talking about him a little. You know how it is.

Please write back. If we ever get this thing off the ground, we're going to really say something and I want you to be part of it.

Love and miss ya,
Martha Frehler

P.S. try to think of a title for the paper. I was thinking of calling it
NATURE
AND
FREEDOM

Dear Denise,

I'm in first period. I got your letter yesterday and this is the only chance I have to write. I've got so much homework I can't turn around without worrying. Yesterday I got called into the dean's office. She hassled me and I hassled her and it was one big hassle.

The paper idea fell apart. First of all it would cost over $600 for the first copy. Then as soon as they find out who is doing it we'd get thrown out of school. Something in the Student Handbook. That's what Dean Johnson said. Shit, I wonder what happened to freedom of the press?

It snowed here yesterday. When I woke up there was about 2 inches on the ground and it was still falling. There was a big snowball fight in the smoking area. Everybody throwing got swats or suspended. They closed the smoking area, too. You try to have a little fun and they get all uptight . . .

My friends didn't go back to school after lunch. When I got home, they (Terri, Frank and Scott) were in the back desert writing "get high" in the snow. Keith was with me and we went out and had a big snowball fight. I got dusted about six times. Then Jack came out and we all jumped him. I went back in the house to find Terri crashed in my room. I built a fire. Keith came in, followed by Scott, followed by Frank. Scott got the guitar and I made tea and we had a little jam session, by the fire. It was a trip.

Anyway, I feel pretty good except for about Keith. He's got me so uptight, I can't believe it. Denise, I wish I never met him.

I don't know how much running away would accomplish. It might wake them up, but it also might just get them pissed off. My honest opinion is that it would do me some good. Let me know what you think.

All the days are the same. I'm always forgetting what day it is, when I'm supposed to go where, people's names. I always have the feeling that there's so much I have to do, but I never know what it is so I don't even make an effort. It all runs together into nothingness.

Sorry, you've got enough to worry about without my problems. I'll make it.

Keep your head up.

Love,
Martha

Dear Denise,

What's happening? Not much is going on here. We're all just making it.

I got the pictures Terri took on New Year's Eve back. I almost cried when I saw one of me and Keith. It looks like we belong together. I know

I'll never get over him. He just sticks in my head. I have this feeling that he sees me like no one else can and if he's not seeing me no one will, especially not me. Does that make sense?

Today he took me home from school. I wondered what was going to happen. Well, we got together just kind of naturally. It seems so right to be with him I don't see how I stand it when I'm not.

Cyndi looked at that picture and I could tell she was kind of hot about it. It's been two years since she even looked at him, so I don't see what the hassle is. She wants everyone that ever liked her to be madly in love with her for the rest of their lives.

Keith came over again at dinner. Then we went into my room and he beat the hell out of me. Actually, I beat the hell out of me, but he was directing my hands.

This letter is totally fucked. I'm sorry I'm blowing it so bad. I guess I'm weirded out and talking out of my ass. Just ignore me. I better close before you can't understand this thing at all. Keep it cool. Don't let anyone or anything hassle you. Tell anyone who's hassling you to get fucked.

Dear Denise,

Shit, there's so much to relate I doubt if I can ever say what I'm trying to say. I hope you can dig what's going on. I hope I can dig what's going on.

I think I've met another one of us. I mean, not me and you exactly, he's me and you at one point in our lives. I can't figure out if that point is in the future or the past. I have no idea what I'm trying to say. Harry is really real. That sounds like a weird thing to call a person. I dig just being there and talking to him. Denise, did it hit you in a huge wave? Like all of a sudden "What the hell is happening?" and you wonder what's going on in your own head?

Cyn and I went over there tonight and we did some coke or whatever. It made me feel insane. I can't type. I better get my head together. It's almost 1 o'clock and I have school tomorrow.

What can I say?
Martha

Dear Denise,

Something happening here. What it is ain't exactly clear.

You remember Harry, from the ski lift? He asked me to come to his house and I did. He spaced me out. He is something different. It's not just that he's a fox or he's nice, it's like he digs what is going down in my head. He understands me better than I understand myself. I went over there last night again with Cyn. We had to leave early because of school and everything. I wanted to stay, but Cyn couldn't dig it because—well, I don't know why.

Then, on the way home, Cyn lays this rap down on me about how Harry's too old and he's just using me. I got pretty uptight about it. I can't believe it's possible. Then cousin Larry (of all people) came over— him and Cyn had been talking. First he's like, "Where's your mom?"

"Work, where else?"

And he lays the same thing down only like, "I'm a dude. I know." I got really uptight and insane. I ran out into the back desert just to get away from them. I don't know what's true.

I wish so badly you were here so you could feel this yourself. It's not just me, it's everybody feeling it.

The enclosed letter is the one I wrote you last night. It's really senseless but I thought you could dig some stoney emotions.

Love and understanding,
Martha

Dear Denise,

I'm sitting here wondering what the hell to tell you. My mind is gone. I'm so confused my insides are churning.

I think I'm sick or dying or something. It seems like an effort to do anything. I feel like I'm getting old. I think the "generation gap" has set in between my mother and me. I can't talk to her anymore. I can't understand her or myself. I spend so much time alone. Even when I'm with everybody in body, my mind is alone. I dream so much these days it's like one long acid trip. Nothing is real, it all slides by me. I can't feel. That's the worst part. My heart has a chill on it all the time. I'm numb and drowning.

I went to Harry's house last night. We didn't hardly talk at all. No one did. It was so quiet. I couldn't open up. The whole night my heart pounded as if I were terribly afraid. I read some of his writing. You know how I feel about my writing. It's my whole self. In my writing there are no lies. Harry's already read most of my stuff. The pieces of his I read were fantastic, in their way, but they've really ruined my picture of his gentleness. Harry was a soft, feeling person, but all of a sudden . . . I can't describe this knowing fear inside.

I feel the Devil in the true sense. I can't let it happen, man, I've got to find me. Where have I gone? It used to be I was so sure of what I was. I can no longer find the truth. Everything is so under layers, nothing is open, nothing clear. I want to see you. I wish it could be right now.

Harry wrote a poem for me, but I didn't read it. I'm scared. God, I've never felt such fear within myself. I'm dying inside, and it's such a long, boring process. Where am I going? Who am I? I can't find you. I want to cry out, but it's like there's a strong hand over my mouth. I haven't said anything ever. I'm dying slowly from something I can't name. I never want to see Harry again, yet I wish he was here now. I hate him and love him all in one breath.

I wish I could express this, the truth of it.

Love,
Martha

Pete's mother is dead. She died Monday afternoon. I've been cooking dinner for him. They're going to send him to Alaska. They might let him live with his brothers but if they look at the records, I'm sure they won't. Last night I stuck my hand against the screen of the fireplace and now I have a million little burns on my hand.

Dear Denise,

I've been trying to write you a decent letter for about a week but I've been so loaded or busy I haven't had the chance. Today was the last day of the semester. Last nine weeks I got an F in history. The trip is I had an A the first nine weeks. C for the semester. My final exam was a mindblower . . . I didn't study AT ALL, test was 12 pages long and . . . I didn't miss one question! I don't know how I did it, but I did.

Now we have five days off: Thursday because of Johnson's death, Friday because the seniors register, then the weekend and Monday we register. I really need sleep. Harry came over while Mom was out of town. The first night he stayed until about 2 o'clock in the morning. The second night he stayed all night. It was really far out. Cyn almost shit when she came in and found us sleeping—pretty funny. Sure was nice to have him beside me all night. A feeling I can't begin to describe. I haven't seen him since.

Had a big hassle with my mom this morning. She was pissed off because I went to Harry's last night and didn't get home until morning. I asked if I could stay home and she started raving about how if I hadn't stayed out partying until all hours I would feel like going to school, which is pretty true and I admitted it. But then Jack asked if he could stay home and SHE SAID YES. That really pissed me off and we hassled all morning about it.

Harry said some strange things to me last night. We talked about loving people. He is supposed to be going to Hawaii but now he says he isn't going for a while. I feel so strange about it, like kinda guilty.

My brother Jack is really weirded out about Harry. He always used to tell me "What you need is a boyfriend" and now that I have one he doesn't know how to handle it. Cousin Larry gave me a long rundown on how older guys are only trouble and bitch, bitch, bitch . . .

I suppose you're wondering about Keith, Denise. I think Keith knows about Harry. If he doesn't, he's deaf. I really hope that I'm not causing pain of any kind. Keith's out of sight, but I just can't be with him anymore. Maybe if Keith cared for me in any way. I guess I'm greedy. I cannot honestly say I'd quit seeing Harry if Keith asked me to. Maybe two weeks ago I would've, but it's too late now. Harry really means something to me now.

Terri and Pete had a big fight this morning. I don't know about what. Terri cried all through homeroom. Pete called her stupid and she couldn't handle it.

I went to take my learner's permit test Monday. I failed it. Isn't that stupid? I guess I'm pretty dumb.

I finally got a hold of some whites and so I'm staying up all night. I'll just crank out pages and pages of pure thoughts and hope you can understand. It's so hard to say things in a letter like this, where you have to make sense. It's really important that you understand all this. I don't know if you feel it or not, but I have been getting some zaps from you. I don't know if you know this or not and if you don't, I'd appreciate it if you didn't say anything. The thing I'm going to lay down on you is a very personal matter and you must never, ever breathe a word of this to anyone, especially your mom: Cousin Larry wants to make love to Terri. Cyn is trying to get Terri to do it, but she doesn't know Terri's heart and Terri doesn't want to. I'm really afraid they (Cyn and Larry) will hurt Terri bad. She's so tender inside. This goes back to me and Harry. I love him very much and we made love. This is how the whole thing began. Maybe that's not how it is, but I think I'm right. You know how Cyn's gone through a lot of guys and still hasn't found the right one. I have gone through comparatively little hassle in Cyn's eyes (Cyn doesn't know the whole saga of Keith). All she can see is that I was sitting there picking my nose and Harry walked into my life and we fell in love. Well, she doesn't think I should find love so "easily" when it is so hard for her. Anyway, when I told her Harry and I made love, she expected me to relate some terrible experience, but Denise, it was so beautiful. I couldn't hide the joy. I smile from my soul when I think of it.

So, Cyn is uptight because I had something she didn't. And suddenly she wants to sleep with the guy who happens to like her at the time, who happens to be Cousin Larry, almost thirty. (Yes, Harry is almost same age that's my point.) Cyn got to talking to Larry and he wanted to make love to her, but even though she had wanted to go through with it suddenly she said no, she won't but Terri will. When Cyn told me all this, I told her if Larry touched Terri I'd fucking kill him.

So tonight (with all this knowledge) I was at Harry's. He got a new apartment up by Western so I can just walk over there. I had told my mom I was going to Cyn's after school but I decided to go to Harry's all day instead. So while I was gone Terri came looking for me and Mom said that I was at Cyn's. Terri called Cyn's and of course they said I had never been there. Terri told Mom and she went berserk. She knew I had gone to Harry's and she knew I was lying to her. So she sent Terri and Cousin Larry to find me. They were on the way to Harry's when Larry said he had to stop by his apartment and get something. So he took Terri to his place.

Anyway, they came and got me at Harry's, which pissed me off. I didn't know about what Larry had just done. I came home and explained to my mother how I ended up at Harry's instead of Cyn's and thank God, she understood and let Keith come over. I rapped with him and Ter for a while. Terri told me and Keith about Larry. I could tell Keith wanted me. (I don't mean to sound conceited or whatever but that's what I felt.)

Around ten o'clock Terri and Keith left and right after that Steve called. (Remember Steve? The guy I was hassling with over Christmas?) Steve knows I dig speed and he said if I could get a ride out to his house he'd turn me on to some. Like a miracle, Cyn came in and she drove me over there and Steve gave me six hits. I came home, took one, and sat down to communicate all this to you. So here I am.

I know this is a hell of a lot to lay on you all at once. I feel as though I've just written a fucking book. Denise, please understand this crazy letter. I want so much to let you know everything because you are part of me and I love you. You made me so happy today in your letter when you said I was going to be a great writer and even my letters were "a work of art." I really needed that.

I'm sending all the love here (and there's a lot) to you in this envelope. Pass it out to everyone there for me.

I hope I didn't bore you with all this. I think everything is said.

     Goodbye,
     Martha

Dear Denise,

High! I made it to first period, a miracle! I got a package from O.D. two days ago. He sent me some of that German hash. Cyn and I smoked it after school and it sure is bad! I almost couldn't do dishes. I've got to write him and thank him.

Want to hear a mindblower? Remember Simon Drake, the lounge singer? He wants to take Cyndi out! She doesn't know it yet, but he told me at Caesars the other night when I was picking up my mom. It's a bit icky because he's literally twice her age but they're both playing the same game. No one else knows about it except Simon and me. He's come over to my house on his last two dark nights (while Mom's at work) and Cyn just happens to be there. Last night I wasn't even home and they were there! I don't care, as long as they're happy bullshitting each other.

Pete got a job working at *The Sun* (newspaper). The hours are bad—all night four nights a week. He worked last night and today he looks dead.

Day before yesterday Harry was off work so I went over there after school. We walked to the park and screwed around. He laid some heavy things on me. We were talking and he told me he wanted to see me much more often, like all the time. He said he wants to hoard me all to himself until he leaves. I'm freaked out at this but in a good way. I can't believe how nice it is to love him. I am a lucky bitch. All my friends hate Harry. I wish they could know him like I do.

I have something really important to tell you that I've been worried about for a long time and I put off writing you about it because I just don't want to think about it myself. But it's been on my mind so much I just can't go without telling you. I'm a little worried that I might be pregnant right now. I know that must really hit you hard but not as hard as it hits me. Man, I'm scared. I do know one thing, if I am, I can handle it. Just pray I don't have to. Please don't tell anyone, not even your mom. Please try to call me if you can.

Dear Denise,

This has got to be a fast letter because I'm terribly pressed for time. Things have taken a phenomenal change—mass confusion! First, about this summer—it is imperative that you come here *as soon as you get out of school*—before, if possible. It may be the last time I will be able to see you for I don't know how long. I'll try to explain later.

Terri ran away from home and is living at Pete's house. Her parents are totally unreasonable, according to Terri and Pete. It seems (from what I can get) that Terri's parents put her on restriction for drugs, bad frame of mind, etc. so Terri blew up and left.

Scott and Greg still work at the gas station, Pete at Robo Wash. Terri and him are getting tight playing House. Cyn is going with a guy named David, an SOC fox. She only hangs around with the SOCs now. To each their own.

Now, about me. I spent the weekend at Harry's. It was really mellow but something I was very much afraid of has happened. Last night, before I left, Harry asked me to move in with him for the summer, maybe longer. He's got work in Detroit for the first few weeks of summer and wants me to come with. My head is screwed. I had so many other plans with other people (music, writing, Canada). You and I alone have so much to do together. That's my main hang-up. I wanted to go it alone or with you for a while. I love Harry, but I'm so confused I could die. I tried to call you last night but no one was home. Please write.

Dear Denise,

Thanks for the letter. Just received it. Gerald (old man across the street) won $15,000 playing craps two days ago. Him and his girlfriend Diane went to San Francisco and left their dog and their kid Debbie with me. She's six. They were supposed to be back this morning. It is now 5:30 at night and they aren't home yet. I hope nothing happened. Debbie starting to drive me crazy, but I think I can handle it.

Harry decked Pete in the parking lot Friday morning and then Pete beat the shit out of Terri at lunch. An hour later I saw them walking arm in arm. I wash my hands of the whole mess. Anything that happens to them, they deserve. I can't sympathize with either of them because they could change things but don't.

Saw two great movies at the drive-in last night with Debbie. "The Harrod Experiment" and "Slaughterhouse 5." Both great. Be sure to see them if you get the chance.

Hey-O Denise,

Right to the trouble: Last night Harry and I got in a huge fight. It was my fault and I know it. I kept saying he didn't love me anymore. He wouldn't say anything. I was crying and everything. I think all I really wanted was a little attention because he had been working and talking about dealing all night and I felt pretty ignored. Like, hello, I'm alive! I have a job! I know it was a stupid way to get attention. I said I'd go to my mom's, but went in the living room and watched TV. (This was really late at night.) I heard something in the bedroom and went to see what it was. Harry was completely dressed and packing his things. By this time I was crying so hard I felt like I was getting sick. (You know when you cry so hard your stomach gets all churned up?) I kept saying no, no, no. I'd go over and try to hug him and he'd take me over and set me down on the bed and continue packing. After a bunch of this he finally laid down with me. I was still crying, he was still dressed. I was afraid I'd cry myself to sleep and he'd leave so I was hanging on to him real tight trying to stay awake. He said that he loved me too much to hurt me and I said he'd hurt me if he left and he said he was loving me as much as he could. He said he had a heart too and I was really hurting him. I called him from work tonight and he sounded far away. Then he came in to the office, gave me some dinner and a book I didn't want to read. He still acted kind of far off. I walked him out to his car and before he left I asked him if he was going to leave me. "I don't know."

Dear Denise,

I don't know what I'm going to do. I really have a big problem. It's called my butt. I have gained (get this) 10 pounds and everyone is noticing it. Cousin Larry came over and asked me where "skinny" was.

Mark told Harry he'd get him an audition for a dealing job at the El Cortez. It's a dumpy joint, but there're a lot worse in town. I hope Harry gets the job so maybe he won't be so grumpy all the time.

Did you see my mother? Her and Mark said they were going to your house for vacation. I wish I could've gone, but I don't think they really would've wanted me along even if I could've gotten time off work. I'm not getting the grades I thought I'd get. My homecrafts teacher (bitch) said that even though I turned in all my projects on time and they're always the best, I still couldn't get an A because of absences. It pisses me off. She's not judging me on my work, she's judging me on whether or not I sit under her nose all day. I wish I was as good as you in school. I'm not cutting it. Shit! It's terribly depressing to go for years thinking you can do it if you try and then you try and find out maybe you can't.

Sundays are slow here, so I don't have much to do. I just finished reading "Alice in Wonderland" and "Through the Looking Glass." Harry gave me a book to read about it. Here's a quote from it. Alice says, "There's hardly enough of me to make one respectable person!" (This is after she drinks from the bottle and shrinks.) Harry's book says, about this, "And the question is thus raised. How can a person be defined? Can he be so numbered as one person? Is he just one person only when he is very small?"

Personally I think this cat is full of shit.

Devil and darkness!
Martha

Oregon Trail

After the assembly at Hug, Wendy drove us by Ty's car so I could pick up my stuff. He and Rust might have gotten in Ty's car but wanted to come along to the airport, to have more time to say goodbye. To me or to the Tesla, I couldn't tell. Anyway, we could afford a little intimacy, driving electric. Ty and Rust explained the Oregon Trail Generation to Wendy on the way to the airport. "We're optimistic like Millennials but opt out like Gen X. We're not as cynical as Gen X, and that's the problem. We want to believe in change but we can't."

Rust said, "Deep down we know it's bullshit. You have died of snakebite, you have died of typhoid."

He said, "It's about cognitive dissonance and the impossibility of empathy and the impossibility of ethical consumption under capitalism and coming of age with the internet. Like Claire's dad, his generation really thinking they're gone tunnel down in some hole in Death Valley and the world's gone end and then they'll reemerge."

I said, "In their defense, Death Valley makes you think that."

"I know, power, rage, the sublime, blah blah blah. Helter Skelter's just the same old racism and misogyny when you think about it. It's like schools: they're hardening, yeah? A lot of those girls were given to Manson and no one cared."

"We're spectating," I explained.

"Sounds confusing," she said, missing her exit.

"And that dickhead somehow ended the counterculture?" Rust was yelling now. "Maybe—don't matter! I'll probably die of wifi. Elon Musk's gone arocket us to Mars. What I wanna know is how much do those guys trust their bodyguards, their helicopter pilots? That'll be the last of the *Homo sapiens*, lady—I mean, Wendy—Zuckerberg's cutthroat helicopter pilot and his family eating radioactive crickets in New Zealand. Not me. I'm not gone last. I'm barely here as it is. I'm not killing a man, I'm not drinking a puddle through a damn straw."

Ty said, "It's a generation defined by its hopelessness and alienation."

"Aren't they all?" asked Wendy, missing Departures.

As we circled the airport I began to pretend to worry I'd miss my flight home. "This airport's very confusing," I assured Wendy. "I got lost in it yesterday."

After circumnavigating the facility three times, Wendy pulled up to the curb at Departures. I thanked her profusely for being a first-rate escort. A hot air balloon floated to the north. I pointed it out to my friends and made a break for it. I hustled through the airport, stressed, exhausted, stinking and damp, but amazed once again by how easy it was to move through the world on my own, utterly unbothered even by the breast pump in its tote. Beyond security, I winked to the miner and the bear and the bighorn as I passed each, then boarded my plane just as they called my name over the PA. The last to board, I was informed. I slipped apologetically into my window seat, displacing two white men. They resettled, and together we all waited to pull away from the gate.

Lise texted me positive travel vibes, because, she said, *I know you're a nervous flyer.* I wouldn't say flying makes me *nervous*, just that I hate crowds and became extra don't-tread-on-me in airports post-9/11 and this perfectly understandable if antisocial disposition occasionally becomes a full-on panic attack when relocated inside a steel tube obviously held in the sky by nothing but wishes and fear. I felt guilty for not telling her about the Tecopa house, and knew that I would not tell her for a very long time yet.

Instead I stoked the fires of love for my biologist with the bellows of our correspondence. I liked how he could be anyone in text message. Love in text message was sapphic, if Sappho's fragments had been designed to be addictive. After multiple texts, the plane had not pulled away from the gate. My tardiness had cascaded into another delay, something to do with our place on the runway. There was some master queue somewhere that I had displeased. The plane hummed. A text from Theo—*safe travels!*

Out my small window, more hot air balloons had risen. I would ascend with them, southbound, Lake Tahoe on my right, the Great Basin on my left. How I'd miss them. I'd fly to Vegas, a cursed city I do my very best to avoid, and make my connection. Then I'd fly home, to the country of marriage.

I started to feel a little claustrophobic.

My phone chimed, another text from my biologist.

When I say *my biologist* I mean Noah, who got a BA in environmental humanities from Chico State in the nineties and knows plant names. Noah lived in a van, wanderlusted up and down the West Coast, rock climbing and surfing or seed harvesting for BLM when he needed money. We met about a year ago, when he came to a reading I gave in Oakland. I saw him standing in the back and knew.

I'd thought it would be hard to fall in love again. I mean Love love. To be honest, the idea was terrifying. I worried the capitalists were right, that Love was a thing in a jar. Maybe I'd spread mine too thin. Gave the milk for free. But then I met Noah and the milk was plenty. He was tall, Jewish, smelled like campfire. A tiny burn hole in his jacket. Gentle mumbles requesting my signature. I liked the feel of his eyes on me, wrote him a wanton inscription unattributed to Woody Guthrie.

Take it easy, but take it.

Instead of going back to my hotel I followed him to his van. We drove to Drakes Bay and waited for the sun to come up. When it came I thought of my parents. I wondered, ludicrously, if this was their way of calling me home. Just then a sea lion popped its silken, chonky dachshund head up through the water, looked at me, and nodded. I thought, *Did they send you, California sea lion?*

The sea lion nodded again emphatically. I asked Noah, "Did you see that?"

"Saw what? That sea lion egging you on?"

He took me to the airport and then found me on the internet. We started texting all the time. He sent me summits—Whitney, Shasta, Mount Tam and Mount Charleston—and I sent him nudes. Our correspondence left me constantly atingle. Was it love, I sometimes wondered, or just the chemical manipulations of unethical design?

The ancient rituals of courtship were what did me in, by which I mean the phone. The first time Noah called me, I canceled my grad seminar and we talked for three hours, deep into the night my time. Twice, thrice a week or more I would tell Theo I was writing and hole up in my campus office with the door closed and the lights off, whispering on my landline. Noah came through clear as 1998, except he'd inevitably describe for me the blights unfurling across the vista before him where he'd pulled off at some scenic overlook, the ridge he'd scaled to get cell service. Fires, grasses, beetles, man man man.

He told me about the shimmering blue lizards sunning themselves in plank pose on the back way up the Alabama Hills, the juniper retreating from the hanging valleys of the Eastern Sierras, the corpse of an emaciated mountain lion he'd come upon, embalmed in algae at the bottom of a shrinking glacial lake.

I told him to hold on while I microwaved an Amy's in the department kitchen. Thai Pad Thai, usually, sometimes another authorized Amy's purchased by Theo, who did all our grocery shopping. I watched the microwave tray rotate for exactly four and a half minutes, the plastic I'd slit puffing like some high-concept scent pillow above the mummifying noodles. For four and half excruciating minutes I bargained with myself, burned to go back to Noah, to hear his voice, to make sure he was still there.

I returned to my office, ate my Amy's with the plastic coffee lid I used as a spoon or the chopsticks I fashioned from wooden coffee stir sticks, for plastic coffee lids and wooden stir sticks were the only utensils to be found in the windowless department kitchenette and I had not in all these years remembered to bring a set of utensils from home. I described myself eating. Noah made every inane detail crackle with meaning. Lids and Sweet'N Low packets and stir sticks reliably bountiful, countless in number, seemingly infinite. I told him the feeling of opening the drawer of the department kitchenette and watching the stir sticks slide over each other, laying my hand on them and pushing gently, a sensation always found comforting during those four and a half anguished minutes nuking my Amy's without him.

Noah was from Tahoe. Together we mapped a history of near misses, the two of us cometing across the Sierras in barely missing arcs. We drew fated constellations with points at the Merry Go Round in Lone Pine, the Expresso Hut in Lee Vining, the In-N-Out Burger in Auburn. We discovered that we'd sung along to the same songs, stoned, in the same small crowd at a show in Grass Valley, had sunned ourselves on different bends of the same river on the same day: the Yuba, Mother's Day, 2004, Noah downstream after a hike with his mom and dad and brothers, me upstream fucking Jesse on a rock.

It was not lost on me that I loved Noah best when he talked about his parents. Firefighter father, librarian mother. Probably nothing brought me into estrus quicker than the story of his grandmother, her mother, the camps. I felt all this in his two-word text, saw with ancient and absolute Tahoe clarity that I was standing on a threshold to another life.

Please stay, it said.

These thresholds were everywhere. I needed to observe them. Was Noah the threshold or was I? And if me was it me or my teeth?

I unbuckled my seat belt and yanked my tote bag from under the seat in front of me.

"Pardon me," I said to the men seated beside me, though I was already climbing over them. The flight attendant bustled up to me. "Ma'am, we've closed the cabin door. The fasten seat belt light is *on*."

"I have to get off," I told her, lurching toward the front of the plane.

"We'll be pushing back from the gate *momentarily*!" she wailed.

"I can't go to Las Vegas. I have to get off the plane."

"Ma'am, *please*. Please take your seat." I felt for her, this corporate human shield, as I shoved myself past her.

A hum began among the other passengers. A man—one of my former seatmates, I sensed—shouted for me to sit my ass down. Others offered their own advice. I heard but did not turn to see them.

The intercom came on and said, *Ladies and gentlemen we* are *ready for departure but we* do *need everyone in their seats to avoid further* delay. No threat so potent in this new century than *delay*. I saw it on the face of the brown, slim, well-groomed attendant at the front of the plane, his hand still cupped around the little white intercom phone.

I was frantic. I had two voices in my head. One of them was my own and it said, *You are about to get yourself tased by the state.* I said, not at all politely, "Can you let me off, please, now."

The flight attendant paused, considering, then rolled his eyes and replaced the white phone in its cradle. He opened the door of the plane.

The other voice was the goose from *Charlotte's Web.*

An hour of freedom is worth a barrel of slops.

1972

Dear Denise,

Tonight has been a very strange night and I don't think it will mean a whole lot to anyone but you. Things are happening fast. Last night Terri and I went to a play at the university. The play was pretty good, but what happened after was even better. We wanted to go to Caesars but we didn't have a ride so we started walking. These two guys—heads, long hair—pulled up and asked if we wanted to go to the Spirit concert. I said no, we had to be home. They were going to turn us on to a joint but they couldn't find one, so they gave us three hits of speed instead. We started to walk off and they said, "Do you want a ride?"

Remember that night I told you about? On the bus coming back from LA? Well, I got a flash of that. I started to say no, but Terri said, "Sure." They were in a truck so I had to sit on the one dude's lap. The conversation went like this:

Him: "So you have to be home early?"

Me: "My mom's pretty protective."

"I would be too." (Smile.) "Yeah I really would be."

(Weird look at him, then I smile.)

Him: "So you've lived in Vegas your whole life, huh?"

Me: "How'd you know that?"

"I just know."

I asked him if he'd ever seen the high rollers gamble at Caesars. "$1 million on the table, and they don't even think about it!"

He says, "Just think of all the people you could help with that money."

My mind is completely blown. I'm thinking, Wow, this guy I'm afraid of is a real person! Maybe a good person. By this time we are almost to Caesars. He takes my hand and kisses it! I start to pull away, but I don't really want to. I wanted to stay with him forever.

We are pulling into Caesars now. I felt like saying, "Take us with you." But Terri got out, so I just hugged him and let them drive away thinking what a bitch I am. I blew it.

At Caesars we took the whites they gave us and went to fish some change out of the fountain to buy a burger. When my whites came on I began seeing things clearly. Lay this on your English teacher: compare those heads to all the old men who proposition me and Terri at Caesars, the self-proclaimed "gentlemen" asking us if we want to have a drink with them, the pair who offered us $200 to blow them. We saw about ten people of our generation dressed decently and being mellow, then at least 200 middle-aged women with their tits hanging out and grown men grabbing on them.

At one point I said to myself, "What the hell is this?"

"Trick-or-treat," Terri answered. And that's exactly what it was.

99% of this town should be blown off the map. Cops, teachers, gamblers, all of them. They're all so fucked I can't believe it. And they say we're "sex-oriented," that we have no moral values! I'm here in my town trying to drink tea and discuss the English language!

Tomorrow's payday.

Pete and Scott got their learners permits, I get mine this week. Ding a ling!

A chick I know got in a car wreck. She was beautiful, but her face is screwed now. Hope she is beautiful inside, ha ha!

Roger (my boss) put a contract through for thirty-five new green houses and he says when they get built we can get everybody working out here.

Terri is driving me crazy. She is what I call a clinger. She won't let me go anywhere alone. I never have a minute to myself. I'm trying to hint around about it but I don't think she's catching on. I don't know what I'm going to do, but I'm just going to tell her if it gets much worse. I don't want to hurt her feelings, but I can't hack her clinging.

The other day Keith was brushing my hair and he kept getting his comb caught in my glasses so I took them off and set them on the floor. He got up to get a cigarette and stepped on them! He broke them and I had to take off from school and pay to get them fixed. He didn't even say sorry. Just, "Why'd you leave them where I could step on them?" and how his foot hurt.

We got our report cards this week. I blew it. I'm ashamed to tell even you what I got but here goes:

History I: F (boo!)
Art: D (I fool around)

Orientation and Guide: D

American Lit: C (because it's after lunch and I always get stoned

at lunch)

Drivers Ed.: B

Pretty rotten huh?

It's 1 o'clock in the morning and everybody is crashed except me because of the whites. We went to Scott's but there were just too many people there and Scott was getting uptight, so we left. It was fun I guess but anything is fun when you're wired.

I want to tell you about Harry but I don't know where to start. Oh well, here goes—

He's got blonde hair just past his shoulders and blue eyes (I think). The first time I saw him I thought, "Give me to that dude." It's not just because he's a fox. I just saw him and I knew he was a mellow person. Lately I've become sorta obsessed with him: He meditates! He says pain is "just a sensation" whatever that means. He can go places in his head. Sometimes he can go into people's heads! Now, maybe this is a bunch of bullshit, but Harry is this type of person. He's from another dimension.

Tonight Vicky, Scott, Greg and I went to see "Bless the Beasts and Children." I had forgotten how far-out that movie is. I have forgotten a lot of things. Like you, me, everyone is so fucking beautiful it's insane. Jesus, we are all the most beautiful people. I can't believe it! We are the outcasts, the outsiders. We are the only people who remain soft in this fucked world. We are what God had in mind when he created man. He meant for people to be like us—feeling true human feelings. Not machines. Not worker bees. Truly alive. Yet we're the people people put down. If only they could feel something other than the pressure of society. Wouldn't that be something? Someday, there will be all the people, all rising together! Man, that'll be beautiful. I don't know if I'm going insane or what but I just had to write and tell someone these crazy ideas. I hope you can get into this rap.

I have an extreme case of the blues. Saturday night and no one is here and I'm very lonely. Harry is at work, Cyn is at work, Greg went to a SOC party, Terri is babysitting, I have no idea where Keith is. That should give you an idea of how together our group is. The group is dying.

I want to get out of here, but I want to stay. Been feeling so down you can't believe it. Since I'm telling all, I guess I better tell you the whole shit. I was with Keith last week. Don't ask me why, I know I'm an asshole, and I KNOW he's an asshole, but I just couldn't help it. I love him and no amount of hating him will change that.

I feel better. I felt like I was hiding something from you. Now you know. I hope you understand. If not why don't you come down and beat my ass? I could dig seeing you even if you were about to kill me.

Pete got a pound of blonde Lebanese hash! So righteous. But I'm worried about him. He's been working nights at the gas station and flunking school. I've been trying to get him to take a night off work and get some sleep, but he won't listen. I don't think he's had any sleep for about four days and he looks like he's been dead for two years.

Went to see Elton John. I wasn't really into the music until Elton started playing "Your Song" and I found Scott because that's my song to him. Me and Scott were standing on our chairs and I yelled "Elton!" super loud and Scott held his hand up in a fist. Then I got on Scott's shoulders and said, "Elton, we love you!" and then Elton looked right at me, held up his fist and said, "Las Vegas, I've come home!" We brought Elton back out four or five times. It was SO mellow!

Big storm today. The door got torn off the main greenhouse, a bunch of windows cracked, part of the roof fell in. We're closed until they can get it fixed, so I had to quit. Roger is pissed, but I can't stand around with my finger up my butt making no money. It's supposed to snow tonight, but I doubt it will. Harry got fired. I guess that's about it.

The Now and the Big Gnar

One way to conceptualize this scene, Noah says, one way to characterize what we're up to, if he had to put words to it, is that we are simply living very much in the now.

In the immediate past I climbed Mount Rose in a Lyft, heart clawing for Noah and for Tahoe. I composed and deleted a series of texts to my husband—

Not coming home rn

I need to stay here

in love with someone else

—and sent finally

Rats! missed my flight. Can't get out until tomorrow

O no that is sucks he responded, adding a pic of our nearly year-old daughter.

If I had to pin it in messianic time, the now begins when I see the lake. (I am not alone in this view.) I see Tahoe and it dawns on me: I left my breast pump on the plane.

In the now, I have the driver drop me at the bathrooms of the state campground on the California side of the lake, where Noah said to meet him. I brush my teeth, splash water on my face, wipe out my armpits. I change into dry clothes. I drop my bag in the sand, leave my soggy shoes beside it and walk barefoot to the pier where he said he'd be. I see him at the end and he sees me, does a kind of slump to the side with his hips and his head, visibly gobsmacked. Love has lit him from within. If you've been lucky you know what I'm talking about.

At the end of the pier he pulls me to him. "I'm so glad you came," he says into my hair.

I say I'm glad too, feeling him, his skin warm as stone in the sun. I study his laugh lines, jealous of every single person who made them.

He says I don't seem glad, and that that's okay. "Considering . . ." careful ellipsis like a stone skipping across the water.

"If we're going to do this, I'm not going to pretend I sprang forth fully formed from your helmet." I apologize; say I'm tired, haven't slept.

Noah says, "We seem to have found ourselves acting out a couple of tropes."

"Yes—" I try. "And those feel very far away from where I am now. I can see us from a great distance. I don't know why I'm telling you this."

Noah takes my hand. "What do you see," he says, "from the great distance?"

I look at our hands. I admonish myself into the now. Inside I scream, *Pay attention, you lucky motherfucker! Look at his perfect god-damn hand holding your lost and wretched hand!* Whatever happened or happens, this did. Is.

"It's like . . . for a long time it seemed like we were all doing what we were going to do. The tenses blurred. That's how it *was* and *is* and *will be*. If certain things were going to happen, they would have already happened."

We kiss, wanting and unashamed.

Noah says, "Things are happening now."

I push my finger into my palm to check. They are.

IT'S WONDERFUL HERE, in the now. I completely see its appeal. In the now there are no mass extinctions, no mass murders, no masses by definition. The now is pure particle. There is, however, the trouble of the teeth. I've grown fond of my vagina's teeth, but I can't deny that they're the ultimate cock block. Now, if you have a very heteronormative definition of sex, as in: sex = penis + vagina, you may at this point in our story be confused. As I've said, Theo and I had an open marriage. For years I took liberal advantage of this policy, gladly welcoming all sorts of things into my vagina, among them penises, fingers and devices made of soft, deathless plastic. But after the baby was born, and the vagina dentata came in, vaginal intercourse got dicey. And here I have to say I did not miss it. Now that I had a baby, I didn't need it. The Innocents loved anal sex. Many of them had taken Women's Studies 101 as their diversity or gone to prom with a lesbian. Most had heard the Good Word about the vulva and all of them knew better than to admit to being threatened by a toy. I'd spent my cuddleslut period having more orgasms than ever, and *that* is why the foremothers marched.

So don't mistake me, we both come, here in the now in the van.

Noah's orgasm is pleasingly straightforward in its summoning and accompanied by copious, garlicky ejaculate I swallow. But before that, during, a peculiar urge overtakes me. A yearning for Noah's semen against my cervix. Maybe I'm ovulating, I don't know, but for the first time ever, I wish my teeth out.

After sex I sleep and sleep and when I wake it's morning. Noah's made oatmeal, rolls a joint. Sex again and then he asks, "Now what do you want to do?"

"I wish I could take a bath with a whole bag of Epsom salt poured in, maybe find some hot springs." I'm thinking a soak would brine the teeth, soften them up enough for Noah to slip in and out of me unscathed. I tell him I am ready for the now, need it, have always been here, that all else is dust, that death is a friend of mine, that according to the latest research I have all mother's pain in me and her mother's and him too that we came from their spines and and and.

"Can I ask?" he asks. "When's the last time you saw the *ocean*?"

He had—has—a way of saying that word, *ocean*, an italic yearning. I want him to say my name the way he said *ocean*.

"Too long," I admit.

"The ocean will hella ground you in the now."

I like the sound of that, can almost feel the waves grinding me into sand, my vagina dentata pulverized by the ecstatic sea of the present. We have more sex, then procure sunglasses, caffeine and gasoline. We drive from the Sierras to the coast, Noah naming every mountain, every tree.

Theo calls, voicemails, emails. I text him back.

I am fine

I am safe

I just have to be alone rn.

I will call you when I am ready.

I do not say *I will come home.*

Do not say *I just have to get this out of my system* because I do not want it out.

STEINBECK COUNTRY, KEROUAC COUNTRY, George Lucas's ranch around here somewhere. I get us a hotel room on sea cliffs, peacocks and wild turkeys stalking the grounds. Noah puts the hotel's eye mask on me, gives me a welcome rough fuck in the ass. We shower and take a walk. We smoke a joint on a ridgeline, trace the fire scars on the hills, hover in the gusts on the bluffs above Drakes Bay. We are on some other time, emerald hummingbird time, blue agave time.

"This is the place I would choose if I could choose," I say, choosing.

THE SEMESTER BEGINS. I email my dean, propose several innovative student-centered approaches to distanced learning. I propose a twenty-four-hour creative writing intensive. I propose a MOOC. The dean doesn't buy it. I take a leave of absence.

Theo sends me an email re: $. The hotel says there's been an issue with my credit card.

No worries! Noah's buddy—tech guy backstroking in a money bin of Bitcoin speculation—has a little farm above Big Sur.

"These are *not* ponies," brags the buddy, arms outstretched before a field of bored stocky ponies. "They're miniature Icelandic *horses*. They have *five* gaits: the walk, the trot, the canter, the tölt and the flying pace."

Noah becomes their shepherd, tends the Icelandic horses and a herd of ornery Rastafarian-looking dwarf sheep the size of large cats. I am astonished by his competency and discipline. Before long he's running the place, expanding the pygmy goat play structure, milking the micro cows, mucking the teacup pigs' pen. I work a few hours in the brunch shack, handing guests the matchbook-size menu and fielding questions about our sole and signature dish: quail egg omelet with microgreens and espresso.

At sunset Noah and I hit the hot tub then roll around together in the woods or in the van. After, I nap and wake to the renovated farmhouse aglow. The buddy, Andy, is what E. B. White called "a very young pig—not much more than a baby, really." He has a sizable yet barely readable library of hiking guides, veterinary manuals, Libertarian treatises, signed locavore best sellers in hardcover and paperback, self-help "systems" to "track the past, order the present, design the future." For dinner Andy summons uniformly delicious things from the internet with his voice. Over dinner we drink a bottle of wine each, everyone loose and warm when the boys begin to jam. Their sessions stretch into the night, moving through phases like the moon. Three songs in, Noah looks to me like Dylan doing "Like a Rolling Stone" at Free Trade Hall. If they'd stop there he could have me any way he wanted. Andy too, vagina dentata be damned! But on they play, swiftly departing the sensual realm and off to the land of tiresome boner-killers.

I find myself another bottle of wine and drink it on the deck or on the walk to town. At the bulletin board in front of the library I find a flyer for donation-only classes at the Yoga Yurt and begin going to Yin with Flora five nights a week. I get a library card. I win a Guggenheim and, when Andy asks Noah to "run the numbers" on free-range Christmas mini hams, I spend most of it on teacup pigs. When it's dead in the brunch shack I go to the barn and read library books to the pigs. Thanks to this and buxom Flora's guided meditations—*I am safe enough*—language returns to me, not writing exactly, but wordy drawings I leave around the farmhouse for the boys to discover and compliment. I rediscover grown-up music, especially rap, and though I know my pain is but a smidge of any of these artists' pain, listening to rap in the woods I feel the whole smidge. I take my wedding ring off, drop it somewhere in the dark, beetley forest and let my white tears flow.

I take a blanket and my favorite teacup pig (Wilbur, whom Noah instantly rechristens Pig Willie Style) on a leash into the woods and read there all day. I come back bug-bit, with sticks in my hair. I don't shower much, am full-on Medusa at the beach watching the boys surf when in the sand I feel the warm drop of my long-gone menses.

Pig Willie Style and I hike to a grassy thatch in the dunes and he watches in concern as I squat there for privacy. I pour water from a Nalgene over my fingers and press them inside myself to investigate, afraid the teeth will be gone. But they're there, softly throbbing and laced with bloody gobs.

"They're there," I reassure Pig Willie.

We leave the free boys to surf and take the van to a pharmacy. In the sandy bathroom I fold a brand-new neoprene menstrual cup inside me. The teeth hold it firm and elegant. Natural, the way Ty describes math. I feel them through the course of the day, supporting the cup as it fills with my dark jelly. I like its weight—I feel full, pleasurably so, and when I post up in the bathroom to remove the cup at the end of the day it occurs to me that the teeth might somehow *let go.* I try and they do. The neoprene cup emerges.

Furthermore, rather than cramps I notice a warm tingle has been shimmering through me. I practice this trick, pulsing the teeth with a combination of breath, pelvic floor strength and something else, more of an unaction, some deep fossil-bed part of me relaxing. I ease the teeth open, I zip them back up. It feels tremendous, like the wildest dreams of every woman who fell for the jade pussy egg scam.

That night I fuck Noah and Andy both in a DILD. The next day, while Noah tends his flock, I let Andy finger me in the bathroom of the brunch shack. I'm cleaning the bathroom when Andy delivers a cube of paper towels, which he doesn't ever do. He doesn't even know where they go. I point and he leans close to get them on the shelf. He smells like the Nike flagship store. "You smell good," I say, lion's breath on his neck.

He kisses me. "I'm going to finger you," he says.

"You are?" I say, delightedly taking my gloves off.

"I am."

I will the teeth open. "You're certainly welcome to try."

I watch Andy's face for evidence of evisceration, but he looks happy, goofy, grateful. I beg him off and give him a handy for his troubles.

That night Noah says he wants to take me out on the ocean.

"Why? I can see it from here."

"You gotta get out *on* it. It's like the woods but better." He borrows Andy's boat and a picnic basket packed with a jar of Afghan Kush and three bottles of wine.

On the water he seems moody. I worry Andy has blabbed. Noah and I haven't talked about ethical nonmonogamy or unethical nonmonogamy—we haven't really talked about much, it occurs to me, a thought as shallow and dissolving as sea foam.

Another: I wonder if Noah could become violent?

I breathe, urge the teeth back and forth inside me where I sit, remembering I can become violent, too.

He cuts the engine. "This is what I wanted to show you." He points overboard, to blooms of bioluminescence glowing in our wake. At once I feel completely safe, as if no one who knows how to find nocturnal bioluminescence in the sea would harm me. He strikes me now as solemn, reverent, so much so I worry he might propose.

Atop the shimmering bay, Noah announces he's changed his mind about the now. He wants to know everything, every dark throbbing part of me. "Tell me your big gnar."

"Tell me yours."

He pulls away. "You already know mine," he says.

I don't, but should. *You fucked around with Andy* is my best guess. I brace for him to say it. But a handy is no one's big gnar. "Tell me again," I say. "It'll be powerful for you." He breathes in deeply. "It's extinction." Noah grieves a diaphanous moss hanging from the coastal pines, gauzy beards that grow only in the cleanest air. "Half the birds in the Mojave Desert are gone," he says, "and the other half are mistaking solar arrays for lakes and dying there. Your daughter could live to see the last sequoia."

"She'll have to go to a zoo to see a cardinal," I offer, relieved and completely turned on.

He changes course. "Can I ask you something? It's so embarrassing but I can't let it go. I can't sleep. I keep wondering. Why did you marry him?"

"That's not really an answerable question."

"What was your wedding like?"

"Why do you need to know?"

"Tell me anything about it."

"It was expensive."

"Where was it?"

"A lavender farm. More like a hotel with some lavender growing in a field. One of these boutique historic deals with a farm-to-table restaurant and small-batch gelato and silk-screened dishrags and peacocks walking around. Not a real place."

"Like the Little Farm."

"Exactly. A content set. A backdrop for the internet. The beekeeper there has all these followers. That's how I heard about it."

"What was your ceremony like?"

"Why are you asking?"

"What were your vows?"

"We wrote our own."

"What kind?"

"Ambivalent atheist vows."

"What did they say?"

"Mine said basically, 'I'll try.'"

"Did you?"

After the wedding I bought lavender everything, diffusers and cleaners and soaps. I hung sachets on the doorknobs. I planted lavender in the garden but couldn't wait for it to grow, bought it potted, already in bloom and cut it (sorry, bees), dried it and hung it in our windows. I bought bouquets from the farmers market and hung them over the doors. "I was trying to repel a hex but knew the hex was inside me." I bought lavender douches and sprayed them inside myself, the undutiful daughter, the fat twin. "None of this is my big gnar, by the way."

"Your mom is."

Warmer.

"What was her name? You never told me."

"Martha Claire."

"You're named after her."

"Yep. I got my name and my brains and my pains from her."

"What was she like?"

"She was big on surrender. She liked to say, 'This too will pass.' 'Resistance is futile' from *TNG*. She said it rubbing my back at bedtime. After she died, I left the West, haven't had a home here since." I told Noah about Ohio, arriving nauseous in Columbus, vomiting on the sidewalk above a half-scale replica of the *Santa María* anchored in the stagnant Olentangy River, about buying a two-pack of pregnancy tests, taking one in the bathroom of the Kroger's and the other in the bathroom of a bar, about borrowing money from my sister, about the abortion, about taking my first cab afterward to my sublet in Ohio State's undergrad ghetto, where I soaked through pads watching *The Sopranos* and thinking *men are weak*.

Noah laughs. His laugh, I can still hear it.

What I really thought was that I'd made a mistake. "The move, not the abortion."

"Why?"

"I thought she wouldn't be able to find me. I worried she wouldn't know where to look. The last time I talked to her was when I told her I was moving to Ohio. I told her that she did a good job. That I never wondered whether she loved me. That I knew I'd been born at a good time."

"What did she say?"

"She said, 'Iowa's just so far away.'"

I have a good cry. Noah holds me a long time, then rolls us a joint. I tell him he was right about the ocean. He says, "Can I ask you something else?"

"I get nervous when your questions require affirmative consent."

"Did something happen to you?"

"You will have to be more specific."

"Because you don't seem . . . into, or don't seem to *like* . . . me . . . *in* you? And I guess I've just been assuming . . . it's because you'd . . ."

"Been raped."

"Yes."

"No. I mean I have, I told you about that. But that's not why."

"Why then? If I can ask."

"You can ask. You're asking. I do want you in me. I, like, think about it all the time. And sometimes I think I want to have another baby with you. You or someone like you. But that's off-topic!" I glug some wine. "I'm going to tell you the truth. The truth is . . . I have these . . . teeth. Inside me. This ring of teeth. A mouth. It's a mythic thing women get."

He looks stricken.

"You probably think I'm crazy. You could feel them to see—"

"No."

"Yeah, gross. Sorry."

"Don't be sorry! *I'm* sorry. I didn't mean 'no,' like, 'gross.' I meant no, like: I don't think you're crazy."

"You don't?"

He got very tender, very careful. He said, softly, "I think that . . . if you think that . . . is happening, then . . . that is happening."

Maybe I don't have to stop everything before it starts. Maybe this man can pull me back into my body. "I'm on my period," I warn him.

"Great," he says, and plunges in. I breathe. It's heavenly, to receive like the goddess his abundant Ashkenazi *jīng*. I breathe and no one is lacerated. Except Theo. But Theo has become only a signal contained in my phone, itself a poison thing pulled from the ground by slaves, gone from my hand to the glove box of the van, silently receiving photos and videos of our daughter, whose first birthday I miss.

1971

Dear Denise,

Me and Keith broke up again. He ignored me all day. He can *KISS MY ASS!!!* It took me a whole five hours of tears to figure that out. I still love him and everything, but I'm sick of getting a bit of love dangled before my eyes like a tidbit before a dog. I won't (repeat *won't*) kiss his ass anymore!

Now for the local gossip. Greg spent this weekend in the mountains, with Tom, Steve and the Dunbars and they all dropped acid. Greg really dug it. I'm glad to have them back.

Cynthia and Greg still like each other and Pete still likes Vicky. Did you get a letter from Keith (alias: THE BASTARD, just kidding ha ha!)? He said he wrote you. Well, I guess that's all, see you soon!!

Later,
Martha

Me and Keith are completely broken up. He can shove it up his ass. We just broke up tonight. Man, he was such a pecker about it I can't believe it. You would have to be here to understand the situation. I clean, sew, and work my ass off for him and he never has a kind word for me. It burns my ass.

A super-lot has been happening. Greg's getting a van and some land. I got suspended. I got busted for smoking pot. Two days later I got caught with cigarettes. Then last night me, Dickie, Scott, Greg and Brian D. got loaded in Dickie's pool and we were pretty well fucked up when we went to the dance and I got caught at the dance completely loaded. All the faculty are really on my case. It's been pure hell just keeping my mouth shut and staying out of trouble.

Mom was really cool about me getting busted. All she did was cut off my allowance for two weeks.

After getting kicked out of the dance we all walked up to Albertson's. Scott and I were walking ahead of everyone else, singing James Taylor. That was far-out.

I wish I liked somebody. Even if they didn't like me it would be better than not feeling anything.

> Later and love,
> Martha

Denise,

I had to open my letter and put this in. It's 1:30 in the morning. I just got off the phone with Keith! We talked for 2 hours!!! He just got back from Utah and went over to spend the night at Bobby Langer's house. Bobby lives across town. I just walked in and the phone rang and it was Keith. He said he called three times earlier but I wasn't home. I said no, I wasn't home. None of his beeswax. We just talked about what we were doing and that shit until Keith said, "Know what?"

"No, what?"

"I'm drunk."

"Oh."

"Know why?"

"No, why?"

"How long have we been broken up?"

"About a week, I guess."

"Seems like a year." Then silence.

I said, "What the hell are you talking about?" but I knew.

"I'm trying to forget you but it won't work."

"Oh." I'm about in tears.

"Martha, do you still feel for me?"

I didn't know what to tell him. I half love him and half hate him. "Ask me that question when you're sober."

I'm hoping he won't remember. Anyway, I just wanted to tell you that before I mailed this. Maybe you can make some sense out of the whole thing. I can't.

> Bye,
> Martha

I just wrote you to tell you I have absolutely nothing to write about. Except this: we went to *Jesus Christ Superstar* last night. Me and Keith and Pete and Barb and Jack went together. It had to be the greatest thing I've ever seen. I was sobbing by the time the thirty-nine lashes came around. I can't even describe how fantastic it was!

Yes, Keith and I are back together. I can't stop thinking about him. I think I'm mentally ill. Love is a fucking hassle.

How I Like It

In the morning I ask Noah can we hit the road and he says hella. After breakfast we say our goodbyes. Noah walks the farm with Andy, who offers to board my passel at discount. Sadly, I bid Pig Willie Style and his brethren adieu.

On the road I gave it some thought—this question they all like. I like it in the woods. I like it in the van. I like it on the beach. I like Noah's hand up my dress in front of a movie theater that has pizza and beer. I like it with pizza and beer. I like it with fries, gyros, tacos from the truck parked by the paper mill. I like it with baklava, like licking honey off your fingers. I like it in the mountains, I like it on the coast. I like it in the wild, and if not the wild then at least near water, at least under a tree, at least smelling of campfire, of whiskey, of weed. I like the idea of fucking a rock-climber but I don't like it when you go rock climbing instead of hang out with me.

I like it beside not inside a swimming pool, a river, a hot spring.

I like it on the Lost Coast and beneath the Trees of Mystery. I like it real working class. Filthy Carhartts, steel-toes and NoDoz. I like it in Humboldt, up all night talking about *The Graduate*.

I like it when you kiss me and knock a glass off the bar and it shatters.

I like it when we come to our senses and out again.

I like it when you ask about my daughter but not my husband.

I like it somewhere in Mendocino County, at a rest stop in the rain. I like when we pay for things in weed, watch a video of a baby panda finger-painting, a video of my daughter's first steps. I like it with camp-fire coffee and bacon for breakfast and I like to read the *Times*.

Talk dirty to me about why you're a feminist. I like the words *pussy, cunt* and *come*. I like the word *love*—it's treacherous but I do. I like it rough. I like it deadpan. I like it when you make me laugh and laugh and laugh until I can't remember how. I like it by your side, just being there, just feeling you breathe. I like it when you pick me wild-flowers even if I had to ask. I like cut lilacs in the bed because the previous spring we'd been walking together and I guess I stopped and smelled them and looked so alive smelling them it made you want to be alive too, kind of.

I like it when a word goes meaningless from prayer, a word like *death,* a word like *daughter*, a word like *wife*.

I like it after rich bitch yoga in a strip mall.

I miss my husband sometimes, that's how I like it.

I like it when I say what are we doing? And you say *I'd say we're just drifting here in the pool*. I like you smoking a cigarette with me. I like it better with a blunt. I like it when you say what we need to do is acid up at Malakoff like in "Slouching." I like it at the Diggins like

Didion never was. I like it during morning meditation, from beneath a handkerchief smelling of Nag Champa.

I'd like my mother to visit. She's found me twice before. First, she came through a skylight. This was in Columbus. I went to bed saying, *I need you*, and that night she came in through the skylight over my bed and said, *This is just information*.

Next she came as pain during childbirth. My doula said, *Breathe*, and I said, *But I'm so tired*, and someone said, *So rest*.

Rest, my mother said. *I'll meet you on the other side*.

I liked OxyContin the time my mom gave me some of hers. I liked it a lot. It made me feel melted and borderless. After my c-section I liked Percocet, needed more at my follow-up. I washed my hair and enunciated the magic nouns—*professor*, wife of a *doctor*—got the pills and thought, a shimmer at the corner of my eye, of taking them all at once, my fearsome matrilineage, then I flushed them.

Jesse, I do not want to hurt the baby or myself. I am not choosing darkness but darkness is choosing me. I am on this dingy beach at Malakoff Diggins. I need waterfalls, hanging lakes tinged pink by tailings. At least the deep worshipful divots where the glaciers used to be. Donner, Marlette, Tahoe's open eye. I see it draining down through the foothills, into Reno and out, disappearing into the Great Basin from which no water escapes, unless you count as escape transmutation into hay, steak, sagebrush, mustangs, bighorns in the Ruby Mountains and beyond those the little town of Ruth.

Here I am with another heartsick lover beside a stinking, almost-gone pond. Gray reeds and cigarette butts and wads of garbage. Smoke from whatever wildfire wherever. I needed us naked, swimming in sun. I needed clean water. But summer's over. There is no such place anymore.

I look east across the hundred-mile desert, over range and prairie. The sky gets lower and lower. In Iowa cicadas drip screeching from the trees. In Michigan it is winter. Five o'clock and dark. Toxic plumes and algae blooms. Lead in the water, fire retardants in the breast milk. Theo getting Ruth from the nanny.

In the now my mother shows me.

I LIKE IT IN SPARKS, sad and drunk before noon in a Mexican restaurant on a rainy day. I like it in a booth with an inflated Corona hovering overhead. I like it when the poet says is this a message, finally, or just another day?

I like it when Noah says, "I can't do this anymore . . . it doesn't feel right . . ."

—oh yeah. "I'd like another, please—sí, Corona."

I like it when Noah cries, when I cry, when anyone cries.

"I really thought we were going to ride off into the sunset together," I say.

"I know you did."

I want to hate him. I eat chips and try. But I like him best not liking me, love even his widow's peak, its ambivalent crest and healthy boundaries.

"I get it," I say, not at all getting it. "If I were you, I never would have let me into my van."

PULL MY HAIR. Be kind to all plants and animals and children. Leave me alone. That's how I like it.

I like it in Ruth, Nevada, in the sacred vestibule of the Mormon church. I like it when it rains in the desert, when it rains in the mountains, when it rains on the coast. Basically I like rain. I like it hungover and heartbroken the morning after a rain, sage smell rising, Noah carrying my tote bag to the airport.

"Careful, it's heavy."

"What's in here, rocks?"

Special ones. That's what I'm into.

Kiss me hard in the airport parking lot, aspens gold and trembling. Release me to the terminal where everyone can see. The teeth inside me pulse with longing and lostness. That's how I like it. That's where I'm at.

1970

Dear Denise,

A weird thing happened to me today. For a long time nobody liked me. Judd never wrote. Bill wouldn't talk to me. And Brad Neilson gave me dirty looks all the time. But today I fainted in P.E. and Brad helped me into the hall. Then Bill put his arm around me at lunch. And Judd wrote me a letter telling me how much he loves me! Speaking of Judd, enclosed is a picture of him. Please return it.

Have to cheer at a game tonight. Blah! Don't ever become a cheerleader, it's a drag. Better go now. Bye.

Love + Peace,
Martha

P.S. Write back

Dear Denise,

What's happening? I've got good news. Don't tell Aunt Nancy but I'm going to save up my money until I have $35 then I'm going to get a two-way plane ticket to come and visit. I'll call or write and tell you when I get it all saved up.

We went to Rancho to see Viet Rock. It was an anti-war play. They sang some songs. My favorite one was called the "Brand-New War

Machine." It goes, "Have you seen the brand-new war machine? It looks real clean but it's evil..." something like that.

L & K,
Martha

P.S. Say hi to everyone and write back.

Dear Denise,

I just came back from my "end of grade" school trip. The whole class went to Disneyland. We also went to a whole bunch of museums. It was fun. We passed right by your house! I tried to get Mr. Busdriver to stop, but he couldn't. We didn't get home until 12:30 at night but when I got out of the bus, sure enough, there was Brad, Tony & Monty (they didn't go on the trip). Tony took my suitcase, Monty took my hatbox, and Brad took me. They walked me home.

Don't tell anyone but on the bus I was with Monty's little brother, Jeff. The first night of the trip Jeff was with Cynthia, the second with Marcy (a friend of mine) and the third (on the bus) with me. He really hurt me bad. Cynthia too. Oh well.

I better go now.

Love + Peace,
Martha

Hey Dee,

Cynthia likes this guy named Kim Smith. She was supposed to meet him at the jayvee basketball game but she was out on the field having a smoke. I was already stoned so I went in the gym and Kim was sitting by himself, waiting. I went up and sat with him and waited for Cynthia. I had just washed my hair and it really looked pretty and smelled like love. Kim started playing with it. Cynthia came in. She sat between me and Kim. After a few minutes, he got up and sat above me and started braiding my hair. Naturally Cynthia got mad. I admit it was bad to take him, but he liked me and that wasn't my fault. After a while, me and Cyn made up.

Friday night Kim was babysitting his sister's kids and he called me. We must've talked for two hours. It was really mellow. Saturday I went downtown with Cyn. On the bus home there was this guy who was a real freak. He had a silver cap on his front tooth. I decided to tease Cyn. I went over and sat down next to Joe Cool and whispered in his ear, "Kiss me baby, my tonsils itch."

Sorry I haven't written for so long. I've been busy (with Kim, of course). I think this is the first time I've ever wrote two letters and been going around with the same guy in both of them. Amazing! Just between you and me, I think Kim is going to ask me to go steady. I hope so. Sunday night Dern asked Cynthia to go steady. I've been hinting around a lot lately and I think Kim is finally getting the hint.

Dear Denise,

I've got to tell you what happened last night. Last night Cynthia and I were over at my house and Mike, Jay, and Steve (seniors) came over in Jay's car. They asked us if we wanted to go to the Garble House with them. The Garble House is this old house that is supposed to be haunted by some old man. Well, we went down there and man, was it ever scary! Me and Cynthia and Suzette almost peed in our pants when we got out of the car. The house had a big front yard, all dirt, with an old, broken down fence. We climbed it easy. You walk up the steps to this castle door with a lion knocker, really heavy door. Mike pushed it open without knocking and we walked in. Big spiral staircase. We walked up the stairs into complete darkness before we saw the roof's ripped off. We looked around a little more and then went out back. There was a big swimming pool and horse stables! After that we went down to Winchell's and sat around and talked. The house was fantastically beautiful but obviously haunted. Me and Cynthia decided greed is a disease. Mike said we're weird.

Love and miss you,
Martha

Loafing Along
Death Valley Trails

And so once again I boarded flight 4325, the very same midday Reno-to-Vegas commuter flight I'd forced my way off months before, same Los Angeles–based flight crew. I recognized them during boarding, when I handed my extremely expensive ticket to the flight attendant I'd shoved. Worse, the attendant recognized me. Her colleague, the angry one with the exacting facial hair who'd opened the door for me, frowned my way as he patrolled to close the overhead compartments. I got a little panicky but took a Dramamine and fell asleep.

I woke forty-five minutes later in Las Vegas, a city I had promised myself I would never again step foot in, as long as I lived. I staggered groggily through McCarran—the only airport where I have ever heard the intercom say, *Sir, alcoholic beverages are not allowed on the jet bridge.*

The airport was playing "Leaving Las Vegas" by Sheryl Crow, as always. I'm not complaining. "Leaving Las Vegas" is a perfect song, although the airport people, in cahoots with the all-powerful tourism bureau no doubt, ruined it by cutting the final lines:

> *No I won't be back*
> *Not this time*

I chanted this lopped-off coda to myself as I bought a Cinnabon at Cinnabon, found the gate for my connection and waited to go home. I had tried to book another flight, any other to avoid connecting in Vegas, but it wasn't possible, the ticket agent in Reno had said, not on the same day, not so close to the holidays.

"No worries!" I'd told the agent, handing over my credit card and in fact brimming with worries. That I'd be unable to escape that city, that it would grasp me as it had my foremothers and sisters. So, it was the city's hand I felt close around me when the monitors announced my flight home delayed an hour. I tried not to panic, browsed a gift shop, bought a book called *Uncommon Characteristics of Common Wildflowers of the Mojave Desert*, and returned to the gate to read it. Our new departure time came and went. Folks pawed frantically at their phones, beating the rest of us to the cold hard truth of our situation. Soon enough an announcement admitted the flight delayed again, this time indefinitely, by a storm in Chicago. People called their people and cursed Chicago. I considered calling Theo. He was expecting me.

I considered messaging Nate, still a bouncer at a bar on Trop where we met fifteen years ago, though by the looks of his social media he now also trained UFC fighters and sold tubs of supplements. I

226

recalled Nate's huge and expressively curved dick, which I had used over the years to commemorate UNLV vs. UNR sporting contests and to annihilate the emotional aftermath of my brief visits to my family.

I did not call Theo, but neither did I message Nate. For this I rewarded myself with a trip to the international terminal for a massage and a pair of Uggs. Noodly and slick with oil, I wore the Uggs out of the store, walked in them from terminal to terminal, sheepskin wombs I used to ward off the babies all around me. I ducked into a bar and in no time was fairly drunk. The bar had plenty of TVs. It was almost Christmas, the local news all toy drives and house fires. Outside was the Strip, the physical manifestation of every bankrupt ideology of the twentieth century. Though I could not see it, I heard the young city's psyche crying out from deep in the bowels of its gaudy icons, struggling for breath inside the tightening fists of the rich men who owned them. As I've said, I was quite drunk. I could not help but wonder what sort of ill culture births, almost overnight, a vice capital of such grotesque scale and such shallow memory? What future could there be in a city whose sparkling lore was all violence and infrastructure? Hoover Dam, atomic bombs. America's most rapidly warming city, the news said. "Planners here are searching desperately for a replacement for pavement." Furthermore, I learned from *Uncommon Characteristics* it was true what Noah said about the birds of the Mojave—half gone, what's left mostly corvids.

Finally, a message: my flight canceled. *Act of God* the text from the airline said. I admit I interpreted this completely routine fuck-over by a tax-dodging monopoly as the hand of Fate. Las Vegas makes you think this way. Ask anyone not from here who lives here how that happened and I guarantee you'll hear a harrowing saga writhing with the cruelest twists of fortune, highly questionable decision-making and the very worst luck. Drive off Strip in the morning, before school, witness the city's daily migration, a beleaguered shuffle of women and children from one unstable housing arrangement to another, their luggage a distant cousin to the matching wheeled sets loaded and unloaded by shuttle drivers and bellhops all across a city where the population regularly doubles with visitors. See these belongings on their backs and piled on shopping cart wagons and stroller rigs. A decade after the massive upward redistribution of wealth that was the Great Recession, this city running out of water was still in survival mode and always would be.

Yet I knew it as well to be a city alive, ribald and shameless, embracing of grime and sex, each body therein a site of filth ready to receive the purifying fires of the sun. Maybe that was just me. You have to be careful in Las Vegas—the place will be whatever you need it to be. For me it was a thirsty city joyously screaming the song of the unbearable now. For me it was my mother's city, and for this reason I had to get out.

I wanted there to be a place for me. That is what I'd said on the phone to Theo at the beginning of this day, the day after Noah broke my heart in Sparks. I'd said, "Maybe could you put me in a place?" I told him about this idea I had of sitting and looking out at a lake, a wool blanket draped over my legs. Theo thought there could be such a place, but it required prior authorization. We'd have to make a place ourselves. He promised to look into cabins on the lake. A "Yellow Wallpaper" scenario, that felt like now, my shoulder already in the groove. I thought of calling Lise, but knew she'd say if I had been to visit our mom in any of her "places" I would know there was no such "place" for me.

Maybe not, I thought. But also—driving a rented car (the cuboid model driven in commercials by husky rapping hamsters) over the mountains toward Tecopa—*maybe so.*

IT IS UNREALISTIC TO EXPECT even fossil water to pull you back into your body, yet this is a frequently documented effect of very hot springs. I admit I had impossible needs driving out to Tecopa, needs inflamed through Spring Mountain pass and down into the Joshua tree forest on the other side, combusted by a passing glimpse of the Christmas Joshua done up as it is every year in sacred trash, its arms draped in garlands and tinsel, tines speared with glittery ornaments.

According to my book, the Joshua tree, *Yucca brevifolia,* used to be cunnilingued on the regular by the ridiculously long tongues of giant ground sloths. I'm paraphrasing. Its sloth lovers extinct, the Joshua tree now finds itself in a loveless marriage to a common, dirt-colored moth. My book called this a miracle.

I pulled up to the public baths in Tecopa, open twenty-four hours and bicameral, separated by sex. As girls, my sister and I often followed my mother into the women's side, eager to gawk at the secret bodies in the waters there. These were bodies you could read, stories on the skin in sun and scars, stories of pain, deformity, malignancy, the evidence of many operations. I remembered the awe I felt for those old naked women, my neighbors. I never saw bodies like them anywhere else—as marked, as resilient, as expressive. You could see time on them, their rippling fat, wrinkles, their hair everywhere. I remembered vividly how each woman seemed impossibly sturdy, an effect perhaps of the refraction of light through the mineral water, or of their big old bushes. Their bodies were the first books I read and those books were mostly about work. Child-rearing, housework, yard work, waiting tables, prospecting. Markings of birth about the breasts, thighs, belly and—though I did not know this then—inside. Most deformed of all were the feet, mangled by one long story—centuries long—in which a girl brings a man a drink.

But now it was the middle of the night and just me at the baths. I stuffed some bills in the coffee can at the entrance and went in. I turned off the lights and undressed in the darkness, feeling my body, reading by Braille the scar threaded across my lower abdomen, smirking above my pubic hair. I stroked my stretch marks, a weathering of shimmery purple across my stomach and thighs and hips.

The water's murmur bounced off the cinder blocks. I sank into the scalding pool and floated.

I wanted to take everyone I knew and float them in the hot springs, starting with everyone hurting. Everyone clenched against winter. Everyone bent from work. Everyone on their feet all day. Everyone floating outside their body. I wanted to look at death, to know it, to feel in my bones that it came for me, yes me, so that I might act accordingly.

It is not uncommon to fear dissolve while floating.

It is not uncommon for lost people to return in dark skies and minerals.

Cancer served me very well. It was as though I got grabbed ahold of by the neck, like God grabbed me by the neck and said "You want to look at your life and, uh, get it back in the productive mode? You want to really live it, or do you want to continue to rape, pillage and plunder?"

I wondered, watching the steam rise all around me, up and out the open roof of the bathhouse and toward the insane stars.

THE FIRST THING to leave you in the desert is time. Dawn found me sleeping in the backseat of the cube in the bathhouse parking lot. My soak had brought on the sleep of the dead, even though it was freezing and the back of the Cube was surprisingly cramped for such a dumbly bulky vehicle.

I checked the time—a few more hours until my rescheduled flight to Detroit. I might have gone by the Tecopa house, might have checked on it, but instead I drove up the road, past the tufa caves, to Shoshone. In front of the Crowbar I was greeted by a nine-foot stalk rising from a massive dusk-violet agave. *Agave deserti*, commonly called the century plant, another misnomer. It sends up its stalk not after one hundred years, as most assume, but a measly thirty. Its bushy yellow panicles spread open to the desert air and then it dies young. Oldest trick in the book.

The diner side of the Crowbar was open, but the bar wasn't yet. Still I begged my waitress to make me a Bloody Mary. After some hemming and hawing she made it a double. I slurped it down with a pair of runny fried eggs, two flaccid strips of bacon, coffee and toast. The waitress—a salty mother of four from Amargosa Junction—suggested I visit the museum next door. I downed another Bloody first.

"Can I help you?" An old lady docent propped up on a stool behind the cash register at the museum eyed me.

I glanced in the back to make sure the mammoth was still there. "I'm fine," I said. "Just looking around."

I could see what she saw: a day drunk in brand-new Uggs. The soak had cleansed my soul but the rest of me was filthy, ripeness radiating from my crotch and armpits, my hair gathered into a single unforgivable white girl dread. She parted the shades of the window by the register and peered out to the parking lot, to the cube with no food or water inside it. She tried to figure me out and did: tourist with a purse full of rocks.

"We have maps," she offered. "Do you have a map? They're free. *You'll* need a map." Emphasis mine, probably.

"I pretty much already know where everything is," I said. "I used to live here. My mom used to run this place."

She asked my mother's name. I told her.

"Yep," she said. "I know who you are."

I can't tell you how good it felt to hear that. I bought a rock and one of the books by the cash register, a new copy of Caruthers. He's in all the gift shops out here. The docent rang me up and then an idea struck across her face. She sprang up from her stool. "I was in the archive the other day and found something your mom wrote."

She stepped into the back office. "You can share it with your big sister," she called, "wherever she ended up." She thought I was Lise.

She returned with a purple mimeograph. I glimpsed the title of the short-lived newspaper my parents put out. She folded the page and slipped it into Caruthers.

"How's she doing, your sister?"

"Honestly she's kind of a mess," I said. "Walked out on her husband and baby."

Dottie, her name tag read.

"Yep, well." Dottie shrugged. "It's a messy business being alive."

BACK IN THE CROWBAR, the bar was open and dark as a cave. I sat at the bar and read the obituary my mother wrote for my father. The picture accompanying it was darkened by ditto ink, but I knew it by heart. My father standing beside the road sign at the Tecopa turnoff. Lise and me barefoot, her in his arms, me in the dirt. We look like tourists but we are the very opposite. This is the only place we've ever known. The ground is strewn with hazards: stickers and goatheads, mesquite thorns. Scorpions. Rattlesnakes. You can almost see them. My mother took the photo, told us where to stand and how. She kept the original in her jewelry box under her chips. Was it so much to ask, to walk beside them one more time in the place where the Family gave way to our family?

IT WAS. I drove back over the mountains to Vegas, returned the Cube to the rental car center and dragged myself and my belongings toward the line for the airport shuttle. Waiting there, I received another sign. *This Way to Rideshare Pick Up Zone.*

As the poet says, I could have made it mean most anything. What I made it mean was: get an Uber and have it, them, take me to Red Rock, the off-Strip casino themed after the ecosystem it paved.

My sister Lise was right where I left her, weaving through slots in a sexy-referee outfit, tray balanced on her hand as if a part of her. She looked me up and down like one of her tiresome regulars. "Make sure you're playing or I'm fucked," she said when she came back with my free drink, nodding to the security camera overhead. She knew where they all were and where they were was everywhere.

I *played*—Vegas for spending money—and Lise brought me drinks. I thought what a sad marvel it was that casinos had rebounded so well, given how most of us now walked around with little casinos in our pockets. I drank until I thought, Good for you, casinos! Thanks for having me! I drank until the end of Lise's shift, telling her my big gnar in what fits and fragments the corporate surveillance allowed.

She was tender and pitying as one can be while remembering a dozen slot junkies' drink orders, said finally, "I'm sorry you blew up your marriage for an overeducated JewBu who didn't love you back."

"It wasn't *for* him," I tried.

"I get it." She hugged me with her free arm. "JewBus are hot. Leonard Cohen, Goldie Hawn. You always had a hard-on for the dead Beastie Boy."

"I liked him before he died."

"But you liked him more after. They're easier to love, the dead ones."

At that she had to scoot.

I DIDN'T MENTION the likely demolition of the Tecopa house, not during Lise's shift or on the drive home. Her apartment building was built in a Las Vegas vernacular best described as rooms-by-the-hour meets doomsday prepper, the complex encircled by a high cinderblock wall lined with crispy obelisks of dying juniper doing a bad job of masking the barbed wire on top. I was reminded how expensive it was to be poor. Lise's thin-walled, roach-infested apartment cost more than I paid for my four-bedroom foursquare in Ann Arbor. For what she paid in rent she could have gotten her own house, or at least rented a place that was clean. But she had debt, student loans and bad credit, and a more affordable place would not have her. "I just don't make food here," she said as she flipped on the kitchen light and the cockroaches scuttled under the fridge, annoyed.

I showered, which took forever, filthy as I was, then dressed in some of Lise's clothes and joined her for a smoke on her balcony. She'd changed out of her uniform but still had her makeup on. Her feet were propped on the balcony's flimsy railing in my Uggs.

"So this is what brand-name Uggs feel like," she said, her toes wiggling approvingly.

She'd arranged for us to have dinner that night with Lyn and their joyfriends Dre and T.

Lyn arrived at the restaurant fully baked, ordered platter upon platter of vegan meze. I cried and stuffed my face with grape leaves while Lyn gave me a pep talk. "I love you, Claire, but all this bullshit, all this pain, for *what*? 'The American West?' Marriage? To be *chattel*? No way, José! Oh em gee, what a racket! Marriage should be abolished. It's a trap! It's property law, as in you are the property. Adults can love adults! We can share property with whoever. That's why we have contracts—hello! No bosses, no masters, no husbands! Read *Lucifer the Lightbearer*! Read Emma Goldman. Read *The Ethical Slut*. Marriage is a *church*!" I detected our mother's disgust in that word.

I told Lyn I'd read *The Ethical Slut*.

Lise said, "Read it? She's living it!"

"I'm living *The Awakening*," I corrected. "And a little bit of *Charlotte's Web*."

Lyn said, "You know, I hope you get free, Claire Bear. As you know, I was mindfully single for a long time. Slutting it up, like you. But I was still insisting on vulnerability and intimacy and honesty and porousness from myself, none of this"—their hand circled the sad clock of my face—"pioneer girl bullshit."

"Don't be dumb," said T. "We're getting married. We're going to have a Wiccan ceremony for the whole polycule."

Dre nodded avidly. "It's going to be dark and it's going to be *divine*!" Dre was my favorite, their gorgeous equine face, their long Jesse fingers with nails painted robin's-egg blue. The three of them cuddled in the booth, Lyn basking in the love-light beaming at them from both sides, conceding that they'd wear medieval garb and do a three-way Celtic hand binding.

That reminded me. Lyn's father, Ron, had died in a motorcycle crash outside Denton, Texas, in the fall. On his way to Florida. Probably quick, the Texas cops had told Lyn.

"I'm sorry," I told them.

"Fucking *Texas*," Lyn said. "Fucking *Florida*."

We were quiet for a time, then Lise held up her phone, the portal from whence all bad news springs. "Darren says G-ma wants to see us tomorrow."

"Fuck that," said Lyn. "I've got plans." They were going with T and Dre to Dre's parents' for Christmas Eve dinner, then to T's parents' to open presents, then home for sex and a good night's sleep before they went up to Mount Charleston on Christmas morning to eat mushrooms. "You're welcome to come to the mountains," Lyn said.

"We have to see G-ma," Lise demurred.

I said, "Who's we?"

G-ma, our grandmother Mary Lou Van Osbree Orlando Frehler ("Grapes Grandma" to Ruth), still lived on Fairway Drive. My aunt Monica's house had been foreclosed, so she and her son, my cousin Darren, lived in the Fairway house, too. Both were addicts, but G-ma refused to live anywhere else.

"I get it," Lise said on the drive home from dinner, "she only has one daughter left." Aunt Mo had been prescribed opiates for her Crohn's disease around the same time our mother got hers for her Lyme disease. Soon enough they were snorting it, their sisterhood invigorated by their shared commitment to getting high. People think addicts are dumb because being high makes you seem dumb, from the outside, but from inside you're brilliant because you had the ingenuity to get high no matter what and the courage to leave everyone else behind. Well, not everyone. They got my cousin Darren hooked on that shit when he was fifteen.

I admit these were the broad strokes. Truthfully, I didn't know what all horrors had gone down in the house on Fairway Drive since I'd moved away, what all horrors continued to go down. I didn't want to know.

"It'll be grim," Lise admitted. "Worse than last time. Darren's on bad meds. Every time I go over there I have to go straight to an Al-Anon meeting after. But . . . it's Christmas!" This was a decades-long private joke referring to our favorite bad movie of all time, a holiday rom-com starring Keira Knightley's midriff in which "It's Christmas!" is offered as rationale for all kinds of bonkers and borderline sociopathic decisions. We watched the movie that night, our tradition, after which Lise called and asked Darren to tell his mom and G-ma that we'd be coming by the Fairway house tomorrow.

We spent the morning before the visit shopping for them at WinCo. SlimFast, milk, Kix, eggs, ground beef, Hamburger Help Me, a pallet of Diet Pepsi, cinnamon-scented pine cones and chocolate oranges for their stockings.

"I'm kidding," Lise said, tossing the chocolate oranges back on the shelf. "There are no stockings."

I schlepped the groceries up G-ma's driveway, where the Datsun 280Z Lise had been born in sat balanced on a rusty jack. Yard art, trash, flower beds full of beach glass and seashells, crab grass overtaken by cane and sprinkled with shards from a busted window patched with cardboard. Lise knocked, and a brigade of little yappy dogs sounded the alarm. Scraggly terriers and a one-eyed Chihuahua climbed the couch to the front window and snarled at us through the cardboard.

We stood there with them barking at us for a long, long time. I peered into the porthole in the front door where a doorknob might've been, were the entire scene not a menacing, surreal extravaganza of poverty, pain and neglect. Instead of a doorknob the door was held closed by a blue satin ribbon. The dogs yapping away. I peered in the window, saw movement, somewhere, blinding flashes. Then the face of a corpse filled the window, its skin ashen, yellow-gray, sunken eyes rolling, smacking lips collapsing in on toothless gums.

I staggered back, stopped myself from crying out. The skull face smiled, knew me.

Aunt Mo opened the door, bewildered in her bathrobe, colostomy bag bulging at her hip. I stepped through this doomed threshold uninvited. The dogs snarled. The smell.

Darren had told no one we were coming. "Karma's a bitch!" he shrieked, taking the cube of diet soda into his bedroom and slamming the door.

Lise shrugged, hugged G-ma and ghastly Aunt Mo. I could not bring myself to follow suit. Mo retreated behind the shredded comforter nailed up to replace the door someone—Darren?—had ripped off its hinges. Every surface in the room, I knew, was covered with pill bottles, ashtrays, stoma bags, unread newspapers and unopened mail. When I was a kid it had been art supplies, sewing, decoupage during *Oprah*. I missed Oprah, missed my aunt, there in her house.

G-ma showed me where she slept, an alcove off the kitchen that had been Aunt Mo's sewing zone when she worked as a seamstress for the casinos. I remembered her working late into the night embroidering uniforms with logos, stitching the names of high rollers on satin jackets. Now they give out plastic swipe cards.

G-ma showed us her current project, a mess of doilies crocheted with obscenities. *Shit happens. Life's a bitch and then you die.* "The little old ladies on Death Row won't sell them," she said.

"She means the senior center," Lise explained, "on Decatur. G-ma was 'disinvited' from the craft fair over there. But I'm gonna get her set up online once I get my new phone. WE'LL SHOW THOSE UPTIGHT OLD BIDDIES, G-MA! YOU'RE GOING TO MAKE A MILLION DOLLARS ON ETSY!"

"I don't do it for the money," said G-ma smugly.

Aunt Mo's embroidery spools were still on the pegboard on the wall, lustrous cones of thread in rainbow rows. The rhinestones of G-ma's Willie Nelson pin winked in the light of the TV. Something else flashed, two prisms in the windows throwing rainbows on the walls. My aunt Mo taught us to sew in this room, me and Lise and Darren. I remembered the hum and chug of the sewing machine, how it tried to lurch away when I pressed the pedal. I looked around for the trunk bursting with bolts of fabric, but it was gone. The sewing machine, too.

"He pawned it," said Lise, reading my gaze.

The house was freezing. "Is the swamp cooler on?" I asked. G-ma couldn't hear me. I went around the corner into the kitchen to investigate and found a hole in the ceiling where the swamp cooler had been. Beneath it, the oven was open and on. I sat with G-ma under her electric blanket and watched a show she loved about murder. I held one of her hands, skin soft as suede with blue veins traversing ridges of bone, each witchy finger weighted with sterling silver. I wondered if my dad had made any of her rings, touched his lapis between my collarbones.

Darren didn't come out of his room for the rest of the visit, except to take a shower. "Be fair to him, Claire Vaye," G-ma said at a commercial break, the pipes screeching.

"To Darren?" I shouted. "You mean in my book?"

G-ma shook her head. "To my buffalo."

"She means Theo," said Lise. "This is her nickname for him. Really for all large, dark, hairy men."

G-ma raised her eyebrows, making her appetites known.

"She calls Grandpa Joe a buffalo too," Lise said. Grandpa Joe was my G-ma's abusive fourth husband.

Darren emerged from the bathroom, soaked. He'd apparently showered with his clothes on. He looked at me with scorn, then stomped back to his room. His room had been my mom's. Before he slammed the door I saw briefly inside it, saw the guitar chords she'd drawn on the wall, a bed with no bedding and a horse blanket over the window, the only light the anemic glow of Darren's phone.

I said, "I can't be fair, G-ma. I don't even know what that means."

G-ma said, "Eh?"

"SHE SAID SHE CAN'T BE FAIR!" Lise shouted.

G-ma said, "Why the hell not?"

"I hurt too much," I said.

"Eh?"

"SHE HURTS TOO MUCH!" Lise shouted.

G-ma considered this, tapped her lips with her index fingernail painted pearly amethyst and brittle as a beak. She rose slowly and beckoned me into the bathroom with her. I thought she had to pee and needed help, but she swatted me when I tried. She wore head-to-toe denim every day, jean jacket, jean skirt, because, she said, Neil Young had once complimented this very ensemble. He had put his hand in her pocket, she was saying now, showing me the pocket, putting my hand in it. She shakily raised one booted foot up onto the closed toilet and with much effort lifted her heavy denim skirt. She showed me her fishnet stockings and the adult diaper beneath. "Beauty must suffer," she said. She had, she said. She'd been smacked around quite a bit in her day, not just by Grandpa Joe, who'd used a knife just once. I said thank God he was an ex-con and not allowed to have a gun. She said we girls could be shocked all we wanted but she was of the opinion that she had deserved a smack here and there, since she'd been stepping out. I tried to disagree—"We're not doing that anymore, G-ma"—but she kept on peeling her fishnets down, then tugging her diaper, by some witchy dexterity not snagging her rings. In Nebraska, she said, her father had been a preacher. Did I know that? Yes, he'd been a preacher and yes this was the Dust Bowl times when she was a little girl and yes daddy had let the men in his congregation have their way with us, with me and my sister. My great-grandfather offered this, I gathered there in the bathroom with *Law & Order* blaring in, as a type of therapy for adulterers and would-be adulterers in his congregation. Considered it his calling to invite men to rape the younger two of his four daughters. That's why the sisters didn't get along, G-ma said. She moved through all this quickly, far more quickly even than I have put it here, as if she was annoyed to have to catch me up, there, straddling the wobbly toilet with her denim skirt hiked up and her fishnets around her ankles, peeing standing up the way she'd taught me in Zion, her piss golden brown and mighty. "And that's how I came to Las Vegas."

G-MA COULDN'T WALK FAR, so Lise offered to walk her dog, the one-eyed Chihuahua who answered to the name Bobby Flay. The terriers were assholes, Lise said, "Not my jurisdiction. Look at the anal glands on this one."

I fled outside with her, grateful for the excuse.

Lise, Bobby Flay and I walked the tarry road past yards gone to dirt, crumbled breeze-block, men rolling under and out from under cars. They eyeballed us. Maybe that was my imagination. I waved to an abuela in a lawn chair. She did not wave back.

"Who are you kidding?" Lise said, tugging Bobby Flay along. "You think these people are saying to themselves, 'Why, there's my neighbor in the two-hundred-dollar Uggs. She sure is one of us.'"

As if in rebuke, two kids, a brother and sister it seemed, biked up to pet Bobby Flay and talk to him in Spanish. The girl had huge chestnut eyes, Ruth eyes.

After they took off, Lise said, "I want to have a kid. I'm not gonna! But I want to . . ."

I said she could have mine.

She stopped. "You're being an idiot."

"You don't know the half of it," I said. I told her about the Tecopa house, told her everything. "I'm sorry I didn't say anything sooner," I said. "I don't know why I didn't."

We'd circled the neighborhood back to Fairway Drive.

"So the Tecopa house might be bulldozed. That's what you're saying?"

"Probably it already is."

"And you knew about this months ago. And you're just romping around Cali with some brocialist? Why didn't Mikey get in touch with me? I'm friends with him on Facebook."

I shrugged. "Because I'm the oldest, I guess."

She yanked Bobby Flay up the driveway and began to untie the ribbon looped through the hole meant for a doorknob. The nasty terriers went berserk. G-ma began shrieking at them to *shut up shut up*, Aunt Mo too, even Darren. I could not go back in that house and I did not want Lise to go in there, either. Before she could, I gave her the article I'd been given at the museum, the obituary.

"What is this?"

"Read it."

She left the door closed, did not go in. She handed me the leash and we walked to the curb. I sat, picked up Bobby Flay like a baby deer and nuzzled him, reading over Lise's shoulder. The terriers shut the fuck up at last.

DEATH VALLEY—The great deserts of the West have a past that is filled with the meandering lore of heroes. Men who came from somewhere else to carve a legacy out of this vast beautiful and terrifying land.

Families like the Chalfants, the Fairbanks, the Browns and the Lowes. The Lee family left a long line whose members still populate the somewhat tamed but ever-changing desert. They saw riches and opportunity while wandering through this immense country—and all of them found themselves awestruck by the sheer presence of God.

These legends, somehow or another, never got their feet unstuck, and began marrying and producing little ones, who called

Inyo County home, and, several generations later, folks would whisper, "She's from the Lee family, you know."

And all these heroes, who gave their names to our mountains and valleys, met the equalizer in the end. Death came to call and no one could refuse.

Another hero of Inyo County has passed away recently. He did not come from one of the "old" families, but he left behind a small tribe of his own. Paul Watkins, miner, musician, writer, geologist, heavy equipment operator, artist with a crystal or a piece of turquoise, con man, orator, ladies' man, died on Aug. 3, 1990, at the age of 40, following a six-year battle with cancer and leukemia.

I waited while she read on through our mother's telling of our father's story. His first visit to the desert, *bumped along with his two brothers and three sisters in the back of the family station wagon.* Helter Skelter. Our father's turn as *star witness for the prosecution.* The van fire. Music. Jewelry. Mining.

Although Paul was "just a little guy" he was much admired for his strength and agility. I overheard this conversation in the bar one night:

Supervisor: "Yea, get little Paul. He's a con man but he sure can mine."

Foreman: "How you gonna con a rock?"

His first marriage, to *a Las Vegas girl.* His book and its aftermath. *At the ripe age of 25, lacking anything better to do, he took up womanizing, and, due to his good looks and way with words, he was quite successful.* The dissolution of the first marriage.

It was during this time that I met Paul. He was tending at the Crowbar in Shoshone when I came in. I was absolutely floored. Love at first sight.

I returned to my job in Las Vegas and could not stop thinking about this man, whose name I did not even know. Finally, I drove to Shoshone and feeling more than a little foolish, found Paul and introduced myself to him. We were married two years later. In 1984 we had a daughter, Claire Vaye Watkins. Paul began working for the county road department, the Caltrans. Paul hated both jobs with a passion and we both began to drink more and more. I found myself pregnant again.

The cancer. The trips to LA for diagnosis and treatment, courtesy of volunteers piloting "Angel Flights." The outpouring of financial and moral support from the community back home. *I often wondered where I'd have been if I was in a city and a stranger to my neighbors, as I so often had been in Las Vegas.*

The remission.

The Visitor's Center. The paper. The Chamber of Commerce.

The cancer's return. Bone-marrow transplant and chemotherapy. Graft-versus-host disease.

After ten months of this grueling ordeal, it became obvious Paul's life was coming to an end. After a week-long struggle with the huge medical institution, I was able to fulfill a promise I had made to Paul—that he not be left to die among strangers in the hospital.

The discharge to Malibu, to die *surrounded by friends and loved ones.*

Paul gave away his special stones and gifts to those he had wanted to. He talked at length with his two daughters, bidding them farewell . . .

He died peacefully while holding my hand at 3 p.m. August 3, 1990, at the young age of 40.

Goodbye, sweet Prince. May you find the God you've sought for so many years.

"Where'd you get this?" Lise asked through tears.

I told her.

"So you went out there—yesterday? And didn't bother to check on the house?"

"Essentially."

"Didn't even *drive by*?" Without waiting for an answer, she scooped Bobby Flay from my lap, hustled up the driveway and chucked him into the house, shouting "I'M BORROWING YOUR TRUCK G-MA!"

To me she said, "Get in. My car won't make it over the pass."

IT WAS CHRISTMAS EVE, the only night this city is still. It had always been my favorite Las Vegas moment, the orangey glow of the streetlights on the wide asphalt avenues, sometimes snow falling. It wasn't snowing now.

Lise did not seem soothed by the silent city. She was quiet but trembling, wouldn't look at me. Hypnotized, I watched a bolo tie (Grandpa Joe's?) sway from the rearview mirror until the city disappeared behind the range and I could feel her breathe again. We passed the Christmas Joshua tree. Willie Nelson came on the radio. "On the Road Again," the song we used to sing in this truck with Darren and G-ma on the way to Zion. It seemed to me our sleeping bags should still be in the bed. I turned to check but the bed was empty.

Lise glanced at me.

I said, "What's the last thing you want to hear when you're going down on Willie Nelson?"

She was unamused.

"It's Christmas," I said.

"You stole that joke from David Sedaris," she said. Then, "G-ma's right. You're hurting Theo."

"You talked to him?"

"He's my brother."

"I'm glad you're talking to him. I'm glad he has someone. Glad you have each other."

Lise said, "I want him to be in our family still."

"I'm not trying to be rid of him."

"But you're going to divorce him?"

I said I didn't know.

She whipped the swaying bolo off the rearview and flung it at my feet. "Well," she said, "you should probably fucking figure it out."

STAMPMILL ROAD, the road to the Tecopa house, the so-called Watkins ranch, is less a road than a gravel wash choked with tamarisk. On our approach we met a new blockage, some strange form. A gigantic iron arch, upon inspection. Some Mad Max Burner deal welded of mining equipment, rusted tools and car parts. It probably spewed fire. A 1980-something Mercedes was parked beneath the arch, blocking the road. The car was filled to the windows with dirt. "Artists or tweakers?" Lise asked.

She parked the truck and we heard dogs barking. Plywood, chain link and barbed wire ringed what had once been our nearest neighbor, someone too old then to possibly be alive now. Whoever lived there now, their dogs did not sound happy and they did not sound small.

I said, "Maybe we should go back. This is somebody's house."

"It's ours," Lise said, approaching the compound, which truly looked like a kiddie pornographer's doomstead, or worse. Lise located an illuminated doorbell inset in a mannequin's belly button and rang it. We heard voices on the other side of the chain link. The dogs swarmed behind the gate, a pack of huge loping hounds with moppish lap dogs underpaw, mutts all. They barked like mad but their tails were wagging, I saw now. Behind the dogs, eventually, emerged a woman. Thank God, a woman! A pretty one, even—a ruddy white Pre-Raphaelite with brunette ringlets whispering away from her face, maybe twenty. We told her who we were: her former neighbors, in short. That we'd once lived down the road they'd blocked. She unlocked the gate, let us in, then cinched the chain closed behind us with a heavy-duty padlock.

I said, "You sure are locking up tight."

"It's for the dogs," she said.

"Coyotes?" asked Lise. "They got a few of our dogs when we were kids."

"Coyotes," she confirmed, "and people too." She patted the eager collie mix aswirl at her feet. "Long story."

She led us along a narrow path. The labyrinth seemed mostly trash and bamboo in the darkness, though in the morning I would see that what I first registered as a run-of-the-mill Mojave Desert junkyard was an elaborate cloister of sculptures and paths made from casino debris and discarded Vegas kitsch. She led us to a plush red carpet laid over what felt like gravel and then through a gauzy sort of tunnel of prickly plants, then a boneyard of dead neon. Lise took my hand from habit.

At some point we were indoors, though it was not easy to tell when that happened. The house, or cabin—it had no trailer creak—was maximalistic to the point of mania, at once decadent and trashy, every surface bedazzled, too much to take in, phantasmagoric, a never-ending dinner party. I gave in to the blur of colors and textures and structures, focusing finally on the table beneath a humongous chandelier, where our hostess invited us to sit.

"It's Tiffany," said a voice belonging to another woman—person—a queenly femme person I had not noticed, poised regally at the far end of the table in a completely sincere caftan.

Lise complimented the chandelier, said it looked familiar.

"Used to be in the lobby at Caesars."

We learned more about where we were, an art farm called Villa Anita, an ever-changing and extemporaneous livable sculpture built by a collective of mostly women artists, two of whom sat with us: Deena, the Pre-Raphaelite who'd let us in the gate, and the magnificent Carlotta, older than Deena by at least three decades, and divine. The two were lovers, I sensed. Also, that Carlotta was in charge. She summoned an androgynous mothlike person, J, from the studio in the back of the cabin where they'd been making jewelry.

J was maybe also Carlotta's lover, I thought, listening to their happily codependent patter. "Baby," Carlotta faux-beseeched J, "drinks, please—wine and beer!" J complied gamely. Meanwhile, Deena took a fluffy lapdog named Tito into her arms and went to fetch someone called Erin from "somewhere on the back forty." Soon she returned with Erin, still wearing their welding mask. The group fed us, brought us drinks, told us stories. Carlotta was a fashion designer and photographer. They shot billboards, owned a nightclub—"I pioneered putting girls in cages!" Carlotta once cut Mick Jagger's hair. She and J flipped Debbie Reynolds's house for $80,000. Erin had lived in a tree in West Virginia for a year. Carlotta was once invited to a lunch with Michael Jackson, who was considering hiring Carlotta to design him some clothes, but there was a very young boy at the restaurant with Michael, so Carlotta and assistant turned around and left.

They took us through the years they spent transforming a foreclosed railroad tie house into Villa Anita. They made it up as they went along, a maze of bottle walls, bottle cottages, gardens and groves, revamped trailers, outdoor showers, horse trough plunge pools. They let the objects lead the way. If they came into a fishing boat they tipped it skyward into a cathedral. Whenever they went to Vegas they filled a Hertz truck with Las Vegas detritus. Used to be, in the seventies, that they'd have to haggle with the thrift stores, but now managers begged them to trundle away what they couldn't sell.

"We've been rolling in junk since the recession!" Carlotta crowed.

Erin had been Carlotta's assistant until bugging out to Tecopa. Now she painted and made Dalí–meets–Noah Purifoy sculptures "in the desert yonder, at sites never to be disclosed and unlikely to be come upon." J came out to Villa on a recommendation from an art professor, made jewelry and grew food. Deena came because of Instagram and ran the social media accounts for each in the happy pack of dogs rescued from the sides of various Mojave highways: Tito, Yenta Placenta, Moose McGillicuddy, Dhillon aka Dill Pickle, Betty Magoo of the

Long Island Magoos, Guido, and Dwight White or, more formally, Mr. Poodle, Mr. Puffs, or Clarence T. Puffs Esquire and several other honorifics I now forget. The outer spheres included various nomads and healers and volunteers from the internet, we were told, but those sitting around the table—Carlotta, J, Erin and Deena—were the core Villa Anita family.

That's what they called themselves. Lise and I glanced at each other every time they said it. Before we could get a sense of whether this was a family with a capital F, Carlotta offered to put us up for the night and I accepted.

"Some weird people come out to your old homestead," Deena offered, leading us to our quarters in the bottle cottage. "We've been protecting it for you."

After she left, Lise said, "What are we doing here?"

"What's your problem?" I said. "These freaks are offering us their bottle cottage. Be gracious."

Lise took in the bottle walls, the brown and green glass like gels tinting the moonlight, the dirt floor, the absurdly suggestive velvet nightclub furniture, Erin's trippy paintings and sculptures screwed to every surface including the ceiling. "Is this a good idea?"

I shrugged. "They're on Airbnb. How bad could they . . . *be*? Anyway, it's not like we can go down to the house in the dark. Let's stay the night, have breakfast. We'll go down to the house in the morning."

After a moment my sister consented. "We'll make a ceremony of it," she said.

"Perfect," I said, though I could think of nothing worse.

1969

Hi.

It's me again. How's everything on your part? Everything is groovy on my part. I have just had a dream about Milan Pompa. He is cool, but does not like me. It was a bum dream and I woke up crying. But now I am happy. Weird.

If you can't ask Nick for a picture send me his address and I will do it myself. How do you like this paper? I think it is boss. It is the exact same pink as the flamingos at The Flamingo. At the present it is 12:00 at night. I just woke up from that bad dream about Milan P. I wish I could tell you about all the neat people at school. Here is one: Mr. Harris. He is a teacher. He is so boss you can tell him anything.

Well, see you later. Remember to send Nick's address. I'll tell you more about more people later.

> Love + Peace,
> Martha

Dear Denise,

Raining. Please hurry with Nick's address. I have the letter wrote and everything! Oh, by the way even if Nick doesn't like me I still want his address so I can change his mind. If you're jealous and don't want me to have a boyfriend then don't send me his address. How are YOU?

How is Jerry? How is Aunt Nancy? I like a boy named Richard. He is almost the cutest boy in the whole world. Next to Nick! At school we are having a contest to see who can write the best poem. Mine is about John F. Kennedy. I am going to win. Got to go now. See ya!

Bye,
Martha

Dear Denise,

Please pay no attention to that last letter. I have decided that I don't want anyone but Richard. He loves me and I love him. Isn't that boss? How are you doing with Jerry? Why does he go to a different school? Do you have Phases at your school? We do! Here is what phases I go into next year: English 5 (there are 5 Phases), Math 4, S.S. 5, Science 5. How about that? Your cousin is a genius! (Ha, ha, and ha.) Well, I got to go now. I haven't finished my homework.

Love + Peace,
Martha

P.S. Tell Nick what I said about Richard.
P.P.S. Good luck with Jerry!

Dear Denise,

Have you met Mom's new boyfriend Gene? He looks so cool! He has a scar on him from his chest to his back. Far out!

I hope David picks you. If you ever see Nick tell him I said "Hi." The last day of school was cool. Everybody had squirt guns. I squirted Milan Pompa and he poured a hat full of water over my head! Then I hit him.

There is a boy at our school named David that everybody likes but he likes a girl I know (Cynthia Scott). I don't try to take him away because Cynthia is one of my best friends.

Guess what? It has been raining for three days!

Tell Aunt Nancy that if she thinks all I talk about is boys she should read some of your letters. Sending two pictures. The one that says "the gang" is the gang. The other one is Milan Pompa. (It's a bad picture of him.)

Say "Hi" to Nick, Ronnie, every boy, and Aunt Nancy.

Love,
Martha

Dear Denise,

School starts Tuesday and everyone is kind of depressed. 7th grade, blah. Went shopping today and got a suede skirt, a pair of boots, a pair of moccasins that come to my knee, a pair of red shoes, a pair of light blue shoes, and a purse.

Mom and Gene got married in a drive-thru. I couldn't go but they showed me pictures. Got to go. Say hi to everyone.

Love and peace,
Martha

Dear Denise,

I've got to tell you what we'll do at the river. (We is Ronnie, David, you, and me.) The first day there we'll go down to the pool hall and the pool. When we're at the pool Ronnie picks me up and throws me in. Then you come over to the edge and David pushes you in and you take Ronnie and David with you. The next day, just the four of us go on a boat ride. We are half way across the river when a storm hits. We get through that then we go water skiing and skinny dipping. After that, you and David go into a cove and Ronnie and I walk along the shore, holding hands (among other things). On the last day me and you sit around and cry while the boys are depressed. That night we leave. Pretty good, eh?

Why am I so ugly? Debbie and Cynthia are so much cuter it's not even funny.

Debbie is conceited. She acts like she's the greatest. I'm hardly ever around Cynthia, so I don't know about her. Debbie says she is but I don't think so. Say hi to everyone. I wish I was there.

Miss ya,
Martha

Dear Denise,

How are you? I am fine. Lots happening here. We are having race riots. A boy in English got killed on the Westside last night. Even as I write this there are things on the radio about it. Just now they're saying two more kids were killed at Rancho (black boys).

Today my boyfriend (Tony de Bonio) came to class with a big bandage on his head. When I asked him what happened he said he was walking home from school and some colored kid hit him with a chain. I almost cried. Then at lunch he came up to me and Eddie (Garcia), put his arm around me and said, "I'm not going to have you walking home alone. Wait for me after school." Then he walked me to class.

Love and peace!!!
Martha

Tecopa

C hristmas morning. A feast had been prepared by the internet volunteers (a pair of sunburnt British girls and Garrison, a nineteen-year-old Sigma Chi freshly dropped out of UNC Chapel Hill) under the supervision of Carlotta's niece, Mari, a recovering addict with Jesse eyes and six months sober. Over a perfectly sludgy pour-over I gathered that Mari had been a contractor in another life. She was the only one at Villa with any building expertise, but that wasn't why she was here. Her habit had almost cost them the family business. Digging holes at Villa Anita was part atonement, part ersatz rehab.

Lise was antsy, in no way down for coffee, breakfast, a spiked nog or two, watching the family (Family?) open their presents, learning more about the cane grass and tamarisk overtaking Villa's early sculptures.

Improving them, Erin insisted, emphatically and at length. Finally, sopping with nog and mimosa and stuffed French toast and sausage and orange chocolate from someone's stocking, I followed my sister down the hill to the Tecopa house.

Once, our dogs found a rattlesnake in the garden here. My dad cut the snake's head off with a shovel then brought us out to see. Lise was crawling. She was as curious then as Ruth is now. She took the dead snake in her hand. I've heard the story so many times I'd swear the memory was my own. She took the severed end into her mouth and began to suck.

Where our house once was, only a stone chimney rose from a pile of rubble, rat shit and trash. Shredded insulation and shattered glass. Much had been stolen or scavenged, yet strange dioramas sat preserved. The spice rack. A box of warped records, a box of crumbling books and magazines. Stunning rocks everywhere. Lise and I trudged through the debris awhile in silence, risking exposure to hantavirus to gather the special ones.

I wanted to say: You and I have loved each other and her and been loved by each other and by her, them, in all these houses, through all these memories which were once moments, real and felt even if forgotten. We have loved and loved and been loved despite the fissures and losses, violence, cruelty, smallness, deficits in money and time and attention, despite the betrayals and indifferences, the distance and weather, despite developing different definitions of certain words. *Death, expensive, cold*. How? I wondered. Because the skinny twin was kind, pliant with forgiveness. Because she absorbed the fat one's failings, made them her grace. I thought, *There was not enough to go around*. Such a handy phrase to describe such mean circumstances. Here came another: *I was born at a good time*.

We made no ceremony, had no ritual. I stepped on a sheet of cor-rugated tin that had once been a wall of the darkroom and a rattle-snake went berserk underneath. Lise and I screamed and scrambled up the far ridge with our rocks.

Catching my breath, I said, "I think I'm gonna stay here."

She tossed a tired glance down at the trash heap that had been our first home. "And do what?"

"Bear witness?" I said. "Grieve?" In truth I was thinking of Mari, the little orb I already felt athrob between us.

Lise shrugged. "I guess that's what this place is for."

After a time, I told her, "I saw the redwoods."

"With what's-his-face?" she said, squinting into the canyon. "Were they huge?"

"So huge. They grow in a circle."

"What circle?"

"The big ones shoot up babies all around, from their roots I guess, and then when the big one dies—gets killed, in the redwood's case, cut down for extractive—"

"Keep it moving."

"Right. When it dies all its family is there, circled around the empty space. Grieving in a circle. The parent tree, it's called."

Lise said, "Too much."

"We put our tent right in there. Me and what's-his-face. I thought it would feel cozy but to be honest I felt kinda trapped. I kept think-ing how they're stuck there, the redwoods."

"*They're* stuck there," Lise said. "But we're not." She gathered her specimens to herself and stood up, as if to illustrate. "Your shit does not scan." She set off down the ridge.

"Where are you going?" I called out after her.

"Home," she called back. It took me a moment to grasp that she used this word to mean Las Vegas. "I have to get G-ma her truck back and I have to go to work. I don't want to live here anymore."

She walked up the hill past Villa Anita to the truck still decorated with stars and stripes G-ma had painted on there after 9/11, and drove away. Though it was midday, a crown of coyotes appeared on the opposite ridge. Together, we watched her go.

That night I heard them howling. I got up to record them and discovered I'd left my phone in the truck. I lay in the bottle cottage and listened. At first I'd mistaken the howling for sirens. I remembered how many times in how many cities I had heard sirens and wished them coyotes. The yipping howls became sobs. They really were sobs, I realized, and very near, not coyotes or sirens but a woman crying close by. She might have been sitting with her back to the bottle cottage, thinking she was alone.

It was Mari.

The next day after breakfast, Garrison introduced me to a bong he kept hidden in a work boot in his trailer. He'd built it out of a water bottle, a lug nut and an empty tennis ball canister. He was a natural teacher, offering extensive instructions for the device's care and use, with demonstrations. "Technically it's a gravity bong," he said. "You can call it a gravity bong but we"—Garrison spoke in the first-person plural a lot, like he had a few of his Sigma Chi brothers rolling with him at all times—"we just call it *the geeb*."

"The geeb," I coughed, having cleared it.

Garrison nodded in admiration. There was some worry on his face, too. Perhaps he was reckoning with the fact that I was someone's mother. Maybe I was imagining that.

Just then the softest knock came at the trailer door. Mari. Garrison silently offered her the geeb and Mari silently obliged, an oft and intimate ritual, I could tell. I revised: Mari was Garrison's *we*. And now, thanks to the life-changing magic of cannabinoids, we three were the *we*. Together we took to hitting the geeb before and after breakfast, working all day digging holes for we knew not what or sorting junk for Erin's sculptures, then soaking at sunset. At night we'd hit the geeb once more before bed at a picnic table on the back forty before Garrison inevitably drifted off in the direction of the Brits, leaving Mari and me alone.

Mostly Mari and I talked about Villa Anita. It was like living in a very big fort, we decided, playful, ecstatic, chaotic, mysterious to me still. Where the Watkins ranch was open to the desert, fenceless, embracing the canyon, Villa Anita was fortified against it. Inside, Villa (as the volunteers called it) was a bonkers honeycomb of paths and secret rooms. Actually, a word like *rooms* was not especially useful here, given how difficult it was to tell if you were indoors or out. Someone somewhere had a lot of money. Priceless oriental rugs lay atop ripped-up casino carpet lay atop dirt. The bathroom I used had a poor man's Chihuly skylight and a gravel floor, its walls a collage of tarp, billboard panels, beer bottles and cane grass, which Erin called the new adobe. I said cane grass was an invasive. J said there was no such thing as an invasive and if there were we'd be one and I should try not to garden like a fascist.

The place felt exuberant and illicit, like a brothel in a ghost town. Nothing was where I expected it to be, especially not light switches, doors, floors and doorknobs. It slowed me down, made me a beginner again. Reaching, I discovered architectural orthodoxies deep in my muscles, felt how often my body honored someone else's code. I regretted spending so much of my life in buildings designed by banks.

Sometimes it felt like being in the built-out imagination of my most alive self, and sometimes honestly it felt a lot like a cult. Carlotta made me cry a bunch. Sometimes I was naked a long while before I realized it was no longer the time to be naked, that naked time had come and gone. Needless to say, I was high the entire time.

There was no such thing as trash at Villa Anita. The family had not thrown trash in the county dumpster for more than twelve years. Erin and Mari showed me how they insulated the trailers and cottages with plastic, Styrofoam and other eternal materials. I felt my standard objections start to flare—ants, cancer—and then fade away. They didn't make sense here. Erin taught me to make adobe bricks and bottle walls. J taught me to heal stressed plants with my root chakra. A visiting shaman named Skandar did a crystal sweep and got my levels right.

Two other important rules at Villa Anita: objects were sentient, and there was no such thing as being lost. Garrison, who had lived in Villa for nine months, discovered a chamber he'd never been in before, its walls made of mattress coils and car parts turned into planters now poking up cactus. If you put something down it might run away from home to be part of the art. This happened with Mari's things a lot. But she'd come into things as well. The universe provided. For example, her park ranger boyfriend had found some mushrooms while picking up trash at a backcountry site and Mari was safekeeping them. "Psychedelics tend to find me when I need them," she said, sending a rush of blood to my vulva.

I told her Foucault did psychedelics in Death Valley. "His trip had a big impact on his thinking."

No wildflowers this year, Mari said her boyfriend said. No rain. I said I missed the smell. It came from creosote, she said her boyfriend said. Creosote is ancient, I said. Creosote survived the nuclear blasts, she said her boyfriend said. I said none of us survived the nuclear blasts, that her boyfriend sounded like a dud, that we should eat his mushrooms at the hot springs without him.

At the hot springs Mari said she missed pills. I got very DARE, did my Sackler rant about growing up in the blast zone. I said, "My mom died from that shit."

She said, "For real?"

"So that's how that ends. If you're wondering."

"Wise words from someone who's been clearing the geeb on the regular." She floated on her back, nipples rising to the sky. "Anyway, that's how all this ends, isn't it?"

"It's different when you choose it. You leave all these people behind on purpose, you reject them, abandon them, then they're stuck here, alone. It's the worst kind of loneliness."

"Shit is selfish," she admitted.

"And you can't know how final it is. It's like I think on some level, in some warped way, I thought they would be out here. Down there." In the water, I guess I meant. "But they're not. She is never anywhere. They never say what I need them to say."

"I think the worst kind of loneliness isn't when you're alone but when you're with the wrong person." She raised the joint pinched in her fingers—rolled of fluffy dank buds Garrison had procured from the Timbisha dispensary. "All that was in another life. I'm clean now. No hard stuff, no pills, no needles. Just mushrooms, flower, water and sky."

I floated beside her, watched the stars overhead. Grateful. Wantless, I promise. I wanted only my baby, and if not her then for the waters to urge me to Mari, and for Mari to please please please touch me.

ABOUT A HUNDRED PEOPLE lived in Tecopa, and every one of them, it seemed, took the waters at sunset, whether at the public baths, the private baths, or the wild springs Mari and I preferred. There was no cell service in Tecopa, and I never heard anyone wishing there were. Spaces without cell service were like wildlife refuges for idiosyncratic thoughts, I opined stonedly as we rode bikes past the public baths to where a sun-cracked sign began, "These ancient hills . . ."

We picked our way along the path to where the water rose from the rock, hot and healing. Mari said, "The path is not the route to the springs but a part of the springs."

Ideal soaking began before sunset and continued into nightfall, obeying no clock but the sky. Wind rippled through the marsh grass and blew steam from the water. We dropped our clothes in the dirt.

"Hot springs can cause abortion and are thought to have served this function in the past," Mari said.

"Also in the present," I added.

I watched her big black bush surface toward purple mountains ancient and indifferent. I floated on my back, felt my nipples harden against the wind.

She taught me where the vents were, that they always moved, to feel to find them. I did, pressing my feet to the hottest rocks I could bear. I thought about how rarely we let pleasure lead the way. For most of my life it seemed my body had been molded by various structures—tight waistbands, bras, foot-binding high heels. How often had I invited—paid for—some wire to dig into me, and for what? If it was buoyancy I was after, all I had to do was come to the hot springs and float free, for once, and do it daily. I let myself be held by the fossil water.

Mari pulled my hand into a hole. She pressed my fingers and hers into the silky mud there. It frightened me a little. She instructed me to pull up a fistful of it. Gently, Mari and I smeared the green-gray mud on each other's faces.

It seemed essential to become accustomed to drift. It seemed the wild springs were an inoculation against the oppressive beauty standards of patriarchy. Maybe they were practice for death. I know that in the water we were the opposite of deathless. We floated naked and vulnerable as manatees. Our skin tautened as the mud dried. My mother had put it on our dogs' noses when they were bitten by snakes. My father had hoped it might cure his cancer. I have a photo of him slathered with it, cross-legged on a blanket in the sun, waiting. I wanted a God like that, some way of knowing this place that evaded the internet, the park rangers, the anthologists, a wordless knowledge. The feeling would be intense, Mari warned. "It's the empathic extraction of any number of invisible venoms."

A long, long time ago, I said, all of this was Lake Tecopa. Then Lake Tecopa leaked through the canyon and into Lake Manly, which we now call Death Valley. A story my mother had told me many times. With the help of the park ranger's psilocybin, long-gone memories returned to me. "They taught me to swim here." I remembered stretching my whole body toward them, my parents. I saw the stars and felt their hands beneath me. From the bottom of a vanished inland sea, nothingness tightened in me. A sensation of sublime insignificance, of almost orgasmic loss. Fellow bathers came and went. They whispered, gossiped, stroked each other in secret.

In a secluded eddy I asked Mari, "Do you feel that?"

She said she did.

I said, "We should probably kiss."

"I can't," she said. "I just couldn't."

Then we did.

When exiting the wild springs, I took care to observe not merely the ecstatic cold, but that this ecstasy lived at the intersection of the wind and my own perfect, dying body. I practiced not wanting more but my teeth always did.

On Sundays monks came down from the mountains. They draped their saffron robes on the reeds around the wild springs and played their radio too loud. It seemed there was a place for me.

THOUGH THE INEVITABLE DETERIORATION was mild in the wider genre of utopia-to-dystopia implosions, the scene at Villa Anita went south almost overnight. Carlotta and Erin asked me to pay them Airbnb prices for the nights I'd been in the bottle cottage—an extraordinary fee to which I agreed, occasioning another email from Theo re: $.

Soon after, Mari and I returned from the wild springs on a windless day, itching mud mite bites at our ankles, and discovered a Park Service truck parked outside the compound. At the gate was a paper bag filled with my belongings.

Mari went inside and came out a long while later with her eyes red and puffy. The park ranger had read her diary. Carlotta had deemed me "volatile" and "insecure," bad for Mari's recovery and a bad mom.

I said, "The owner of fifteen dogs says I'm a bad mom."

Mari apologized. "She says you gotta go."

"Go where?"

She considered, said hold on, went back into the compound and after a long while returned with a sleeping bag, a tent, two gallons of water and a box of granola bars.

"I'd get a stick," she said while locking the gate. "For the coyotes."

"What stick? There are no trees, Mari!" But she was already gone.

I found a length of rusted metal pipe and considered vandalizing the park ranger's truck.

It was February, freezing and dark, the waxing crescent moon behind rare clouds. I wasn't going to hitchhike to Vegas—that's no solution to any problem ever. So, feeling brave and white and territorial from my wounding, some latent Libertarianism in me perhaps inflamed from being jilted by a federal employee, I walked down Stampmill Road in the dark. There, I layered on all my dry clothes and pitched my tent under the salt cedars near the trash heap I still thought of as the Tecopa house. In the dog-smelling tent I took an inventory: Uggs, Caruthers, toothbrush and toothpaste I'd bought from the gas station in Shoshone, my wallet, granola bars, jugs of water, keys to I didn't even know what anymore. I arranged these beside the sleeping bag and hung my towel, still damp from the wild springs, on a branch of salt cedar.

The coyotes went berserk that night. I lay awake listening to them yipping closer and closer, clutched my pipe in my sleeping bag as they sniffed around the tent.

I woke well before dawn and while I did not remember sleeping I knew I'd had a bad dream about childbirth. Pain ran through me, as if from the teeth inside. I wondered where their roots went. My water jugs had frozen solid. I held one to my pubis, quaking, waiting. When the sun finally came up, I said, "Thank you." As in *for another day on this rock*.

I WALKED THE CANYON, saying aloud every nightmare thought I'd stuffed down inside me back in civilization. I let everything that was wrong with me bounce off the canyon walls. Me and others. I ranted at Mari for not wanting me, at Noah for not being there beside me. I conjured him a new girlfriend, younger, brilliant, without child. She only made me want him more, want him so bad he appeared as my thoughts in his voice saying *J curve,* saying *tamarisk.* If only Noah would walk beside me in the date grove at China Ranch, or swim with me at dusk in the Shoshone pool with bats swooping overhead, he'd see plainly that he loved me back.

I tried summoning the beloveds: Noah, Ruth, Theo, Lise, anyone. I had no phone so I used the old ways. I regretted not loving Theo better, said so in the canyon. I apologized to him and to Ruth for the ways I had "prepared" for her, that is, by buying shit. I apologized for the care and grief and attention I poured into various pieces of plastic, the deliberation I had taken in their purchase, the grotesquery of this agreed-upon ritual, what a doofus I'd been for doing that as a way of getting ready to receive her when all along I should have been doing this.

I was doing the best I could with what I had. Or was I?

Days got warm fast. I spent the hot part of the day in the tent, reading, crying, masturbating, napping. My favorite chapter of Caruthers was, predictably, chapter thirteen, "Sex in Death Valley Country." It began, "Sex, of course, went with the white man to the desert . . ." Here I learned how my trailer school came to be.

Once Shoshone faced the desperate need of a school. There were only three children of school age in the little settlement and the nearest school was 28 miles away. Parents complained, but authorities at the county seat nearly 200 miles away, pointed out that the law required 13 children or an average attendance of five and a half to form a school district.

Like other community problems it was taken to Charlie, though none believed that even Charlie could solve it.

The time for the opening of schools was but a few weeks away when one day Brown headed his car out into the desert. "Hunting trip," he explained.

In a hovel he found Rosie, a Piute squaw with a brood of children.

Rosie's children were five, six, seven and eight. "Rosie was a challenging problem," wrote Caruthers:

She would have taken no beauty prize among the Piutes, but when along her desert trails she acquired these children of assorted parentage, Fate dealt her an ace.

With the few dollars Rosie wangled from the several fathers for the support of their children, she lived unworried. She liked to get drunk and the only nettling problem in her life was the federal law against selling liquor to Indians. So she established her own medium of exchange—a bottle of liquor. Unfortunately she spread a social disease and that was something to worry about.

"Rosie has Shoshone over a barrel," Joe Ryan said. "If we run her out, we won't have enough children for school."

Then there was the economic angle—the loss of wages by afflicted miners and mines crippled by the absence of the unafflicted who would take time off to go to Las Vegas for the commodity supplied by Rosie.

Charlie arranged for Ann Cowboy to look after Rosie's children and called up W. H. Brown, deputy sheriff at Death Valley Junction and told him to come for Rosie. Brownie, as he is known all over the desert, came and took Rosie into custody. "What'll I charge her with?"

"She has a venereal disease," Charlie said.

"There's no law I know of against that. . . ."

"All right. Charge her with pollution. She got drunk and fell into the spring." Then Charlie called up the Judge and suggested Rosie have a year's vacation in the county jail.

The paths that radiated from Rosie's shack in the brush like spokes from the hub of a wheel, were soon overgrown with salt grass. She served her sentence and returned to Shoshone and the paths were soon beaten smooth again.

Eventually Brown declared Shoshone out of bounds for Rosie and she moved over into Nevada. There she found a lover of her tribe and one night when both were drunk, Rosie decided she'd had enough of him and with a big, sharp knife she calmly disemboweled him—for which unladylike incident she was removed to a Nevada prison where the state cured her syphilis and turned her loose—if not morally reformed, then at least physically fit.

That's all Caruthers has to say about Rosie, except that one of her "patrons," a known "total abstainer," left her $50 in his will "to buy whiskey."

I walked to China Ranch for food and to the wild springs for wanting—wanting Mari, wanting Noah, wanting Ruth, wanting to know what I wanted and why and wanting it now. Instead I got aspiring influencers from LA or, often, a grisly, undertoothed local soaker with a pet wolf named Osiris. Osiris's dad worked for the Nature Conservancy. In one of his unwelcome history lessons he informed me that what I called the wild springs was in fact a trough scraped into the marsh by a backhoe hired by a pharmaceutical company in the eighties. I was half listening. When eventually it became clear that he needed something from me and perhaps that something was my name, I admitted it to be Ann Cowboy.

"A real pleasure to meet you, Ms. Cowboy," he said, gifting me one of the bikes racked on the back of his van. It was a bad fit for me, one of those absurd adult tricycles, but it had invincible tires and seemed it would carry me as far as the Timbisha dispensary in Amargosa Junction and back.

It was hellishly hot the first time I set out for the dispensary, so hot Mari's park ranger gave me a ride. It was pushing a hundred and ten or I wouldn't even have accepted. The ranger, A. Adams his name tag said, tossed my trike in the back of his truck before he realized who I was. We rode in silence until I said, "Here," indicating the dispensary, a shipping container set in a gravel lot before three rows of Quonset huts ringed by razor wire.

A. Adams sighed and pulled over. "They promised the Parks they wouldn't do this."

"Oh? Did those mean Indians break a promise with the U.S. government?" I got out and slammed the door behind me. A. Adams pulled away, both of us forgetting my trike in the back until I ran out to the highway and waved him down. When he circled back I tried mightily to get the tailgate down and then once it was down I wrestled with the trike for an eternity before finally climbing up into the truck bed and body-slamming the trike to the ground. I stumbled down, slammed the tailgate closed, and when it fell open I slammed it again.

The dispensary had a total of two strains, an indica and a sativa. The prices were astronomical. Veganic, the signage boasted.

"Vegan, organic *and* humanely farmed," said the Native guy behind the counter. He was huge, wore a headband and a flamboyantly tie-dyed sweatshirt (sweatshirt!) reading MAY THE HÓZHÓ BE WITH YOU. "Shade-grown here on-site."

"Shade-grown? In the Quonset huts?"

"That's right," he said, "in the *shade* of the Quonset huts. We even have fans in there to simulate the wind."

He rang me up. "Cash only." When I griped that the ATM fee was extortion, he stared at me in serene silence that I took to mean, *Reparations, Karen*.

If my parents could see me now! I thought, smoking weed on the side of the highway at the entrance to Death Valley National Park on marathon day. What pioneers those old hippies had been! I gave thanks to all the rappers who marched for my freedom to enjoy a blunt in the shade of a salt cedar and behold the spectacle of the ultra-marathoner in all his palpable pathology, the pinnacle of Progress sitting on my trike unwashed, watching the runners with an inner monologue voiced by Jim Breuer: What are you running from, man?

I rediscovered my love for smoking in the desert. Being high was a delight, obviously, but I loved the physicality of smoking just as much, couldn't get over the mundane magic of pinching a little fireball between my fingers. Smoking at my campsite, I felt as pure as an early human. Barely upright. I found I could commune with my mother by smoking. I felt her as kinetic memories rising in my gestures, her gestures if you replaced the Marlboro Lights with veganic prerolls.

I rode my trike to Shoshone, bought food and toilet paper and calling cards at the gas station, got drunk at the Crowbar. Sometimes before I got drunk I took a calling card into the pay phone in front of the bar, closed its accordion door for privacy and called one of my old therapists, the woman one. Sometimes, after therapy, if no one needed the pay phone, I called Lise. Together we tried to remember the first things that burned away before everything was on fire.

Sometimes I called Theo. "Where are you?" I always asked. "Living room," he always said. Still I envisioned him at our dining table, hunched beneath his cross to bear. One time he said, "In the garden."

"I miss my plants," I said.

"Which ones?"

"The ferns. All my houseplants. The aloe. The lavender, the begonias. My little Japanese maple on the hill," I said. "The black walnut."

"Begonias are dead," Theo told me. "Spiky pink things? Yeah, dead. Hydrangeas are dead. Houseplants, too." As for the black walnut, he spent his summer evenings raking them where they dropped on the lawn, trying to scrape them up before they rotted into a tarry stain wormed with maggots. He said, "I won't visit the black walnut in the tree zoo."

Somewhere, an air horn farted. "Game day," Theo said wearily. It was fall then, late where Theo was. I saw him raking black walnuts in the dim. It wouldn't be dark there like it was dark here. There there were porch lights and streetlights and a string of café lights stretching across the backyard. Or there had been when I left, so many months ago. Surely Theo had winterized. During these conversations

I frequently had to remind myself that while I was on my Oregon Trail, Theo had kept on existing.

"Where are you?" he asked, then answered. "The bar."

"You should come out here," I said. "If you're done with trees." Theo was silent, then said he had to go.

For a time, our story ended there. Theo in the garden, me in the desert.

A FEW DAYS LATER I walked to the Tecopa post office. I wanted to stop living like a coyote. My phone was still gone and I didn't miss it. There was no service and I didn't want any. I sent Theo a postcard. *This coyote has clawed her way back from the grave* with my new address. About a week later I opened the P.O. box to a rockslide of forwarded mail. The volume was wrathful, included slips for several packages that turned out mostly to be books. I made space for these packages' woeful carbon footprints, but truthfully, I'd never been so happy to see so many unsolicited galleys.

The only package that wasn't a book was even better than a book. It was a shoebox full of letters. Theo had sent them, but before that my mother had. My mother had written the letters to her cousin Denise decades ago, when both of them were girls. Denise had sent them to me in Michigan months ago, after reading my clown motel novel. All of this I learned in a short letter from Denise to me taped inside the lid of the box, mostly apologies for not sending the letters sooner, and for not sorting them.

Yet I find the letters *have* been sorted. They're in chronological order, the earliest, on personalized stationery reading MIRTH FROM MARTHA, is dated April 1968. I do the math. My mother is ten.

Hello Dee,

Nothing happened today. A boy named Keith called me he didn't say much. What's going on up there? Do you think Nick still wants me? Nick is so handsome his belly button fell off! Do you see him often? I really miss everyone up there. Oh well, that's beyond the point. I talk to you just like I talk to my friends.

My birthday was the 28th. Cynthia's was the 21st. Chris and Kathy gave us a party on the 24th. It was a lot of fun. We played a game called Kiss, Slap, Hug. I can't explain it, so I won't.

Cynthia likes Kai Neilson. I like Brad Neilson. They are cousins. I kissed Brad. Cynthia kissed Kai. For my birthday I got this stationery some perfume, a ring, some other paper, two dollars & a new outfit. I have the books about pop music also. They're good.

Say hi to whoever said hi to me. Also to everyone else. Got to go.

Flower power!

Black is beautiful!

White is wonderful!

Green is very groovy!

Watch out for Blue Meanies!

Bye,
Martha

P.S. Write back. Mirth means joy.

Your Misery Was Nothing

As I read and reread my mother's letters, the heat broke. Fall came to Tecopa. The pain faded. The teeth inside me loosened and came out with my menses. I'd pour my deathless neoprene cup out onto the dirt and watch the earth swallow the blood, a tooth or two left behind. I felt the space inside me where they had been and it was velvet.

Lise came out for a soak on her days off. She'd gotten a second job and was looking for a third, trying to put a dent in her impossible debt.

"Lyn says since I'm already in default I should join the strikes, but I feel like it's only a matter of time before they bring back debtors' prisons. Now that I think of it, for a lot of people they never went away."

"Did you bring my phone?" I asked.

"Darren." She shrugged. "I left G-ma's truck unlocked and he drove it into the McDonald's. Not to. Into. He's fine—I mean, he's in jail and the truck's in impound—but he's alive." She shrugged again. "So no, I didn't bring your phone."

We soaked. I meditated on driving a truck not to but into a McDonald's. Lise brought more news from the city. Someone had been gluing cowboy hats to pigeons. There had been several sightings across Vegas so far, many of a notoriously evasive and almost taunting pigeon known as Cluck Norris, who had recently found a mate. Lise had seen a video and even downloaded it for me. She rose from the spring and dried her hands, then showed me. I couldn't remember the last time I'd felt so honored. I watched a pigeon in a red plastic cowboy hat strutting around a parking lot. Another in its flock, a female, wore a pink hat. They were perfect, the hats, the birds, the proportion, the body language—pigeons like smug yet impotent mobsters, same gait as every man my G-ma had ever brought around. I couldn't stop watching. *The fucking birds have hats on, bro!* a voice on the video said, awash in wonder.

"PETA hates it," Lise said. "They're no fun."

As night fell, we speculated about how long the pigeon project would take, how many pigeons you'd have to capture, how many hats one would presumably have to glue (PETA had particularly objected to the glue) to how many pigeon heads until one was seen in the wild and documented, let alone *two*. A decade's work, easy! It was something Rust would do. I thought about the things my girl-mother had said in her letters about love. I thought of my element. I thought, it goes almost without saying, about Ruth.

I guess, to answer your question, Dad/God: neither. I do not want to continue to rape, pillage and plunder. But neither do I particularly want to get back into the productive mode. I want to be always moving on and coming home.

I TOLD LISE about the Mormon church in Ruth, Nevada, with Jesse. It was Christmastime, spruce garlands and poinsettias everywhere. In an alcove, a baby tucked in a manger. Our bodies slotted together on the floor between the pews, our sweaty flesh rubbed raw on the carpet. Jesse whispering that we should never be apart, not ever. I agreed. He proposed. I accepted. We returned to the rec room, lit from within and hungry for cake.

I said, "'I kept waiting for God to grab me by the neck.'"

Lise said, "By the neck?"

"That's what Dad said, about cancer. On this CD I bought. On this iPod I lost. 'God grabbed me by the neck and said, "This is your life. You want to live it? Or do you want to rape, pillage and plunder?"' The plunder is where I struggle. I just take and take and take. That reminds me."

I gave her our dad's lapis. I gave her our mom's letters knowing she'd never have the time to read them.

THEO GOT DARREN out of jail and G-ma's truck out of impound. Lise drove it, crumpled and limping, out to Tecopa to bring me my phone. I plugged it in at the Crowbar. One message waited: Andy, regarding my teacup pigs.

I thanked Lise profusely over many beers. When she dropped me off, I slurred, "I need one more thing."

"What is it?"

"Will you take me to A Little Farm?"

That night I stumbled with my charged phone up to the coyote ridge to get cell service so I could call Theo and say thank you.

We started talking almost every night. Sometimes I howled, sometimes he did. I read to him from journal entries I'd written in the blank pages of Caruthers. I said, "I feel on display there. Like living on a soundstage."

I braced for him to say his doctor words. Instead he said, "What else?"

"I watch myself from above, unconvinced." I struggled to read my own mad handwriting. "It says here, 'Make peace with the middle class' but I don't even know what that means." I tried to breathe. "I think maybe I could love you from afar."

"I know you could," Theo said. "I have no doubt about it. The question is how far."

LISE AND I BUILT a pen for my Guggenheim's-worth of teacup pigs and took a U-Haul to Big Sur to fetch them. She only had one day off so we had to hustle. On the drive up, apropos of nothing or perhaps because we'd just got first glimpse of the sea, she said, "*I sort of wish I didn't love him because then I could be free.*"

I was astonished. "Did you read them all?"

She nodded, then added without apology, "And then I gave them to G-ma to read but instead I guess she burned them."

"*Burned them*? How?"

"Oven," Lise said. "An utterly Mary Lou thing to do. At first I flipped out. I kept thinking, *That was the only chance I'll ever have to know her!* Then I realized how dumb that is. My body is her body. My language is her language." She did not seem bereft.

I did not feel bereft either. For once I did not feel it.

TURNED OUT the teacup pigs were regular pigs. "I guess they were babies when I met them," I mused to Lise as she wrangled the monsters into the U-Haul.

Andy apologized for the "miscommunication" but sure did not offer me my money back. No matter! From him I wanted one thing and one thing only.

"Have you heard from Noah?" I asked as behind me Lise unscrolled the door of the U-Haul, the pigs protesting mightily at being shut in. "What's happening with him?"

"Bro, you won't believe it," Andy said. "He got engaged! Going to law school."

I didn't believe it and didn't need to. I had by then my own belief system, one that needed very little of actual Noah, whoever he was. It occurred to me that I was barely asking about Noah. Maybe I didn't know a Noah. Maybe I'd made him up. My Noah lived in Joshua Tree, pollinating Joshua trees with a five-bristled paintbrush. My Noah lived up in the last sequoia. He would never love another, and the sequoia would never die.

"Good for him," I told Andy, fake gracious as could be. "I'm so glad to hear he's walking his path."

BACK ON MY PATH IN TECOPA, I learned the hard way not to take the pigs for walks. Pig Willie Style got off-leash and the coyotes got him right away. I buried him in the family plot, built a stone marker and read from Caruthers.

The Tecopa Hot Springs were highly esteemed by the desert Indian, who always advertised the waters he believed to have medicinal value. In the Coso Range he used the walls of a canyon approaching the springs for his message. The crude drawing of a man was pictured, shoulders bent, leaning heavily on a stick. Another showed the same man leaving the springs but now walking erect, his stick abandoned.

The Tecopa Springs are about one and a half miles north of Tecopa and furnish an astounding example of rumor's far-reaching power. Originally there was only one spring and when I first saw it, it was a round pool about eight feet in diameter, three feet deep and so hidden by tules that one might pass within a few feet of it unaware of its existence. The singularly clear water seeped from a barren hill. About, is a blinding white crust of boron and alkali. There Ann Cowboy used to lead Mary Shoofly, to stay the blindness that threatened Mary Shoofly's failing eyes. When the whites discovered the spring, the Indians abandoned it.

Later it became a community bath tub and laundry. Prospectors would "hoof" it for miles to do their washing because the water was hot—112 degrees, and the borax content assured easy cleansing. Husbands and wives began to go for baths and someone hauled in a few pieces of corrugated iron and made blinds behind which they bathed in the nude. A garment was hung on the blind as a sign of occupation and it is a tribute to the chivalry of desert men that they always stopped a few hundred feet away to look for that garment, and advanced only when it was removed.

Today you will see two new structures at the spring and long lines of bathers living in trailers parked nearby. They are victims of arthritis, rheumatism, swollen feet, or something that had baffled physicians, patent medicines, and quacks. They come from every part of the country. Somebody has told them that somebody else had been cured at a little spring on the desert between Shoshone and Tecopa.

Some live under blankets, cook in a tin can over bits of wood hoarded like gold, for the vicinity is bare of growth. It is government land and space is free. Some camp on the bare ground without tent, the soft silt their only bed. "Something ails my blood. Shoulder gets to aching. Neck stiff. Come here and boil out" . . . "Like magic—this water. I've been to every medicinal bath in Europe and America. This beats 'em all."

You finally turn away, dazed with stories of elephantine legs, restored to perfect size and symmetry. Of muscles dead for a decade, moving with the precision of a motor. Of joints rigid as a steel rail suddenly pliable as the ankles of a tap dancer.

Here they sit in the sun—patient, hopeful; their crutches leaning against their trailer steps. They have the blessed privilege of discussing their ailments with each other. "Oh, your misery was nothing. Doctors said I would never reach here alive. . . ."

An analysis shows traces of radium.

From the ridge, the wreckage of the Tecopa house shone in the moonlight. Glittering glass, the rusted coils of mattress. I told Theo about them, and about the plastic yellow slide still bolted to a low branch of salt cedar. I told him how long the plastic would last and how we girls had played in junkyards and cemeteries, climbing trash that would outlast us, the bones of broken machines, a rust-red chassis rolled and half-buried in the wash, its doors perforated with bullet holes. I told him about caches of tin cans and lids with lizards living all through them, the sun-brittle pornography I found in the heap, the copy of *Charlotte's Web* disintegrating.

. . . the woods, the woods! They'll never-never-never catch you in the woods!

The ash of memory coated everything. Tecopa was in my hair, my body, my ridiculous shoes. I said, "It's fucking depressing here. I mean, objectively. Death is all around! But that's what makes you feel so alive." I told him that I'd been trying to practice being alone, not needing so much, taking care. That I wanted to be better to him than I'd been, but not all the way good.

"The wife thing," I said, "I struggle with that. I don't want to be a dirtbag."

"You're not a dirtbag," he said. "Loving people is never a wrong thing."

"Thank you," I said. "I appreciate that. I do. I feel like I made you say it because I needed to hear it so bad. So, thank you. But that's not the way in which I'm a dirtbag."

"In which way are you a dirtbag?"

"I'm a dirtbag because I can't come back."

Theo was quiet, then said, "Maybe we can come to you."

SO, THOUGH I'D SOLEMNLY VOWED never to return to my mother's cursed city, I met Theo and Ruth at the Las Vegas airport. The first thing Theo said, he said in a barely recognizable imitation of Sir Elton John.

"Las Vegas, I've come home!"

"You read the letters."

"I never got to meet her, so."

Theo put Ruth down and she ran from me. I chased her through the phantasmagoric baggage claim. She could really run now. She could really talk. She had her own real body, her own smell. None of it was mine anymore. Never had been. Yet she *was* me, asleep in her car seat, galloping through the dust, wooing the pigs and tumbling into my lap in the garden at the Tecopa house, saying, "It hot, Mama."

"Yes, baby, it's hot."

Theo got them a motel room in Shoshone. He did not invite me to stay there with them but I was welcome to use the pool. I took Ruth swimming every day. She was a natural.

Theo was not wearing his ring and not asking after mine. I sensed between us a moon's newness, a turn, albeit buried beneath an epoch of pain. Still, there was undeniable air between us, fresh and gusting. We took long walks at sunset, bumping Ruth through the dirt in the UPPA.

"Look that *moon*," she said every time she saw the moon, and every time I looked.

I kept my feelers out. What I felt was about a hundred things a day, each with engulfing intensity. I did as the poet advised, I did inside what I had done / in the world. I came to understand every word—every sensation—a message and part of a system of messages. I paid attention. The gist was *let go*. I did. Eventually it made everything better.

I lost my job, finagled a less fancy one, rented a jackrabbit homestead cabin cum Airbnb not far from Tecopa: five hundred square feet on five acres of creosote, a wash running through full of sea-green salt cedars and the purplest stones. My life now is a spell of love and solitude. I sit in the garden with the dolls. I walk alone in the desert. I make stuff with the rocks I find, nameless things meant only for me. I walk up the alluvial fans or in canyon shade until I have a good view of the river, or where the river used to be. I read and write and nap and teach and soak and smoke and sew and cook and fuck around on the internet and with various lovers.

On breaks I get Ruth. We walk into the mountains with plenty of water, hats, shoulders covered, sturdy shoes. We stomp so the snakes feel us coming. We eat dinner on the splintery picnic table in front of the cabin, watch the sun go down and the stars come out. I try to keep my promises. I take her to the Tecopa house. I tell her about the now and the big gnar, about everybody doing the best they can with what they have, choosing darkness, choosing light. When she asks about you, I tell her the truth. You were here, then you were gone. You died the way this river dies, not so far from where it was born. Turned into sky. Jesse, Jesse, Jesse Ray, my dead ex-boyfriend, my son, my stepson, my sister, Mom, Martha Claire. I have a daughter now. She knows your name.

Acknowledgments

The poet in "Vagina Dentata" is Bernadette Mayer. The poet in "How I Like It" is Eleanor Lerman. The poet in "Loafing Along Death Valley Trails" is Andrew Hudgins. The poet in "Your Misery Was Nothing" is Katie Peterson. Thanks to the following people for thinking with me: Anne Carson, William Caruthers, Roxanne Dunbar-Ortiz, Walton Ford, Daniel Gumbiner, Corbin Harney, Jenny Offill, Eunice Silva, Guillermo Soledad, Kim Stringfellow, Michael Ursell, Florence Vega, Brad Watson, E. B. White, and my parents, Paul and Martha Watkins. Thank you, Amargosa River, American Peace Test, Nevada Desert Experience, Basin and Range Watch, China Ranch, Villa Anita, the Shoshone Museum, and the Crowbar.

Thank you to Miriam Shearing and the Black Mountain Institute at the University of Nevada, Las Vegas, the Lannan Foundation, the Michener Center, the University of California, Irvine, the Writing Seminars at Bennington College, Tin House, Writing by Writers Tomales Bay, and the Bread Loaf Environmental Writers' Conference. Thank you, Rebecca Saletan, Nicole Aragi, and John Freeman. Thank you to my family, friends, editors, agents, colleagues, students, neighbors, plants, and the dead. Thank you, reader.

Thank you, Western Shoshone Nation, for stopping the bombs. Thank you, Newe Sogobia, for keeping us though we continue to hurt you.

Thank you, Esmé Ofelia, for making everything better.

"Watkins writes like an avenging angel.
It's thrilling and terrifying to stand in her wake."
—Jenny Offill, author of *Dept. of Speculation* and *Weather*

Fearless, visionary, and with a peerless feel for the absurd,
Claire Vaye Watkins beat an early path to literary stature. She
was named a National Book Foundation 5 Under 35 fiction writer
and in short order won the Story Prize, the Dylan Thomas Prize,
the New York Public Library Young Lions Fiction Award, and a
Guggenheim Fellowship, among other honors.

Her novels and stories probe our feral and unknowable core,
drawing inspiration from the natural world and uncovering a
brutal beauty from which we cannot look away. In prose that is
both merciless and tender, nimble and lush, she reexamines our
troubled legacies and recasts our collective mythologies.

© Lise Watkins

BATTLEBORN
The award-winning and unforgettable debut collection from a once-in-a-generation talent

In ten exceptionally powerful stories, Claire Vaye Watkins takes on the mythology of the American West and fearlessly reimagines it. Her characters orbit around the region's vast spaces, winning redemption despite—and often because of—the hardship and violence they endure. In settings that rove from Gold Rush to ghost town to desert to brothel, and in a voice that arcs effortlessly from the gritty to the human to the sweeping and sublime, the collection

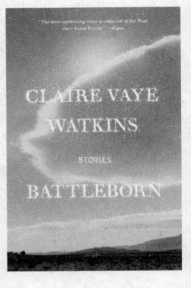

echoes not only in its title but also in its fierce, undefeated spirit the motto of Watkins's home state.

"Dazzling." —*O, The Oprah Magazine*

"[A] breathtaking debut. [Watkins's] stories . . . carry the weight and devastation of entire novels." —**Flavorpill**

GOLD FAME CITRUS
A searing, stunningly original love story set in a devastatingly imagined near future

Drought has transfigured Southern California into a surreal, phantasmagoric landscape. Most of the Southwest has been evacuated. Luz and Ray are holdouts, squatting in a starlet's abandoned mansion and subsisting on rationed cola and whatever they can loot, scavenge, and improvise, their love somehow blooming in this arid place. But when they cross paths with a mysterious child, the thirst for a better future begins.

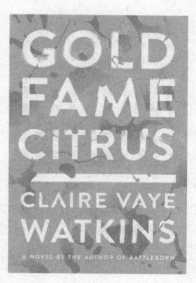

"[*Gold Fame Citrus*] burns with a dizzying, scorching genius." —*Vanity Fair*

"A sun-struck apocalyptic road trip of the California dream . . . working at the intersection between history and myth, reality and sheer imagination. And, refreshingly and believably, it's often very, very funny." —*Vogue*